SON OF THE SIREN

KRISTINA ELYSE BUTKE

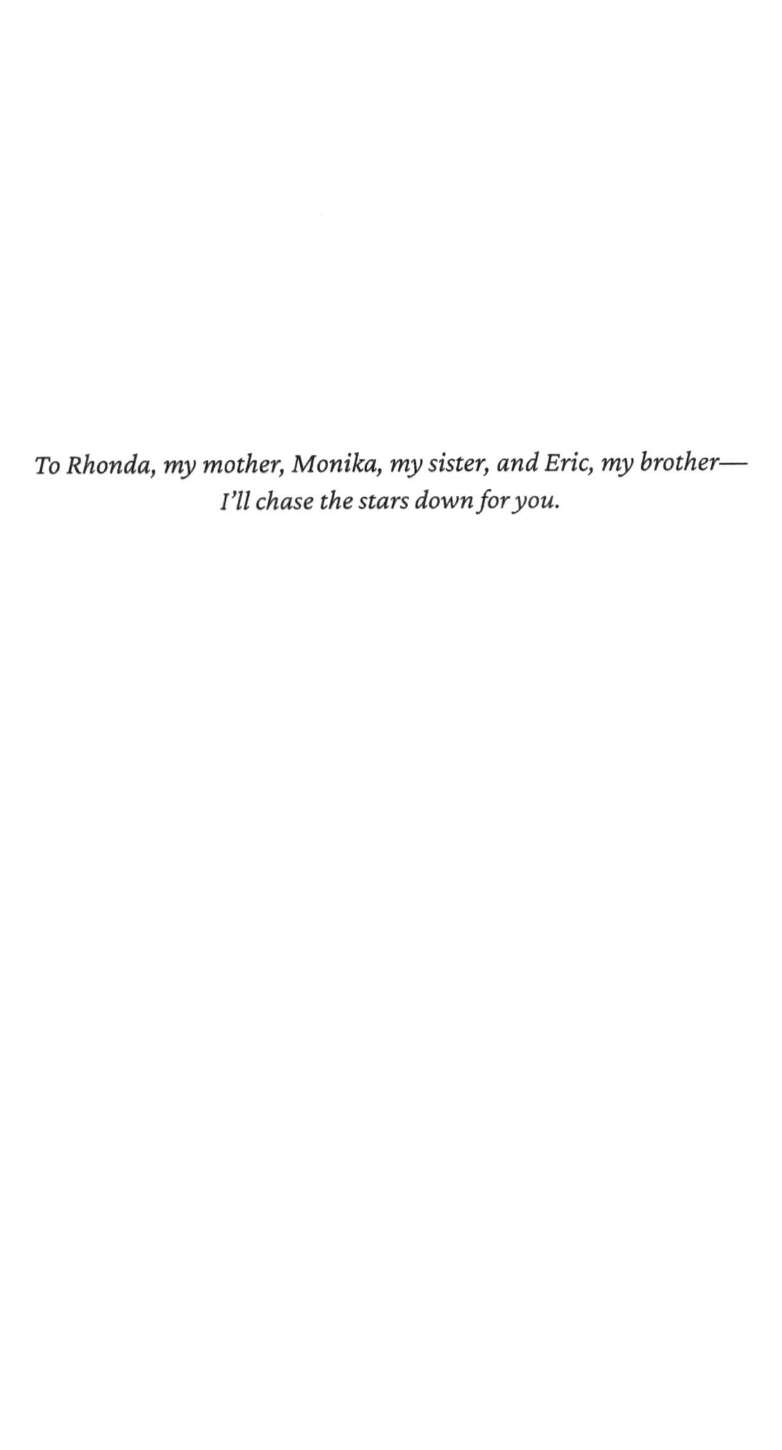

To Rhonda, my mother, Monika, my sister, and Eric, my brother—
I'll chase the stars down for you.

CONTENT WARNINGS

Sexual Assault (forced kissing, unwanted touching)
Attempted Incest (stepmother-stepson)
Violence Against Animals and Animal Injury (hunting)

PRONUNCIATION GUIDE

Lirien (LEER-ee-en)
Aurinda (Or-IN-duh)
Neven (NEH-ven)
Sonalie (SAWN-uh-lee)
Sorin (SOAR-in)
Nina (NEE-nuh)
Kitra (KEY-truh)
Brandegil (BRAND-eh-gill)
Lord Iesin (EYE-eh-sin)
Lady Ariana (AIR-ee-AW-nuh)
Eira (EYE-ruh)
Idela (IH-dell-uh)
Kerrick (CARE-ick)
Bella Morgana (BEL-luh More-GAW-nuh)

CHAPTER I

On the night of his twentieth birthday, Lirien was dreaming he was a golden bird with long, lustrous plumage, when a wordless song invaded his sleep. A woman's voice, rich and beautiful, floated upon the warm summer breeze through the open balconette window, but it wasn't until he felt the gentle brush of her breath against his ear that Lirien opened his eyes.

He was alone in the darkness of his room, but the song caressed him with silky fingers. A tingling warmth traveled his skin before it settled down as a hot knot in his stomach. He felt something like a tug at his waist, pulling him forward.

He didn't remember standing or walking. He was in his bed, and then he was on the beach with the hulking silhouette of the castle and cliffs rising behind him. He thought he was dreaming again, until the cold water washed over his bare feet and, at last, the dreamlike haze within him dissolved.

The singing continued.

The light from the large, snow-white moon cast a strong glow upon the sand, which sparkled as though the stars had fallen and taken root there. Beside him, a mound of red velvet bedclothing had been tossed carelessly aside at the water's edge. Lirien recognized the clothes and the figure in the sea before him, a man slowly stumbling forward against the crashing waves.

The knot in his stomach tightened. "Father! What are you doing?"

The man was already waist deep and Lirien ran in after him, sloshing through with difficulty as his father journeyed farther and farther out.

"Stop! Come back!"

Somehow, over the waves and the breeze, his words reached his father. Now treading water, he turned to Lirien, but too late.

The singing stopped. Long, lithe arms, silvery blue and covered in a smattering of scales, shot up from the water and encircled his father, dragging him below.

In desperation, Lirien dove under, blindly swimming ahead as frantic thoughts pummeled him and the sea floor disappeared underneath him. *You knew someday she would come; you've known all along. It's her, and she's here for you both.* Without ever seeing her before in his entire twenty years, he knew instinctively who she was.

A woman's voice echoing inside his head brought a flash of pain. *Get away!*

Her eyes, two luminous orbs— large, bright, and orange like sunset, orange like Lirien's own —flooded his vision. She was less than an inch from his face. He was so startled he opened his mouth and took in water, and choking, he rose to the surface. And then she was on him, seizing him tightly underneath his shoulders and staring at him intently.

Her hair, of darkest sapphire, another trait Lirien had inherited, was matted against her gleaming skin. Everything about her was longer, larger. She towered over him easily, and her fiery gaze was so intense he could hardly return it. And her face… he would never be able to describe how lovely and terrible it was, or the feeling that came over him when he saw the parts of her that were also his own.

"Let me go." His voice, a gentle baritone, came out flimsy and trembling.

Do not follow. She turned to swim away from him. *You will not see me again.*

Lirien didn't know what else to do. He called her by the only name he knew.

"Mother."

She stopped.

"Don't take him. Please."

A wistful look spread across her face as she gazed into the water. *I loved him. I did. But I cannot help what I am.* She met his eyes. *And because I love you, you cannot follow.*

She dove, a flash of her leg skimming the surface of the water, only to change to feathery finned, kaleidoscopic tail as she disappeared below.

Unable to make sense of his mother's words or what he was seeing, Lirien ignored her command and dove deep. The water was too dark for him to see, but he imagined the hulking form of his father sinking into the bitter abyss. He pushed on despite the pain in his lungs and the pressure of the cold, dark ocean.

He wasn't sure what happened or when he lost consciousness, but when he opened his eyes, it was daylight on the beach. He was sprawled out on his back, his wet nightshirt offering no protection from the sand that scratched his skin.

He struggled upright as his stepmother rushed to his side, clutching his father's abandoned robe to her chest. Several of her guardsmen were scattered along the shoreline, searching the water.

"Lirien!"

He flinched. Queen Aurinda rarely said his name, and the

sharpness of it startled him. She sounded all at once livid and frightened. "What did you see? What happened?"

He couldn't answer her without his own angry tears falling. "King Neven is gone."

LIRIEN DRIFTED through the days that followed like a fly trapped in honey. The atmosphere was thick and heavy with grief, and it took great effort to move through it. He felt removed from everything happening around him. Time could not be measured or observed. All words sounded muffled, distant. He didn't do anything, but things were somehow done.

And when he thought of his mother, he could only think of her in anger: anger for stealing his father away, and anger for the traits she passed on to him. He could hardly stand to look at his own reflection. While his mother had promised he would not see her again, that was a lie. Every time he saw himself, she was there in what she gave him.

His hair, of darkest indigo, glimmered with iridescent shades of blues and greens. His orange eyes shone like the setting sun. His ivory skin shimmered with silvery blue undertones. The small mark just below his right eye, a shining opal fleck, glistened with the hint of a rainbow whenever it caught the light, much like the scales on a fish.

And hidden beneath his flesh, something more disturbing: blood that tasted sweet, blood that was poison. Long ago it was believed siren blood was an elixir of immortality, its taste as sweet and honeyed as the creatures' voices. Quickly it was discovered anyone who consumed the blood would die, and horribly at that, so the pursuit of siren blood was abandoned, save for those who would use it to kill... if the sirens didn't kill them first.

Lirien found out about his blood when he was a child toddling about, when he had fallen and hurt himself, and licked at the wound to find it tasted of spun sugar. When he told his father of the strange flavor, it was quickly deemed poisonous, and no chances were taken should Lirien ever draw blood again. Lirien surmised it was yet another reason he was mostly kept away from the world.

The strangeness that existed in him, what clearly was inhuman about him, all came from her. And he couldn't bear it. He turned the standing mirror in his room against the wall to avoid seeing himself— no, to avoid seeing *her*, looking back.

His existence was an impossibility. He was desperate to know why he lived, why a siren would spare the life of a half-human baby. As a boy, he had asked King Neven about it many times. Neven always responded with, "I will tell you when you're older."

And Lirien, now older, had learned nothing.

But it no longer mattered. He couldn't dwell on his grief or his bitterness, not when he needed to be strong for his family. His younger brother and sisters would soon return home to Ardeth, and given the Queen's state at the loss of her husband, Lirien didn't know what to expect when they arrived.

A gentle but persistent knocking at the door interrupted Lirien's thoughts, and Queen Aurinda greeted him, alone.

Lirien staggered back a step. "Your Majesty?"

In all the time Lirien lived, he couldn't remember the Queen coming to visit him. He was something she had to endure, and she stayed far away to endure him as little as possible. She was never cruel to him, and when Lirien had to be in her presence, she was polite and calm. But overall, she kept a cool, careful distance from him, as he was not her child.

Lirien recovered from his shock and bowed to her. As he held the door open to her, he became aware of the state of the room: his unmade bed, the haphazard stacks of books, his lyre resting on a pile of clothes on the floor, and the mirror he'd turned toward the wall.

"Forgive me." He rushed to pick up his things, but the Queen dismissed him with a wave. She eyed his writing desk, and Lirien quickly pulled the chair out for her to sit. He took his place across from her on the edge of his bed and lowered his head, waiting for her to speak.

It took her some time, though Lirien still had trouble figuring out what time was, exactly. A few seconds were several minutes to him, and he pressed his fingers into his mattress to keep from fidgeting.

He stole a peek at her. She faced his window, staring off to the sea. She was colorless and gaunt. The only vividness left was in her crystal-blue eyes, which stood out against the pink from all her crying.

"You were there, and you didn't stop it." Her voice was quiet but unwavering. She tucked a strand of white-blonde hair behind her ear, and then she looked at him, her gaze like shards of ice.

Lirien's mouth opened, but nothing came out.

"My husband— the most loving, compassionate man — pitied you and took you in, despite what you are: the consequence of what was done to him by that *thing*." Her hand clenched into a fist at her side. "He couldn't understand that as long as you lived, he would never be free of that creature. That your life bound them together. That someday, she would return. And now, look what has happened."

Lirien tensed, his heartbeat quickening. He didn't dare talk back or protest what she said, and so he avoided her eyes.

"No. Don't do that. Look at me so I know you are listening."

Lirien obeyed.

"I have but one command." She reached out, her hand as fast as a serpent's strike, and seized Lirien by the chin. "If you value your life, you will bring back the King alive. Then all will be forgotten."

She shoved his face aside as she let go, rising to her feet.

Lirien stood but would not look at the Queen. A panic grew inside of him. He didn't want her to see it, but he couldn't keep his desperation from leaking into his voice. "Your Majesty, please, I can't do the impossible. She dragged him below. There's no chance he could have survived."

"I command you to do the impossible," she said simply. "You have no other choice. If you don't want to die, you'll find the King and bring him to me."

Lirien's eyes widened. There was no way the Queen would say such things to him unless her grief had driven her to madness. True, she had never warmed to him, never loved him as a mother, but he didn't expect her to seriously threaten him with death.

Lirien's voice wavered as his eyes blurred with unshed tears. "Please. Your Majesty. Think of what you are saying. I know you wouldn't have the heart to—"

"You have no idea what is in my heart." She left, closing the door hard behind her, and Lirien sank back onto his bed.

What did she think he could do? That he could swim into the depths and pluck his father out, after so much time had passed? That if, somehow, Father was still alive, he could force his mother to give him up?

It was a fantasy to believe that Lirien could save the King, however much his heart yearned to believe it might be true. Deep within him, he knew it wouldn't happen. Could it?

He had to succeed, somehow. If not for himself, for his

brother and sisters— he couldn't bear for them to mourn another death. As futile as it would be, he would try.

By the end of the week, Lirien's siblings would return from their journey to the neighboring kingdom of Asherin, ruled by two queens, the fierce warrior wives that drew the admiration of many. Every year the children stayed with their aunts to enjoy the cool, mountainous climes away from the summer heat of Ardeth, while Lirien remained behind to look forward to their return.

There was a reason he could not travel with them, nor ever leave the castle. He bore an affliction, a curse, where if he strayed too far from the sea, he'd transform, and that transformation would kill him.

When Lirien was four, still quite small, but old enough to run around wildly whenever he could leave his tower, King Neven pulled him aside. "It was your mother's warning. Not only are you unable to go too far out to sea, you are unable to venture far from its shores. Your mother showed me what would happen, how you would *change...* You must promise me, Lirien, that you'll never go beyond the castle's outer gate, and stay near the water where you're safe."

Lirien promised, but his father's words— *how you would change* —echoed and bounced around in his head until he couldn't stand it anymore. What did he mean? What kind of change?

In his eighth year, when Lirien was older and braver, he decided to test his father's words. True to his promise, Lirien didn't cross through any gates. Instead, he went down to the beach and ran along the coast until the castle faded from view.

He passed the stone walls of the castle town with its timber-framed houses and thatched roofs, and didn't stop until he spied the crowns of the pine trees growing atop the sea cliffs. He climbed up the jagged rocks until stone gave way to grass and the large forest of Pinemore stretched out before him.

He walked into the woods, telling himself that at the first sign of trouble, he'd run back down to the beach. After all, it was right there below the cliffs. The sea was so much bigger than the forest, anyway, so vast that it was inescapable. He was taking a risk, but he still felt safe.

He didn't pay attention to how long he'd been walking or how far he'd gone until his legs started to feel heavy, like his boots were somehow weighted down. Within a few steps, he no longer felt his right foot, and he stumbled from the sudden loss of balance.

He pinched his toes through the top of his boot and slapped at his ankle like he always did to wake his foot up if he sat on it too long, and his fingers met with something far more solid than flesh.

He ripped off his boot and stocking. His foot had turned white like old bone, dappled with strange indentations, and hard as stone. He stared at the change in horror. It looked as though the pores of his skin were collapsing, leaving round perforations behind. The bleaching of color slowly continued up his ankle toward his calf, threatening to soon envelop all of him.

Without another thought he charged back through the woods, leaving behind his shoe, desperate to get back to the sea. It didn't matter his foot was bare. He couldn't feel the pebbles, fallen pine needles, or roots beneath him. He ran; he hobbled; he fell. He tried to run again. All the while, the transformation continued.

As he hurried as fast as he could, his heart raced. All of the trees looked the same in every direction. He had no idea where he was.

Then, the sound of rustling leaves and the jostling of branches revealed something coming through the trees right for him. A red fox appeared, the size of a small pony. It looked bewildered at its surroundings and said in the voice of a young girl, "Huh. I wonder why it let me out." Then the fox noticed Lirien and gave him a humanlike expression, a look of curiosity and concern mixed together. "Greetings, mortal. Why are you crying?"

Lirien was far too frightened to care that he was seeing the impossible. "I'm lost," he said in between his tears. "I can't find my way back to the sea."

"Maybe that's why I'm here?" She stepped closer to Lirien. "Fae creatures dare not go near the water, but I'll take you as close to it as I can. Don't worry. You don't have to give me anything in return for my help. Now, follow me."

Another sob escaped him. "I don't know how much longer I can walk."

"Hmm. Go ahead and climb on my back." She lowered herself to the ground, and with difficulty, Lirien scrambled onto her, clutching to her fur. She took off at a rapid pace, dashing in between trees and gracefully hopping over heavy roots. All the while, Lirien felt the hardening climb up his stomach toward his chest.

The fox halted where the trees thinned, where Lirien could smell the water. "Here you are."

Lirien nearly fell as he made his way off her.

"I have to leave you now," she said. "I don't know how long I can stay out here with this much salt in the air. I'm already starting to feel it." Before Lirien could thank her, she bounded through the forest and out of sight.

Lirien hurried as fast as he could. By the time he reached the cliff above the rocky shore, his right leg had solidified up to his hip bone. He dragged it behind him, and he had great difficulty bending at his waist.

He sobbed hysterically. He still had to climb down the rocks to get to the beach, and he didn't know how much time he had left before he would lose the left leg and the use of his arms.

He clumsily lowered himself down the rocks, and as he feared, he lost his grip and fell the last quarter of the way down, the softness of his body hitting the stone with a thick smack, and his transformed half with a loud, heavy thunk. To his surprise, his hardened limb didn't smash to pieces on the rocks; his body stayed sturdy. That side of his body didn't even hurt from hitting the stone. The other parts of him, on the other hand, surged with pain.

He lay on the hard earth, a thin layer of white sand dusting the top of it, thinking he was close enough to the sea that he'd be safe. And while his body didn't seem to change any further, his leg remained frozen.

He breathed in and out, his air rushed and heavy, weighted down by his uncontrollable sobbing. Finally, he dragged himself off the ground and plodded over to the shoreline.

He'd had an idea: if he truly were a creature of the sea, then maybe the sea would heal him. He sprawled out on the wet sand and let the gentle beach waves wash over him. It took a long time, but the feeling started to creep back into his waist and leg. He rolled up his pant leg to look, and watched the bonelike hue and texture drain from him slowly, its small perforations disappearing as his skin grew plump and full. The unnatural whiteness to his skin faded and its color returned.

He stayed soaked by sea water until the cold permeated his bones, and trembling, he finally got up and started the walk back to his tower.

He never told anyone what happened to him that day. He

never ventured beyond his boundary again. After that ordeal, Lirien learned that the place beyond the castle and sea was truly dangerous, and he would somehow have to content himself with watching and waiting as the years passed.

And so Lirien, at week's end, watched and waited for his siblings' arrival. The terrible news had no doubt made its way to them on their journey back home, and he both dreaded and longed to see them in their grief.

On the day they were to return, Lirien traveled through the servant passages to the opposite end of the castle. His father had shown him the routes so he could move freely and relatively unseen if he so wished. It's not that his existence was a secret to those in the castle; it was that he preferred to avoid the curious stares and hushed whispers that followed him whenever he graced anyone's presence. Once, when he was younger, he'd heard a group of nobles debate whether he was beautiful or ugly and ultimately determine that he was "just weird."

The servants were better than the nobles, Lirien had decided. They refrained from gossiping directly in front of him, at least, and were always courteous and prompt when Lirien needed something. But they never interacted with him beyond that. Nobody really did unless they were commanded to.

Lirien encountered no one as he hurried toward the grand entry hall. The servants' door, too short for someone of Lirien's height, was hidden along the side of the grand staircase that greeted guests as soon as they entered the chamber. It was one of the castle's most stunning features, massive in size and elaborately carved, the centerpiece of the entire hall. Enormous figures of matching stone rested on marble pillars, flanking the bottom of the stairs at the start of the handrails. Each featured the three heraldic animals of the royal family: a wild swan in flight, a stag rising on its hind legs, and a serpent curling its body into fanciful loops.

The statues obscured the sight of the servants' door. Lirien entered the hall with caution, stepping out as quietly as he could. He slid behind a carving of the snake, hunching his back slightly to peer between its coils.

Queen Aurinda waited at the doorway, looking just as she did when she'd visited Lirien's room— pale and haggard. Armored guards lined the entry, and as the metal-plated oak doors opened, their polearms struck the floor twice to welcome the children home.

The herald announced each of Lirien's siblings, beginning with: "Princess Nina of Ardeth."

The Queen's elder daughter, at age eleven, looked somber like her mother. Her long, straight, pale blonde hair seemed duller, stringier than before. Her warm, peachy skin had drained of color, except for the telltale red puffiness around her golden-brown eyes. She staggered into the grand hall, her pace slow and jerky and completely unlike herself. Lirien's heart sank. She didn't look well at all.

She made it to Queen Aurinda, whose face crumpled at the sight of her daughter. The two hugged, and Nina sobbed quietly in her mother's arms. The Queen remained calm as she caressed Nina, her long fingers drawing a pattern of circles on her back to soothe her.

"Prince Sorin of Ardeth."

He was the elder of the twins by seven minutes, and seven years old. His focus jumped all over the room, his honey-brown eyes wider than normal, and his wavy gilded hair in a bit of disarray. He looked bewildered, gaping at the castle as if entering it for the very first time. He absentmindedly tugged at the edges of his sleeves as he peered around the hall in all directions.

Lirien ducked down when Sorin's eyes searched near him, but he was too late. Sorin found him and trotted his way. Lirien waved his hand and put a finger to his lips— *don't come, please be quiet, I'm not supposed to be here* —but it failed.

"Brother!" the boy shouted.

Queen Aurinda spotted Lirien at once. She wore no expression. Her face was a mask, frozen and unmoving, eyes unblinking. It was the most unnerving stare Lirien ever received from her. Then, to his surprise, she beckoned him forward, all the while saying nothing.

The hint of a murmur rippled through the hall as Lirien came out into the open, stepping in front of the heraldic animals. Sorin flung himself at Lirien, wrapping his arms around Lirien's waist with a sob.

Lirien patted his head. "Sorin," he whispered. "Please, go to your mother. You'll see me again soon."

Sorin looked up at him. "No. I want to be with you."

Lirien hoped Queen Aurinda didn't hear. "Please, go." His brother reluctantly unhooked himself and headed over to the Queen, who seized Sorin's shoulders and pulled him close to her.

"Princess Sonalie of Ardeth," the herald called.

The last of Queen Aurinda and King Neven's children, Sonalie was the most composed of all the siblings. Her face didn't reveal any expression other than the one she always wore — a detachment born of shyness, where she'd avoid eye contact and twirl a long ringlet of yellow hair around her finger.

She was two steps past Lirien when she whirled around and gave him a rapid curtsy. Then she ran off to her mother.

The Queen looked expectantly to the door. "Where is Queen Eira of Asherin? I thought she would be here, given what happened to her brother."

One of the liveried servants who had traveled with the prince and princesses approached the Queen and gave a grand bow. "Your Majesty, Queen Eira chose to ride separately from the children. Queen Idela fell ill, and Her Majesty wanted to tend to her beloved wife before leaving. She should be here within the next few days or so."

"Very well."

Several more servants and guardsmen brought up the rear of the procession, and once they were all inside, there was a final bang from the polearms as the heavy doors closed.

Queen Aurinda threw her shoulders back, then straightened her spine. "Children, come with me now," she said firmly. "We must talk." She led them up the stairs, taking Sorin and Sonalie's hands in her own. Nina looked back at Lirien, giving him a wistful, tired half-smile as she trudged along behind them.

As soon as they were gone, a sudden exhaustion hit Lirien, stealing away his motivation to do anything else but retreat through the passage back to his room.

"Lirien," Nina called him through the door. "You asleep?"

"No." He was lying in his bed in his nightclothes, unsure of the time, staring fruitlessly out the balconette window. He continued to leave it open, thinking he'd hear the singing once more, even though he knew in his heart he wouldn't.

He let Nina in. The light from her candle showed warmth and color back in her face, and Lirien was relieved to see her looking better. She lit the rest of the candles in Lirien's room while he pulled the downy blanket and pillows from his bed. He piled it all on the floor into a towering blob for her to fall into. As soon as the mound was ready, she set her candle on the writing desk and dropped like a stone.

Lirien couldn't help smiling as one of the smaller pillows

flew out on impact. He grabbed it, sidestepping Nina along the way, and climbed back onto his bed, propping himself up against the headboard.

"I'm glad to see you. I was very worried when you first came home. How are you feeling?"

"I mean, I feel awful, but not so bad right now. I just... I can't sleep."

"Neither can I." With the light, Lirien could properly see the clock against the wall: a quarter after two. "Should you be visiting so late?"

"I told the guard I was coming here, and she doesn't mind. She's waiting at the foot of the stairs for me."

Lirien was more concerned with how the Queen would feel, but he didn't push further. "How are the twins?"

"They're sleeping in Mother's room tonight." Nina let out a long, slow exhale. "Sonalie seems to be doing fine. At least everyone thinks she is, except she doesn't understand what's going on. Sorin really wanted to see you tonight, but Mother's clinging to him pretty tightly. He's going to come to see you more often, I bet, now that Father's gone. You look like him."

"I don't know about that." He could only think of how he looked like his mother.

"You *are* like him. Same short wavy hair, same kind of face. Same nose, same mouth, same cheeks. Same mole in the same spot."

"I'll agree with you on the mole. If you can call it that."

"Yours is like a pretty little fish scale. You know, whenever I see you, I always want to give you a tap there. I wonder why."

"Thank you for not poking my face whenever you see me."

"A future queen must learn self-restraint," she said, repositioning herself on the pillow mound. "Anyway. Your colors are all different, sure. But you're the same as Father. I don't know why you don't see it, especially now that you're a grown-up.

You're like a mirror image but with watercolors spilled all over it."

Lirien laughed, the first time in a while.

"At least Father will live on through you. Unless you save him, of course."

Nina's words quickly brought him out of his lighter mood. "Did you hear something about that?"

"Yes, Mother talked to us and she promised us you would bring him back."

Something sank in Lirien as he heard Nina's words. "It's too late to save him, Nina. I tried when it was happening. I can't breathe underwater, and even if I could, I can't go where he's gone. When I get too far out to sea, something always pushes me back to shore. Even if my mother's enchanted him so that he's still alive down there, somehow... she's taken him away into the depths. I would die if I followed."

"I don't want you to die." Nina climbed out of the blanket pile and onto his bed to give him a hug.

Lirien patted her back. "I don't know what to do," he confessed. "I have no hope of saving him. I don't know why the queen thinks I can."

They remained silent for a moment, then Nina spoke. "Maybe you can. You're a human, but what about the other part? If you can't chase Father down, bring him to you. You're a siren. Do what you do best— sing."

CHAPTER 2

As Nina had predicted, Sorin came to see him often over the next couple days. Lirien tried to keep it light-hearted. They played games along the beach: fighting, racing, and drawing pictures in the sand with sticks. Before, Sorin had usually scribbled his name over and over in different scripts and sizes, but now he wrote a single phrase, COME HOME. Every time the water would wash it away, he rewrote it again and again, like an urgent wish. It hurt Lirien to see him this way.

He thought of Nina's suggestion to sing, as if that could easily make everything better. Lirien sang a lot; it was nothing special to him. He had found early on that he was gifted, but even so, it felt like an unremarkable, natural part of who he was.

He sang for the king whenever he'd requested it, and the Queen when she was there to listen. He sang for Nina and Sorin when they asked, and Sonalie when he gave her music lessons. The lessons seemed to delight her the most. It was the only thing that diminished her timidity with him.

Lirien sang all the time, and nothing unexpected ever came of it. There was no mystical power in it, no strange, hypnotic pull on people, no command hidden in the lyrics or melody. He sang because people wanted to listen. He sang to feel appreciated, to be complimented. He was good at it, but there was nothing extraordinary in it.

Out of desperation, he reconsidered the danger of going back out into the ocean. But he was at a loss for what to do. For the next three days, he went out to swim, regardless of risk and futility. He even tried in the middle of the night, around the hour he thought Father had disappeared, as if there was some unspoken, magical rule he had to meet for the king to come back.

Lirien found he could only go so far and so deep until some sort of barrier kept him from making progress. It felt like hitting a defensive wall. When he got close to it, a sudden jet pulled him off course, or a rogue wave knocked him back. Sometimes he blacked out when he crashed into the unseen force, only to wake up half-drowned on the shore.

There was a power out there Lirien couldn't understand, and it made him feel helpless. He assumed his mother was the source, that she had more magic in her than he knew. The power of the sirens was something ancient, large, and primal. *Do not follow,* she had said, and she clearly meant it.

Queen Aurinda was another problem. She didn't visit Lirien's room again, but she hovered close by. Beneath the looming southwest watchtower, she made a habit of passing through the castle's barbican, strolling along it to look out at the sea. She would dismiss the guards to stand alone by the torches, the light making her cold face seem warm as she gazed far ahead in solitude. At times, her face bore no expression, or she cried openly in silence, wiping her cheeks. In rare moments, her eyes were closed and head bowed, and she kept still like that for quite some time.

When she did take notice of Lirien, watching him botch his

attempts at rescue, a look he couldn't place spread across her features, something in between despair, disappointment, and panic. Lirien felt helpless when he saw her. *She really believes I can do it. And I've failed every time.* The shame in Lirien burned brighter whenever she watched him, and the fear inside him grew as he knew every failure was a step closer to his death.

At last, Lirien surrendered to Nina's suggestion. If he was a siren, then he should sing. But it couldn't just be anything. There had to be meaning, an intention behind it. If he put all of his heart into it, maybe it would be enough to call his father out of the waters, just as his mother had called him into them. Sirens had the power to draw others to their side— why shouldn't Lirien have this power, too?

"Whatcha doing?"

Sorin had found Lirien on the third floor of the library, digging through books. The small boy rose on the tips of his toes, clutching one of the rungs of the ladder Lirien stood on. Lirien nearly dropped a book on him.

"Ah, you sneak! I'm looking for some music."

"Are you going to teach Sonalie a new song?"

"No, this one's for me. Or... rather, for Father."

"You going to bring him back? Mother says you can."

Lirien winced. Never before had he wanted to curse the Queen for her words. He swallowed, and said to his brother carefully, "I'm working hard, but... Sorin, you have to prepare yourself. There's a strong chance I won't succeed."

"But Mother says you're magic."

Lirien climbed down the ladder, grasping a book in his free hand. "We don't know if I am. Sirens and other creatures have such powers, yes, but as you know, humans don't. I'm trying to see if my siren side has any magic to it, but it's my human side that might make the magic fail."

"I'm glad you are trying."

Lirien ruffled Sorin's hair. "Trying my best." He wouldn't speak of the Queen's threat to end his life. What would the children do if they learned what their mother was capable of? What could they do?

Sorin eyed the green, dusty tome that Lirien held in his hand. "What did you find?"

"A very special book. See?" Lirien held it out to Sorin.

"*Songs of the Old Country*," the boy read.

"That's where Father said his great-grandmother came from before she married into the royal family of Ardeth. And he loved a song they passed down through the family. I can't remember what it was, so I'm trying to find it."

"What's the Old Country? Aren't all the countries old?"

"They are. But the oldest one of all is Léandor, so that's the one they mean." Lirien fanned through the pages quickly, over and over. "Here. Close your eyes. When you're ready, put your finger on a page. That'll be the one I sing."

"Yeah!"

After Sorin tapped a page, he read the title. "'The Darkling Wood.' That sounds scary."

"We'll see." Lirien scanned the bars of music. Lots of eighth notes written in ascending scales, and a note that the song was up-tempo... that wouldn't work. Lirien hummed through it at a slower speed, akin to a lullaby.

"That sounds pretty! Are there words?"

"Three verses." He paused and inspected the lyrics.

On the heart it rests, two pink, rosy crests,
And their snowy hills below.

On the fertile mound, curling from the ground,
How the darkling wood doth grow!
If you part the lips with a fervent kiss,
Then the rosebud—

"No, not for children." Lirien slammed the book shut.

"Aw, why?"

"Don't worry about it."

"Can we try again?" Sorin grabbed the volume and flipped to a random page. "'The Dark Hollow.' Why are all the songs about dark things? Is Léandor a dark place?"

"Maybe. I've heard the forest of Yanna is supposed to be a little scary." Lirien only repeated what he'd learned from books and whispers.

Sorin handed him the green volume, and Lirien read to himself.

I sing a song sad and profound:
My lover's far from me.
He's travelled low beneath the ground,
To places I can't see.
I searched the wood but found him not
Within the dark hollow.
He's gone to places darker still,
To where I cannot follow.

The lyrics were bittersweet, well-suited for a final farewell. But it seemed a little short, until Lirien examined the score. It was meant to be sung in rounds, with new parts added for harmony.

"No good."

"Not for children?"

"It needs at least four people, and they all come in at

different times, and their notes change slightly so it blends together better." He pointed at each row to show the different voices.

"How does it go?"

"Do you want to try to read it?"

Sorin squinted at the notes. "F, F, G, A-flat…"

"Good work." Lirien ruffled his hair. "Can you read it with the sounds?"

"Nah, I don't hear anything in my head when I say the letters."

"That's all right. It's something you can learn later if you want."

"But you can hear it when you look at it. All of it?"

"Yes." Lirien sang the lead first, then showed him the variances in the other parts. "It might be hard to imagine, but those voices coming in and out at different times, layered on top of each other, that's what makes the song sad."

"Not the words?"

"They're sad, too. But sometimes the words don't carry the meaning, even when it seems like they do. The sound is where the power lies."

"Power? Like magic?"

"It's not something I can explain very well," Lirien conceded. "Help me again? One last try?"

"Yup." Sorin found a random page and read the title. "'The Ocean Dark.' Oh, this book. Dark, dark, dark." He rolled his eyes as he pushed it back to Lirien, whose breath seized when he read the words.

It took you on a blust'ry day.
The wind was cool, the sky was gray.
The cold waves that brushed 'cross your skin,
The tide's embrace that drew you in—

The ocean dark, it was your end.
I took your hand but could not keep
You from the bitter, drowning deep.
Like the moon enclosed by cloud,
A veil of foam became your shroud.
The ocean dark, it was your end.
A voice unheard called you to sea,
And stole you far away from me.
So my own words are what remain.
I sing it now, a sad refrain:
The ocean dark, it was your end.
Farewell my dear, my love, my friend.

Sorin tugged on the hem of Lirien's linen shirt. "What's wrong?"

"It's a bit painful to read."

"Because it's the sea?"

"Yes. And it's not a happy story."

"Oh. Don't sing it for me, then."

"That's fine. But... I think this might be the one." It wasn't the childhood song his father knew. But the emotion of the words and its melody might be strong enough to call him back. Even though it was a song of goodbye, perhaps with enough pain it would penetrate the depths, and he could welcome his father home. Lirien would sing it with all his heart and passion.

THE NIGHT WAS COOLER than usual, the blackish-blue sky illuminated by a bright waning moon. Lirien once again ventured down to the shore around the time he believed his father had disappeared, and he walked out into the sea until the water came up to his knees.

He took a few breaths in preparation. He'd committed the song he would sing to memory, but he felt like he couldn't just start singing it. He had to ready his mind to summon his deepest emotions from their hiding places, giving them shape and form through sound.

Lirien stood still, eyes closed. He listened to the pattern of the waves to settle himself, and, when he could no longer hear the pounding of his own heart in his ears, began.

"It took you on a blust'ry day,
The wind was cool, the sky was gray…"

The waves grew in power as he sang.

"The cold waves that brushed 'cross your skin,
The tide's embrace that drew you in—
The ocean dark, it was your end."

He made it all the way through, with a voice full of contradictions: tremulous and bold, timid and fierce, cautious and foolhardy. With all his effort, it was the best he'd ever sounded.

He opened his eyes, searching the waters where he'd lost Father. He waited and waited.

He sighed, steadied himself, and tried once again.

Then again.

Many, many times, with no change in outcome.

Through the song he grieved, pleaded, cursed, and cried out. Meanwhile, the moon shone steadily. The clouds came and went on their way. The waves rolled in and out and gave up nothing.

He lost awareness of the passage of time. He sensed he'd

been out there too long. But he kept trying, even as his body shook from the dangerous cold that crept into his bones. Lirien remained rooted to his spot until the tingling left his legs and numbness crept in.

"Farewell, my dear, my love, my friend."

He should've known he would fail. It was foolish for him to try. Why was he born to a creature of great magic and power if none of her gifts were passed to him?

He bitterly splashed the water with his hands, shouting to the horizon, "Damn it! Why did you have to listen to her, Father? I'm here. I'm your son! *Listen to me!*"

Something sharp poked him in his back, worse than a bite or a sting. Lirien whirled around, his hand instantly flying to the spot where he felt pain, and his fingers met with blood.

The Queen stood there in the water with him, her hair wild, tears streaming down her cheeks, her face twisted in desperation. In her hand she held a dagger, the tip of it covered in red.

"I'll push it in again, and much more, so help me," the Queen said, her voice shaking.

Lirien's gaze darted to the castle walls, hoping someone would see his predicament, but the Queen had dismissed the guards for her privacy again. "Your Majesty, please, don't!"

"I'm tired of seeing your wasted efforts. Nothing you've done has been good enough."

"I know that! I know. But you can't—"

"Did you think I didn't mean it when I said I'd have your life? Believe me, believe me now! Can I make it plainer, what's at stake if you fail me again?" She swiped the weapon at his stomach, and Lirien jerked back, narrowly avoiding the blade.

"Sing," she commanded.

"I have. It didn't work—"

"It didn't work because it was wrong. You sang without magic."

She lunged at him again, and Lirien took a step back into the ocean, his hands in front of him in a defensive pose. The Queen's knife drew a crimson line across his palm.

Lirien clutched his hand. "Majesty!"

"You're a siren," the Queen said, advancing. *"Sing the siren's song."*

As soon as she spoke, something from Lirien's memory wound its way through his brain. A song in a melancholy minor, with no discernable patterns or words, ethereal and beautiful, came to him in that moment.

He let out a gasp as the melody forced its way out of him. He whirled around to face the ocean, and the music poured out of him like a dam had burst. The power of those notes coursed through him, like a buzz humming through every vein in his body. His vision clouded, his ears were filled only with the sound of the song— and when he finished, he collapsed into the water.

He felt himself tugged at from above, the Queen reaching under the crooks of his arms to pull him back to his feet, the dagger in her hand gone.

Something was wrong. A flush, a ruby glow, colored her pale skin. Her eyes were open wide, almost unnaturally so, yet at the same time glossy and glazed over, her pupils large and dilated. It was like she was staring through his body, her gaze piercing his bones and organs.

"Lirien," she breathed.

He went rigid at his name. The Queen had never sounded that way with him before. Tender, yet fierce. Earnest and urgent and protective. Suddenly he was hyper-aware of every sensation: the icy sting of the water, his legs stiff and cold, and the weight of his fatigue.

"Your Majesty. What is… is there… are you all right?" he stammered, trying his best not to shout, *What is wrong with you?*

She trembled, and the rosiness of her skin crept into her cheeks. Then, her hand flew to her heart. "You... you are so beautiful. *I had no idea.*"

Lirien retreated. Her eyes, what was wrong with her eyes?

She reached toward him, her long fingers shaking. "I've hurt you." She blinked, and a tear dripped down her face. "I've hurt you, and I'm sorry."

Lirien couldn't believe it. In all his years, he'd never heard an apology of any kind come from her. But something about it, the way she looked, the way she spoke— it didn't feel right.

"Come inside," the Queen said. "Come with me, where it's warm."

"I'll be fine." He took another step from her.

She slowly moved in closer, as if she were coaxing a frightened animal out of the corner. Then she grabbed him by the wrists and tugged. "Please."

Lirien shook his head, mostly with disbelief: "please" was a word she rarely used with him.

As the Queen led Lirien back to shore, he managed, "Majesty, what are you doing? What is this? How could you forget what you've said to me; what you've done to me?"

"I made a mistake. I need to take care of you."

The Queen didn't let him go until they made it to the rocky beach. Lirien just wanted to get away from her. "It doesn't matter now. As Your Majesty said, I should go inside."

He struggled up over the rocks, as his body ached and his boots were slick from the sea, but when the land flattened again, he quickened his pace. Despite the weight of her soggy skirts, the Queen was sure-footed and kept up easily.

What is going on? Is she chasing me?

Lirien gave up trying to escape her when she followed him up the spiraling steps of his tower. He stopped just outside the door to his room.

"Your Majesty, I'd like to be alone. Please allow it."

"I will leave you after I look at your wounds. And you will listen to what I have to say."

He relented, using his good hand to hold the door open to her. He quickly lit a taper in his room, the orange light flickering and casting shadows along the wall. He started to pull the chair out from his desk when the Queen came up behind him. She didn't sit but lifted part of his shirt up, where her dagger had gotten him in the lower back.

"Your Majesty, if you get my blood on your hands and should you touch your mouth—"

"I know. I'll be careful."

Lirien held his breath as she drew a line on his back near his wound.

"I think this needs more than a simple bandage," she said softly. "I will send for the surgeon once I leave." She pulled the fabric back down and placed her hand in between his shoulder blades, keeping it there as she spoke. "I'm so sorry. I shouldn't have done that to you."

The Queen's touch unnerved him, so he stepped out of her reach and rummaged through a drawer for a kerchief for his bleeding hand. The Queen eyed him closely, then took the cloth away from him, wrapping it around his palm herself. She moved swiftly but gently, and pressed the kerchief into his palm to soak up the bleeding. Lirien watched a line of red stretch across it, the color spreading beneath the Queen's fingers.

"Your Majesty, you'll get it on you."

"I'll wash my hands."

"Please, I can... I'll take care of it myself." He pulled his hand away from her. She was acting so strange, so careless. What had come over her? His blood was poison, and she knew it.

"You should wash up sooner than later," Lirien warned.

"I will. Just listen to what I have to say first. Sit."

"Your Majesty." He nodded, impatient for her to leave him, and sank into the chair at his desk.

"You must forgive me, Lirien." There it was again, the strange way she breathed out his name, drawing the sounds out as if to savor them. "I wasn't... I wasn't in my right mind when I hurt you. You have to understand, I've been in such despair..." Her voice became lighter, more airy: "But I'm better now."

Lirien voiced it before he could stop himself. "Are you?"

The Queen didn't seem to hear him. She had grabbed one of the thin coverlets from his bed and enclosed him in it. In the absence of a towel, she used the blanket to rub and pat the crown of his head, trying to dry him.

He held his breath as the Queen stepped behind him and worked through his hair, then moved to wiping down the back of his neck. Her movements became less aggressive and slower, more deliberate, as she dipped down under the collar of his shirt. He started to squirm in his seat. Something about the way she touched him then, how she lingered on him, made him uneasy.

When she started tugging his collar open, he stopped her hand. "Please. You don't have to."

"Shh. Let me take care of you for once."

There was an intense pressure from her, the weight of her scrutiny bearing down on him. Her glazed, unblinking eyes looked like horrors in the faint light, feverish and abnormal.

It was the song. It was the melody he sang. That had to be it. The Queen only changed after he finished the final notes of music. What had he done? And could he undo it, somehow?

The Queen brushed the coverlet along his collarbones, then the top of his chest, and then she stopped. The cloth fell to the side as she came around to the front to face him, and climbed onto his lap. She cupped his face, her thumb brushing across his chin, then along his lower lip. "Lirien," she said, the word unnerving. Her face was unbearably close to his.

Lirien flew to his feet, roughly shoving her aside. Then he froze. He'd just laid hands on the Queen. If he injured her in any way, even if it was just her pride, it was considered an offense against dignity— a treasonable act.

Lirien lowered his head to her immediately. "I'm sorry, Your Majesty. I wasn't thinking."

Queen Aurinda recovered quickly but clutched her arm where he'd touched her. "No, I can see I've frightened you. It's too much, isn't it? After all, my affections..." She trailed off in thought; then, in a more assured voice, she added, "I've done you wrong. Your entire life, you've known nothing of my love, so you cannot trust it when you see it for the first time. Therefore, I shall prove myself to you." She gestured to the floor. "Kneel before me."

Lirien's heart continued its rapid, nervous beat as he got on his knees. The Queen's behavior was not her own, he was sure of it. It was the song. Something in the song changed her for her to speak of affection and love toward him, to treat him in such a way as she never had before. He had always wanted love from her, the love of a mother to a son. But this was something different. Something unnerving.

The Queen's posture changed as she raised her voice. "I speak the words; my word is true," she said. This was the Queen's Voice, the voice of authority, of rule, of ceremony. Every consonant was crisp, clear, and assertive, every syllable struck with power. "I speak the words; my word is law. I speak the words; my word is God.

"Bastard of King Neven, I name you legitimate. Bastard of King Neven, I name you firstborn. Bastard of King Neven, you are bastard no more. I hereby name you, now and always, Prince Lirien of Ardeth."

In the absence of the ceremonial sword used for knighting and naming, Queen Aurinda touched her lips to his forehead. "Rise, my Prince."

Something like a sob escaped Lirien as he stood, a sound that could be mistaken for happiness or relief; the sensation of a drum being struck, or a taut rope released. But it was nothing more than the culmination of his anxiety and confusion that burst out of him. Nothing of what had just happened registered clearly in his mind, let alone its significance.

The Queen gripped Lirien's hair and lowered his face to hers. Her mouth was on his, then her tongue pried his lips apart and pushed its way in.

Lirien stumbled back. The force behind the kiss was fierce, almost violent, as if she wanted to consume him. His eyes watered. A tear threatened to trickle down his face, and just as quickly as the Queen attacked him, she pulled away.

She fixed his hair, smoothing it back to how he'd always parted it. "Goodnight, Lirien."

Once she was gone, Lirien sank to the floor. The muscles in his stomach seized, his throat tightened, and he heaved, but nothing would come out. He was empty.

CHAPTER 3

The next day, the Queen's announcement came abruptly. The King was officially ruled dead. The funeral was to commence that very evening, with the bonfire at sundown. Servants rushed to prepare the castle, and a hum of gossip and frantic whispering filled the halls, for Queen Aurinda had not given enough time for any emissaries and diplomats, or even the King's sister, Queen Eira of Asherin, to be in Ardeth for the ceremony.

The palace was to be decorated in brilliant red to honor King Neven, as it was his favorite color. Everyone who could attend the night's ceremony would be wearing the shade, and of course, the royal family would be dressed in their finest crimson garments.

Lirien searched his wardrobe for something to wear. He only had a red doublet, but no breeches to match, and he struggled to pair his clothing together. Even though he was a child of the King and treated relatively well, his bastard status did not afford him the same luxuries as the royal family, and this was evident in the plainer clothing he wore every day.

As he debated over black breeches versus white, holding each up to his doublet, there was a knock at the door.

He jumped, twisting his body awkwardly, and he felt a twinge at the wound in his back, which the surgeon had stitched after the Queen's horrific visit the night before. He knew after what she'd done to him, he'd be fearful of every knock that sounded, dreading the Queen's return.

It was the Queen's right hand, Corva, who arrived, a man of medium stature with olive-toned skin, a trim, short black beard on his chin, and deep brown eyes. "I bring news from the Queen." Corva did not bow to Lirien or address him in a way that indicated the Queen had spread the word of the change in Lirien's status— perhaps the Queen's decision to make him the Prince was just a whim after all. But Lirien was too uncertain to feel relief at the possibility.

Corva explained in more detail the Queen's plans for the funeral. "You are to take one item of significance to the King and place it in the casket to burn. The funeral will proceed from the castle grounds through the town, past Pinemore onto Greensward, where King Neven wished his pyre to be. You will lead the procession along with the Queen and her children."

Lirien's heart sank. "I can't."

"What do you mean?"

Lirien didn't want to explain it. The danger of leaving the sea was a secret he believed only he and the King shared. And he didn't know what would be worse— leaving in the midst of everything or not showing up at all. As far as he knew, the rest of the palace had not heard that the Queen had named him Crown Prince in his tower, so perhaps it would make sense that the King's bastard would be left out of the procession altogether.

"I would like to... be alone with my grief," he managed.

"Very well. I shall notify Her Majesty." Corva halted, then

added in a soft tone, "I am deeply sorry for the loss of your father." Before Lirien could respond in thanks, Corva bowed and departed.

Just when Lirien thought he would be alone, another visitor arrived. One of the Queen's handmaidens bore a bundle wrapped in bronze-colored paper and a black velvet bow. She passed it to Lirien. "The Queen requires you to wear this tonight for the funeral." She left quickly.

Lirien opened the package. A luxurious red doublet and matching breeches of quilted velvet and gold embroidery filled the box. He eyed it carefully. It looked familiar. He pulled the clothes out of the box and held them up to himself in the mirror, and the air escaped him.

These were his father's clothes. The Queen wanted to dress him up like his father. *Can I... can I disobey*? The handmaiden had said "require," not "request." He cringed. It was in poor taste. What was the Queen thinking?

Lirien didn't want to consider the Queen at all, but he couldn't help his thoughts turning to her. The previous night was horrible, what she had done to him... And he knew, deep down, that it was the siren's song that had changed the Queen. It had to have been. Never before had his voice done anything to anyone; never before had his music bewitched its listeners with real magic. It had to have been the melody— that specific, weird, but wondrous tune that wound its way through his mind and out his mouth.

There was more to the siren's magic than he ever knew. He was naïve to think that singing it with intention would summon the desired person to his side, that it was a simple song of calling. He should have known better. It didn't matter that as he sang, all of the will within him was directed toward bringing his father out of the sea. The melody was only meant to do one thing: seduce the one who listened.

Lirien had never considered it possible that another person than he intended would respond to his voice, especially when no part of his song was ever meant for the Queen. Then a disturbing thought entered his mind: what if there was something unvoiced deep within him all this time, something he kept buried and unnamed, that awoke with the siren's song? Did he want the Queen to love him?

No.

...Maybe.

...A little. Yes. But not like this.

Lirien dreamed of a mother to love and be loved by. With his own mother absent, Queen Aurinda was the closest he had, but of course, there was no relationship there. She refused to be anything more than the Queen to him.

Whatever this attention was now, it was nothing Lirien ever desired from her. At the memory of how she looked at him, spoke his name, touched him... his skin went clammy and his stomach knotted. He had to figure out a way to break this horrible spell; he just had to. But how?

THAT NIGHT, Lirien came to the grand entry hall just before the start of the funeral procession to say his final goodbyes. He brought his small lyre with him, a gift from his father that he felt suitable for the ceremony. The King's coffin was displayed in front of the grand staircase with hundreds of red roses surrounding it. The casket itself was woven rattan covered in gilt. It was propped open for display but with no body to burn.

Queen Aurinda and her children were already there when Lirien arrived. Meanwhile, the courtiers, nobles, and guards filled the hall to prepare for the funeral. It was quiet, yet there wasn't exactly silence at Lirien's arrival. Though no one spoke in their full voices, the whispers at Lirien's presence were audible. Several stared at him, eyeing his clothing curiously, before remarking in hushed voices.

To Lirien's surprise, the Queen raised her hand, silencing the murmuring in the hall. "Lirien, come here," she said to him, her voice soft but sure. She held her hand out to him. Lirien stared at it for a second, then the Queen gave a sharp flick of her fingers. Lirien took her hand, wincing as her fingers brushed across the wound from the night before.

"The bastard you see before you is no more," she announced in a somber but powerful voice. "Tomorrow at noon we shall have a new ceremony, the naming of the Crown Prince of Ardeth. It is my gift to you that we follow tonight's sorrowful eve with something joyous to behold." She led Lirien to his siblings, who stood aside the casket, then turned back to the crowd. "Now, let us begin."

The people's faces filled with shock— eyebrows raised up, mouths dropped open, faces changed shades —but they quickly comported themselves and made a line. They were instructed to take a single red rose from the large bouquets that flanked the casket and toss the flower inside the gilded woven coffin. As they did so, they bowed to each member of the royal family, and for the first time, that included Lirien. Lirien followed the family's cue and nodded his head to each member of the procession.

Then his gaze fell on Nina. Her eyes shined with tears, but instead of sorrow, Lirien saw anger. Her hands were curled into fists at her sides.

Lirien stepped away from the Queen's touch and he spoke in a quiet voice. "Nina, I'm so sorry." The Queen making him Crown Prince meant he had usurped the throne from Nina, who was, until the Queen's announcement, the official firstborn child.

"I don't know what to think," she managed after a moment. "I don't know if I can even say anything else to you right now. You or Mother."

Tonight, after she returned from the procession, he would have to tell her he had no part in it, that it was not what he wanted. But then he thought perhaps that might even make her feel worse... because Nina had always wanted to be Queen, had prepared for it her entire life. That the rule of Ardeth would pass to someone who wanted it not at all might be salt in her wounds.

Before Lirien could finish debating with himself as to what to say, the Queen gripped his shoulder. "You are firstborn. You will place your item first. Go now."

Lirien approached the casket with some trepidation. He felt like he had to say a final goodbye, something deep and profound, as he lowered the lyre inside. He opened his mouth to speak; nothing came. Then his eyes misted up, and he swallowed. "I hope I make you proud," he blurted. It wasn't enough. It provided no closure. But Lirien had no more words. He kissed his fingertips and touched the edge of the casket, then stepped beside it, keeping distance between himself and the Queen.

Nina was next in line. She approached carefully, looking somber. She offered something wrapped in elaborate fabric and ribbons, much like a birthday present, placing it at what would have been the King's feet. She looked to Lirien, then her mother, as though she couldn't decide where she would stand after giving the King her token. She sighed and settled for Lirien's side of the casket, though she did not stand close to him.

It was Sorin's turn to offer something up to the casket. The boy was dry-eyed but his skin had an unhealthy pale sheen to it. He gave up the small figure of a white stag which Father had made for him as a birthday present. "Goodbye," he said, his voice breaking.

Sonalie quickly followed behind. At last, she had cried. Her face was streaked with tears as she dropped in something small that Lirien couldn't make out. She said nothing.

Lastly, two of the Queen's retinue wheeled over a large wooden chest with carvings of various animals upon each side. On the left, the King's heraldic trio: serpent, swan, and stag. On the right, the Queen's: bear, wolf, and crane.

The Queen opened the chest and removed a bundle of fabric that was pearlescent and white like snow, with threads of gold and silver intertwining throughout. For a moment Lirien thought it was a ballgown, but as the folds of the garment took shape, he recognized it from numerous paintings he had seen in the palace. It was his father's clothing from his wedding.

There were whispers from some of the mourners in the room, but the Queen ignored it. She draped the pieces over top everything piled into the casket and rearranged them carefully in a way that suggested a person was, in fact, lying there.

She bore a strange look on her face, almost as though she was confused. She stared at the spot where her husband should have been, as if she was seeing the casket for the first time. Then, with a sudden tilt of her head, a movement that seemed jerky and off, she turned to Lirien and stared him down.

Lirien retreated from her gaze, taking steps back from the casket, almost bumping into Nina.

Corva broke the tension with a bow to Queen Aurinda. "Your Majesty, it is time for the procession to begin."

The Queen nodded to him, but held out her arm to Lirien. "Come with me."

Lirien froze. He thought Corva had delivered his message to the Queen. Or did she simply ignore it?

"I can't," Lirien said, and before the Queen could respond to him, he added in a pained voice, "Forgive me." Then he disappeared through the servants' door and hurried, practically running, to his tower room. He locked the door behind him, fearing the Queen's wrath. But no one came after him.

AT NOON THE NEXT DAY, Lirien kneeled before the Queen, steps away from the throne, while the royal family, the top officers of the guard, and the entirety of the court looked on. His breath seized for a moment as he felt the weight of hundreds of eyes fixed upon him, heavier than the weight of the crown just placed upon his head. Only one thing remained of the ceremony, then it would all be real. Absolutely, incontestably real.

Lirien unfastened the top of his collar and held it open as the Queen removed her glove, dipping her fingers into an ancient jeweled bowl made of burnished gold. It contained the sacred oil long used to sanctify royalty, a shimmering amber liquid with floating fragments of gold leaf.

As her fingers approached him, he flinched. He remembered the night she touched him, lingering too long, her hand on his skin as she forced her kiss. He hoped it was subtle enough the Queen wouldn't notice, but she did, and peered at him, eyes unblinking, as she anointed him. She drew a circle on his forehead to represent the sun, and once more on his chest, as her voice rang through the presence chamber: "One mind, one heart, for Ardeth."

Lirien hurriedly buttoned the neckline of his father's coronation costume and rose to his feet, turning to the crowd before him as the Queen formally named him. "I present to you His Royal Highness Crown Prince Lirien, firstborn son of King Neven, future King of Ardeth."

The applause was immediate, but Lirien couldn't help

noticing the expressions of numerous courtiers: forced smiles, furrowed brows, looks of confusion and appraisal. He understood. He did not deserve, nor was he qualified for, his position. Though he was known to those inside the castle, he had no idea about the rest of the kingdom outside its walls. He didn't know what they knew of him. What kind of turmoil would his legitimization bring?

He looked to the side, where his sisters and brother stood in a line in full ceremonial costume. Each outfit was crafted in a variation of gold, embroidered with sunbursts, rays of white light, and metallic braids to represent Ardeth as a golden realm of sunlight. Only Sorin looked at him, his cheeks rosy and his grin filled with absolute delight. Sonalie was preoccupied with her gown, tugging on the skirt and pulling at her sleeves. And Nina, whose cool, regal smile mirrored her mother's, met the crowd's eyes instead of his.

Lirien looked away from Nina, still feeling guilt every time he saw her, and then Queen Aurinda gestured for him to link arms with her. They led the procession from the presence chamber through the watch hall and into the grandiosely designed great hall, which was set up for the feast and revel.

He could hardly tolerate the Queen's touch, and while he had to escort her, he tried to keep some distance between them, holding his arm aside as much as he could until the Queen reached over with her free hand and pulled him closer, making the link between them tighter.

"Don't avoid me, Lirien," she murmured as they walked. "I forgive you for last night's scene— I assume you were overcome —but you will not deny me your presence again. You shall be by my side. I command it."

Lirien swallowed, managing a feeble, "Your Majesty."

"'My Queen.'"

"Pardon?"

"As it pleases me, you will refer to me as 'my Queen.' And you will take your place in the King's chambers from here on."

Lirien's stomach churned, and he worried his breakfast might come up as the Queen's words reached him. He felt like she was a spider spinning a web for him to fall into, setting a trap to keep him close to her before she would strike at him again. "Father's hardly been gone and you told me to bring him back to you. Why would you give me his rooms?"

"The King is dead. We had his funeral. He cannot come back. When the time comes, you will be King, and you need to understand that role as soon as possible. Do not fight this. Do not fight me, Lirien."

He couldn't believe this same woman who had spent days quietly sobbing to herself, staring out to sea for her lost husband, could speak so harshly of his father now.

She patted his arm. "Take that look off your face. Show your gratitude to your family and to the people. Enjoy this moment."

He hadn't realized they were already at the banquet. The servants pulled out the seats for the members of the royal family, and at the very center, Lirien was made to sit with Queen Aurinda, in the King's former chair.

It did not go unnoticed by the crowd. The murmur began as a dull rumble through the hall, and Lirien squirmed in his seat.

Wearing his father's clothes. Taking his father's chair. Being forced into his father's bedchamber. The Queen was wasting no time setting Lirien in his father's place, and a horrid feeling overtook Lirien as he wondered to what degree.

Everyone went silent as soon as the Queen rose to her feet. "Good people of Ardeth, our most loyal subjects. Today is a remarkable day, one to be remembered for the ages. For with you today is a young man who should not exist— who should not be here."

The crowd couldn't hide their shock. Even Lirien was

stunned that the Queen would so bluntly voice what they must all be feeling.

"What you see before you is a miracle. A child of the sea, a child of the sun. A child of siren and human alike. It was the sin of my pride that kept him from you, as he was not mine. Yet you can see with your own eyes, in spite of how magic has molded him, he is King Neven's flesh and blood."

The Queen's voice faltered. Her eyes grew glassy, as if she would cry. Lirien couldn't tell if she was genuine or if this was all part of the showmanship required of being a royal figure. But like everyone else in the great hall, he was drawn to her words.

She took a moment to continue, her voice wavering. "My husband long desired to see his firstborn legitimized, but in his love for me, he suppressed his wishes in deference to mine. But the weight of my shame for what I've done to Neven, to Lirien, has brought me to this moment. In honor of my husband, I grant his desire— to welcome Lirien as heir. To love him deeply as I have never before. And I ask all of my people, whom I hold dear in my heart, to love him, too."

The Queen's words were a calming balm to the audience before them. In that moment, any doubts or concerns advertised on their faces were brushed aside. As if commanded, suddenly everyone in the hall bowed to Queen Aurinda and Prince Lirien.

Even Lirien's heart was warmed by the Queen's speech, but he did not know if he could trust it. Her behavior, her mood, her words— each flitted from one extreme to the next, and he always felt on his guard. Who knew how she would startle him next?

Indeed, Queen Aurinda was not finished with her surprises. She beckoned for everyone in the room to be seated at the banquet tables. "At this juncture we would traditionally have Prince Lirien give the Oath of Ardeth, which solidifies the people's love for their Prince. I do not think this sufficient. For you to love Prince Lirien, to truly adore him, you cannot do so until you hear him sing."

Lirien felt the blood drain from his face as she spoke those words. She hadn't warned him in any way that this was coming. And of course, he could not refuse her as it would shame her before the court.

With the wave of her hand, Queen Aurinda summoned to her side a lady-in-waiting, who presented her with a single sheet of parchment.

"I have chosen an old ballad from my country of Ilvelend, 'The Winter Rose,' for Prince Lirien to sing, as it will show you the range and beauty of his voice. You will, no doubt, fall in love with him." She handed the paper to Lirien and whispered, "They are not there. Think only of me. You will sing this for me."

Lirien glanced at the score and lyrics, noticing that words were substituted, such as "snow-white hair" for "raven hair," and he had the sickening notion that the Queen truly intended the song to be for her, the Queen with blonde hair so pale that it looked almost white.

The Queen looked up at the balcony where the musicians were stationed and gestured again. The player holding the harp plucked the first notes of the introduction.

Lirien took in a tremulous breath and sang.

"In the dusty white, in the dark of night
Grows the scarlet 'mid the gloom.
Rise, oh winter rose, high above the snows!
'Tis the blood that makes the bloom.
'Twas a maiden fair born with snow-white hair,
And my bride I thought she'd be.
Though she had my heart, we were torn apart—
She was given not to me.

For one final time her lips met with mine,
And she vowed that she'd be free.
On her wedding night she would take her flight
And find her way back to me.
How the cold winds blew as she journeyed through—
How the ice cut like a blade!
On the snowy path, she did flee his wrath—
But he found her in the glade.
She would rather die than she with him lie,
She would never warm his bed.
Though I'd meet her soon, under light of moon,
She had took the knife instead.
When I saw her there, with her snow-white hair—
How the petals fell, so red.
How that crimson rose dyed the pristine snows!
There my love lay froze and dead.
In the dusty white, in the dark of night
Grows the scarlet 'mid the gloom.
Rise, oh winter rose, high above the snows!
'Tis the blood that makes the bloom."

A silent awe pervaded the room when Lirien finished. He scanned the crowd and saw some eyes closed in reverence, others shining with unshed tears, and still some faces smiling from the ballad's beauty. Undeniably Lirien could see they were impressed with him, and perhaps the Queen's words rang true: maybe they could love him as their new prince and heir.

Queen Aurinda stared at Lirien, her bosom slowly heaving, her eyes dark and glassy.

Lirien wanted to back away from the Queen. He had no magic in his voice this time— he did not try for it, anyway — but she looked the same as she had the night she'd kissed him, feverish and transfixed. No one else around him bore those expressions, just the Queen.

She burst into applause and the chamber followed suit, the sound of clapping echoing all over the high ceilings, the sound growing thunderous as it bounced through the hall.

Lirien didn't know what to say or do to convey his appreciation to them, so he started to bow, but Queen Aurinda stopped him. "Now you are Prince. You bow to no one but your Queen," she said in hushed tones.

Lirien settled on giving them a small, polite smile. Then the Queen grabbed the large golden goblet from her place setting and raised it to the room. The wine had already been poured at the tables, so the courtiers and nobles stood and raised their cups in turn.

"To Lirien," the Queen said, "Crown Prince of Ardeth."

"To Lirien!" the crowd echoed, and everyone drank, then resumed their seats once the Queen had taken her place at the table.

Then the ripple of voices began. "Please, please, sing again!"

"Once more!"

"Another, Your Highness, we beg you!"

Queen Aurinda smiled to Lirien in self-satisfaction. "See, they love you." Her hand wandered to Lirien's leg, climbing his thigh. "But no one can love you as I."

Lirien jerked his leg away, rising to his feet, sending his chair back toward the wall with a loud scrape along the floor. As it echoed through the hall, all eyes were on him, then everyone rose to their feet to give him a deep, reverential bow that custom demanded was always due to him from his subjects.

It was too much. "I can't— I can't do this," Lirien stammered to the Queen.

"Lirien. Don't." The Queen's tone was filled with warning, but she kept her voice quiet, as though not to make a scene.

"I can't stay here with you."

The Queen looked as if she were struck, and her eyes glassed up again. "Don't go. You have a duty. To them and to me."

Lirien shook his head. "I can't. Let me go."

He didn't wait for more words from her. He ignored the throngs of people watching him, his siblings' perplexity, and the Queen, who looked as though she would cry any moment. He rushed out of the great chamber and through the halls, making his way to the only place in the entire castle where he felt safe— the southwest watchtower.

He ran up the stairs and halted when he spied the door to his room.

It was completely bricked off.

CHAPTER 4

Lirien stood there gaping at the newly made wall, and then shock turned to horror when he realized the extent to which the Queen would go to keep him under her control.

He felt along the line of bricks. Most of the mortar holding the bricks together was still damp, and he considered ramming himself against the wall and breaking it apart. But what good would it do, aside from buying him a single night more in his rightful room? And perhaps not even the full night. If the Queen were desperate enough to seal off his doorway, who knew what else she would try?

Lirien fled outside and ran to the beach. He needed help from the one person he knew could get through to the Queen; the only person she would listen to, even though it would be just as impossible to reach him as before.

"Father!" he called, as he rushed into the cold, dark ocean.

Something took a hold of him. He felt the strong compulsion to sing the siren's song again, but he pushed it down deep inside of him, fearful of what would happen if anyone else were to hear it. And yet the forbidden melody was there, coiled and waiting in his throat, ready to burst free if he so much as opened his mouth to breathe. He tried to distract himself and seized upon a random snippet of song that popped in his head — lyrics from an old ballad of a woman waiting for her lover's return from war.

He sang.

"Come back to me, whate'er the cost.
Without you I am truly lost."

He pictured his father as he repeated the words, visualizing him rising out of the sea like an ancient god coming to shore after a long slumber below. He sang these two lines again and again as time passed, filling the words and music with his desperation.

Then, he heard from behind him: "Lirien! My Prince!"

Lirien whirled around, startled to see the Queen at the edge of the shore, calling out to him.

"No." Lirien shook his head. "No, not you."

The Queen didn't seem to hear over the din of the waves and her skirts sloshing through them.

Lirien didn't know where to retreat. The Queen cornered him against the endless sea, shouting, "How dare you leave me! Don't you know how that made me feel, to watch you walk away from me again?" Her hands reached out to him. "I care for you. I care for you so much. Why won't you let me show you?"

When she was close enough, she roughly grabbed his collar and pulled him down to her to kiss him.

The moment her mouth touched his, Lirien took her by the shoulders and flung her aside into the water.

Oh no, oh no, oh no, what did I do?

"I'm sorry, Your Ma— my —"

He couldn't bring himself to say it, to call her his Queen. But he couldn't just leave her there in the water, as much as he wanted to.

He helped her up from the waves, but the Queen pulled herself out of his grasp long enough to slap his face once, then twice, then a third time, in rapid succession. She let out a horrified gasp, and that tearful, wild-eyed look spread across her face again. "I didn't mean to— I don't know what came over me."

Lirien's lip throbbed, a strange humming pain near the corner of his mouth. He tasted sweetness there. She'd split his lip.

The Queen frantically grabbed Lirien's wrist and pulled him toward shore.

"Please. Let go of me."

"What if you run from me again?"

"I won't, so please, let me go."

The Queen reluctantly unhanded him, but Lirien kept his word and followed her out of the sea and onto the beach.

"I will call an end to the feast and revel for the night, and send for a physician to clean your wound. This is the second time I've hurt you..."

Lirien wondered how many more times she would.

AFTER THE PHYSICIAN came and went, Lirien did not sleep at all that night. He couldn't put words to how wrong it felt to lie in his father's massive, elaborately carved four-post bed. Its heavy gold curtains of silk, embroidered with looping red thread, shut out all light and encased him in. He already missed his open, simple bed and his balconette window overlooking a sea that stretched for miles.

He couldn't smell the salt in the air here.

None of the items in his own room had been brought to his father's chambers. Even his clothing was left behind in the tower, leaving only his father's indescribable finery, which it seemed the Queen would continue to have him wear.

Lirien found no trace of himself anywhere in this place.

The discovery of a private corridor to the Queen's apartment disturbed him the most, a door concealed within a giant painting of the heraldic animals bowing to the sun, the only evidence of its existence a faint outline in the canvas. There Lirien was, readily available to the Queen at any time she wished, and at some unknown late hour as he lay in bed, he heard a faint click and then watched his bed curtains slowly draw open.

Queen Aurinda stood there in her nightgown and robe, holding a candle.

"You're awake," she said. She set the candle on his night table and sat next to him upon the bed, practically on top of his legs. She took him by the chin, tilting his head up so she could examine his cut. "It looks much better."

Lirien couldn't stand it. He jerked his head from her grasp and pulled his legs back from hers. "Please. Stop touching me."

The Queen winced. "It hurts me to hear you say that."

"You've hurt me many times over."

She lowered her head. "This feeling comes over me, whenever you refuse my love..." Then she gave him a desperate look. "I don't understand why you reject me. I love you. I've *always* been in love with you."

Coldness enveloped Lirien's body and his heart seemed to drop to his stomach. No. The Queen was revising their history. How much did the siren spell distort the truth?

"What do you remember of the night I sang?"

"I heard you sing sad lyrics for the King. And then I... I hurt you. And then you were in the water, and I felt this over-whelming— I don't know how to describe it —*feeling* as all my thoughts were flooded with you. I knew I wanted you, how badly I wanted you. I would follow you anywhere. You realize that, don't you?"

She was missing the most important part. "What about what I sang? The song without words?"

Her voice sounded soft and far away. "I don't know what you mean. I saw you there, in the water, and I knew— my entire life was building toward that moment. All I knew, all I know, is how much love I have for you. If only you would let me show you."

She reached for him then, and Lirien flew out of the bed to his feet.

"This isn't coming from you, Your Majesty. Why can't you realize that?" Lirien's own voice trembled. "It was the song I sang. The siren's song. It bewitched you. You do not love me, and you never have, not even when I was a boy praying for a mother's love from you."

"I cannot love you as a mother," she said, rising to her feet. "You cannot ask that of me. Not when I have so much more love inside of me than that. A love that promises body and soul—"

"Do you even hear yourself? You would never dare to say such things to me, not before the song. You were not warm to me. You did not care for me. You endured me. Nothing more."

"None of that matters now. Don't you see? I am here now, ready to give myself to you." And with that, she opened her robe and started tugging at the ribbons that kept her bodice closed.

Lirien panicked, running to her srnd pulling her robe shut. "Stop this. It will never happen."

To his relief, the Queen kept her robe closed and retied the belt at her waist. "Though you hurt me with such words, the love I feel for you is stronger than my pain. I will leave you be for the night." She headed to the hidden door to her room. "But I can only be patient for so long, Lirien. Soon you will learn how extraordinary my love can be."

She left him alone then.

Lirien didn't trust that she would be gone for the night. She could reenter his room any time while he slept. He needed to find safety somewhere, but with his tower closed to him, he could only think of one other place— the library.

He grabbed the candle that the Queen had left on his night-stand and headed out of his room, down the hall. Once he recognized where the servants' corridors were again, he took them to the library. He ignored the giant hearth, preferring to sleep hidden among the shelves. He chose a plush high-backed chair tucked away deep in the stacks and tried to still his heart-beat with slow, steady breaths. He closed his eyes and begged for sleep to come.

THAT FORBIDDEN, calamitous melody returned to Lirien in the dark. The breathiness of the voice, the strange tug at his waist, the energy that danced in the air. He was swept along by it from one end of the castle to the other, then out to the shoreline. Only this time, he didn't stop at the sands. He kept going, trudging into the ocean, walking until the water was at his thighs, his chest, his chin... and then two arms of glimmering skin, long and beautiful, wrapped around him from behind and pulled him under.

You would not stay away, her voice echoed in his mind.

Somehow, this time, Lirien could see in the water clearly. A strange mass, a dark form, floated slowly up from the bottom of the sea until it was no longer shapeless but the figure of a person. A man.

"Father!" Lirien shouted it under the water, but the words came out muffled and distorted.

The man's eyes opened, a brilliant golden-brown color, his light hair moving to the rhythm of the water. He was only a few feet below Lirien now, and he reached upward to him—

I warned you not to follow. Now you will see.

His mother let Lirien go, but he remained rooted in place. Something held him there beneath the sea, and he helplessly watched the scene unfold before him.

The siren, kissing his father passionately.

His father, in a daze, returning that kiss.

The siren, growing in size...

Her teeth growing longer, sharper...

Her mouth opening, wider and wider...

Her jaw detaching—

Lirien shut his eyes. He couldn't look. He prayed Father felt nothing, that it didn't hurt, that it was quick—

Something forced Lirien's eyes open.

His mother, gone. His father, gone.

Queen Aurinda was before him, her crystalline eyes vivid in the blackish blue of the sea, her pale blonde hair looking bright white in the dark ocean.

She reached out and cupped his face.

Something moved inside of Lirien, a force that seized him, that weighed his body down with unbelievable pressure. He felt no willpower, no control, only instinct.

His body stretched, his bones and muscles ached as he grew in size.

His teeth were burning. Something in him snapped, unhinged. His mouth fell open, his jaw stretching apart, and he bent over Queen Aurinda and—

Lirien bolted out of his chair, his body covered in sweat, his heart beating fast. He wiped his damp forehead and ran his fingers through his hair, glad it was just a nightmare and that daylight crept in through the windows of the library.

A face poked out at him through one of the bookcases, startling Lirien. He recognized his old tutor, Kerrick, looking back at him.

"A rough night, Your Highness?" Their voice came out less humorous and more concerned.

"It's been a while, Kerrick. I haven't seen you since you started teaching Sorin and Sonalie."

Kerrick stepped out from behind the shelves and gave a little bow. A strand of wavy silver hair fell from their otherwise slicked-back, gelled coiffure, and with a dark, red-brown hand, they tucked it behind their ear as they straightened their back to Lirien. "Those two keep me quite busy, Your Highness."

"You can still call me Lirien. I'd prefer it."

"Yes… but it's better if I address you so only in confidence. I can't be seen undermining your new title. It would upset the Queen." They reached into their small leather case, brimming with papers, and from the inner pocket pulled out a kerchief. "Here. Keep it."

Lirien accepted it and wiped the sweat from his brow. "Thank you."

"I'll be teaching you again soon," Kerrick said. "I've been ordered to prepare you for your eventual kingship. There's much to catch you up on. But for now— are you all right?"

"Truthfully, I've had an awful night," Lirien said. He desperately wanted to confide in someone about everything that had happened with the Queen, but he worried about the repercussions of doing so. And what use would it be? Who would be able to help him escape her?

Then Lirien thought of something. "Kerrick, now that I'm Crown Prince... I can make certain demands of you, yes?"

Kerrick raised an eyebrow. "Yes, but nothing that may supersede the Queen's command."

"Who was it that ordered certain knowledge be kept from me as a child?"

Kerrick sighed. They seemed to know exactly what Lirien was getting at. "The King and Queen both agreed to raise you as human, and found no need for you to uncover the... *darker* knowledge of your siren heritage. If you're looking for the *Mysterium Syrenum*, I cannot help you. You are still barred from reading it."

Lirien's hand curled into a fist. "Fine. I won't read the book. But I'm Crown Prince now, and I'm not a child— there must be something you can tell me about the sirens after all these years. All I've heard are pieces of fairy tales and rhymes, nothing more. I know they were once birds that lost their wings and fell into the sea, but I don't know why they exist or what their purpose is."

"Well, I think you already know this, but their magic is only meant for one purpose: to seduce and kill."

"So there really is no way to bring someone back from their spell?"

"You speak of the King," Kerrick said somberly. "As painful as it is, the Queen was right to have his funeral. If the siren took the King, there is no saving him."

"And yet the Queen bade me to return him to her."

"Such a cruel thing to ask of you," Kerrick said, and added in a hushed tone, "Please don't repeat that."

"I tried to bring him back. I did. But it didn't work as I'd hoped. He's gone. There's no way he would have survived the water." Lirien's eyes misted up. "I couldn't save him from drowning."

Kerrick gently squeezed Lirien's shoulder. "Forgive me. It's clear you want the truth. He did not drown, Lirien. Sirens don't simply drown their victims. They eat them."

Lirien shuddered, remembering his dream. Of course. That was what the dream was showing him— his mother about to devour his father. But then Lirien had changed, too, as though he would consume the Queen. That was the most disturbing part of his nightmare.

"What I'm going to tell you will be difficult to take," Kerrick continued. "Forgive me. But sirens, scattered afar though they may be, are born for one thing only— to feed. They spend their lives working on their human prey, seducing them one by one, and when their victim is chosen, they are bound to each other until the siren eats. Then the siren moves on from one hunting ground to the next."

As Lirien listened, he realized that's what his mother had meant in her final words to him on the night she took Father. That she couldn't help what she was. That he would not see her again. She would devour her prey, and move on. Somewhere, she was hunting again.

He felt a twinge of... It wasn't sadness, but disappointment, and a sense of loss.

And yet, something nagged at him. If it were all that simple — siren seduces victim, siren eats victim —why did King Neven live so long? How was Lirien born, let alone allowed to live?

"Kerrick, if she chose my father as prey... did she starve herself for twenty years? Why did she wait all this time to feed?"

"I have always wondered about that, Your Highness. Sirens may rely on the power of seduction and obsession to win over their prey, but they don't mate with them. They devour them. And yet, here you are, proof of what was always thought impossible. Perhaps there was something more there between your parents, more than what we can understand."

Like love.

That's what Lirien's mother had told him.

That's what he couldn't believe.

Kerrick shifted in their seat, crossing their legs. "You are so special, Lirien. If you think about it, you shouldn't even be alive. But the King protected you. Your mother allowed you to be raised until you came of age... she waited twenty years before her nature took over."

Lirien thought on his mother's words, that she could not help who she was.

"Sirens forever crave the flesh of humans and are doomed to forever be unsatisfied by it," Kerrick said. "Sirens only know the desire to possess, to consume. Likewise, their magic— their beautiful song —summons that same compulsion in their victim. No matter what else there was between your parents, no matter that you lived, what happened to your father was inevitable. Your mother could not fight off the compulsion to devour her prey. The King could not fight off his compulsion to be devoured."

Lirien now understood. It didn't matter that he was born of a human father, that he had human blood in his veins. As soon as the siren's awful magic had burst out of him, he'd lost that part of himself. The venomous song, once sung, was beyond his control.

And if the siren's power triggered obsession in those bewitched by it...

Lirien swallowed uneasily as the truth hit him. "She'll never stop."

Kerrick could not know Lirien referred to the Queen. "No, Your Highness, sirens cannot help themselves. They will not stop until they consume their prey."

And what would happen to Lirien? He felt no desire to... consume the Queen. He wanted nothing more than to be free of her, and far away.

And yet, his siren song had worked its vicious magic within the Queen. Could he be sure it wasn't working the same poison within himself, however slowly?

A wave of revulsion mixed with fear washed over Lirien, and he buried his face in his hands.

Kerrick bowed their head. "I'm so sorry, Lirien."

"Is there... is there really no way to stop the magic of the siren's song? Will it always end with the victim being eaten?"

"There's only one way I know of, only one way the old texts make clear. The siren must die. It's too late to do anything for your father. Killing your mother would merely be an act of vengeance at this point, and it would be too dangerous to undertake. I wish I had better news for you."

But Lirien didn't hear Kerrick— not past those four words that echoed over and over in his brain:

the siren must die the siren must die the siren must die

"You've gone pale. You slept away from the hearth, and you're just in your nightclothes. You should return to your room, Your Highness. It would be a shame if you were to catch cold."

Lirien nodded absentmindedly. "Thank you, Kerrick," he mumbled, and staggered away from them as they gave him another polite bow.

But then Kerrick reached out to him. "Your Highness. I just thought of something. But it's incredibly dangerous."

That snapped Lirien out of his daze. "What?"

"I'm going to send a book to you to read— *The Book of Stones*. Take a look at the chapter on havoc stones. They have the power to grant any wish, but... humans can't do magic, so the spell always backfires when a human tries to use them. Yet, you're not entirely human, so it's possible you might manage it..." Kerrick shrugged. "It works better for magical creatures, but not all the time. The stone asks for a hefty price and often grants the wish with unforeseen consequences. Even so, perhaps something could work out for you, if you were to find one."

"Yes, send the book my way, please."

"I can have it delivered to your tower in about twenty minutes or so."

"Ah... I don't... I don't live in the tower anymore." Lirien felt his face flush, the heat pooling in his cheeks. "I am required to live in the King's chambers."

"Required?" Kerrick's face registered confusion, but they chose to say nothing more on it. "Well, then. Give me twenty minutes, Your Highness." They bowed and left Lirien to himself.

Havoc stones.

Lirien didn't like the sound of that, but he thought no harm would come to him for reading about them, or considering them. Once he learned more, he would decide what to do. He'd thought himself willing to do anything to break the spell on the Queen, but now he wasn't so sure. If the havoc stones caused that much chaos, would it be worth the risk?

CHAPTER 5

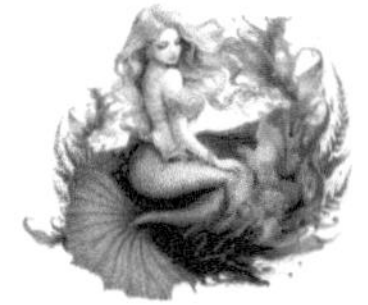

Lirien awaited Kerrick's delivery of the *Book of Stones* in the King's room.

When he'd first entered, he'd looked around the bedchamber for signs of the Queen. He'd debated whether or not he should open the secret door to her room to see if she was there, but decided not to, because what if she was?

There was a knock on the door and Lirien, expecting Kerrick's book, was surprised to see the Queen's right hand standing there.

"Your Highness," began Corva, "this afternoon's luncheon has been postponed for an hour. The Queen is currently engaged with the ministers of the treasury. She would bid you to come but feels you are not yet prepared to handle the responsibility of today's emergency. She says you will, in good time, work with her, but not today."

"What happened?"

"Did you not hear? The Glynnan elves attacked the treasury to take back Alibrandr. I'd thought they'd give up after their last disastrous attempt, but I suppose not."

Alibrandr, reputed to be one of the greatest swords ever

made, a creation imbued with magic. As a child, Lirien had been to the room in the treasury where it was kept only one time. The case that kept it was layered with chains, so much that you could only see the hilt of the sword in its scabbard, and nothing else.

But Lirien remembered the strange energy emanating from the case. It made the atmosphere in the room crisp and clean, like how the air felt just before a snowfall. That sensation lingered with him long after he left the treasury, a taste of the magic within the blade.

"Did they get the sword?" Lirien asked.

"Between you and me, Your Highness...almost. But Alibrandr is safe and locked away from unsavory folk."

Lirien wouldn't dare say this in the presence of the court or Her Majesty, but it never sat right with him that the kingdom of Ardeth possessed a sacred artifact that had always belonged to a different people in a different realm. But humans coveted magic tools, since they could not do magic on their own. And Alibrandr was said to be sharp enough to slice the air into pieces and rend the heavens.

Exactly what that meant— or even if it was true —no one could say. Once the royals of Ardeth had the sword in their hands, they soon discovered that none of them could unlock its true potential. It was reputedly sharp and of excellent craftmanship, but as for cutting through the heavens, it seemed only the elves from the mountains of Glynna could awaken that power.

Instead, Ardeth justified keeping the sword in its treasury to prevent anyone else from wielding it, claiming it was safer to lock it away. If the sword fell back into the hands of the elves again, who knew how they would use it? Would they retaliate? Would they subdue and conquer the realms of the world? With that kind of power, one could imagine anything.

"Oh, and one more thing," Corva said. "For the luncheon, the Queen requires you wear the dark blue." He gestured to the wardrobe in the far corner of the room. "You'll know which one it is, she said. If you do not need me, Your Highness, I bid you good day."

He bowed and left.

Lirien opened the door to his father's wardrobe and found the outfit, the only dark blue suit of clothing there. It was a leathery sort of material dyed a royal blue, embedded with silver studs running up and down the doublet, with a set of matching pants puffed out at the thighs that Lirien didn't care for.

He was sick of being the Queen's dress-up doll, wearing his father's clothes at her behest, being given a role he didn't want. He wanted to rebel against the Queen, no matter how small it would be. Although all of the garments were his father's and he didn't know how much of an impact it would make, he exercised his will and chose something sterling gray to wear instead.

The hour passed and Lirien was summoned to lunch with the royal family. As soon as he entered the hall, the Queen's face registered the tiniest sign of displeasure at the sight of his garments— the corner of her mouth twitched and her eyes narrowed in the slightest way, but it was enough for Lirien to be satisfied.

It didn't last long. He was forced into the King's chair and the Queen's hand went right to his leg, squeezing his knee once, then resting there.

Lirien shot her a hard look. He leaned over to her and whispered, "Stop."

The Queen relented only when it was time for food to be served. She and the children helped themselves to manchet before a main course of wild boar was brought to them.

Sorin talked with his mouth full. "What happened with the elves?"

"Sorin. Manners," the Queen responded, then dabbed her mouth with a cloth napkin. "You don't need to worry about them. They're gone."

"Kerrick taught us a song about them the other day. Wanna hear it?" Sorin didn't wait for a response and launched into lyrics celebrating the Glynnan elves and their mighty sword Alibrandr for all the things it could cut. It was meant to be a repetitive song where more silly things would be added to an ever-growing list to be recited in alphabetical order.

The Queen stopped Sorin just when he got to letter D. "That's very good, but you must understand the elves attacked us today. They hurt several guardsmen and part of the treasury sustained great damage. They are not to be celebrated in song for what they've done."

Sorin sank back in his chair. "Sorry."

"If *I* were Queen," Nina said, "I'd try to negotiate peace with the Glynnan elves. It's been far too long, going back and forth over the sword."

"The sword is dangerous," the Queen said, her voice filled with finality. "We keep it safe from those who would abuse its power. We have done what needed to be done. Lirien, you're not touching your food."

Lirien was in fact hungry, but he had a peculiar reaction to his meal. The meat was flavorless, only a texture on his tongue, nothing more. He sipped his wine, and no longer found taste there, either. It was like drinking water to him, but something less than that.

"Pardon, Your—"

Queen Aurinda shot him a look.

"Pardon, my Queen," Lirien amended. "Does anyone... does the food taste strange to you?"

"What do you mean? It's been tasted for poison already, so what could it be?"

"My plate's delicious," Sorin said.

"Delicious," Sonalie echoed.

"Is there something wrong with the flavor?" the Queen asked. "Here, you there, take this back to the kitchen and bring him a new plate."

A servant took his food away but Lirien raised his hand. "No, it's fine—"

"I insist." The servant left and the Queen handed Lirien some of the bread, her hand lingering over his as she passed it to him. "Eat this while you wait."

It was like biting into a sponge. It wasn't disgusting; it wasn't anything. The Queen carefully watched him eat it and Lirien tried not to respond in any way to draw more attention to himself. "The manchet's fine," he lied.

As Sorin and Sonalie babbled on about some of the birds they saw outside while they were playing, and while Nina was announcing that if she were Queen, she'd build an aviary for the public, a second plate of food was brought to Lirien.

It was the same as the last. All texture, the sensation of being food, but without the taste of it.

"How is it?"

"It's better. I don't know why I thought there was something wrong. It tastes good." Just so Lirien's stomach could at least be filled, he shoveled down his entire meal and finished the drink in his goblet.

As the food settled, the children continued chatting fervently, but Lirien fought off two sensations at once: yearning and disgust. Though he should have felt sated after the sizeable meal, Lirien still yearned to be satisfied, but by what, he couldn't name. And at the same time, he tried to fight off the

Queen's pawing hands, which settled on him every chance she could get.

The Queen wasn't all that careful with touching him—tucking an errant lock of hair behind his ear, squeezing his thigh, gripping his arm —and Nina caught Lirien squirming out of the Queen's grasp just as the Queen tried to put her hands on him again.

Nina stared at the two of them with an eyebrow raised and folded her arms across her chest. Lirien thought she would say something, but she kept her mouth shut. Her eyes lingered longer on her mother, though.

She knows something isn't right. And soon everyone else will see it too, if they haven't figured it out already.

The torturous lunch ended and Lirien darted out of the chamber. With the Queen's attentions during the meal, he knew that she was growing more and more impatient with him. The Queen would likely come visit him that night, and he didn't know how he'd drive her away without involving other people.

He wanted very badly to tell someone what was going on, but he was afraid to, because they would see how he'd had a hand in it. Instead, he formulated a plan to keep her from escalating her affections, and he felt guilty because he'd be taking advantage of his siblings to do so.

He went to the castle courtyard where he knew Sorin and Sonalie would be playing after lunch. They usually shared an afternoon burst of energy that their nursemaid thought best be spent outside.

Sorin and Sonalie zoomed after the nanny, and as Lirien crossed into the yard, Sonalie almost crashed into him. Sorin did, but on purpose, and wrapped his arms around Lirien's waist. "Brother!"

"Hello, Sorin. It's a little strange being in Father's old room.

Can you keep me company for a bit? We can have a sleepover. Sonalie, want to come too?”

Sonalie smiled shyly and shook her head, then went back to chasing the nanny.

“Yeah, that sounds fun!” Sorin cried, letting go of Lirien’s legs. “Can you tell me stories under the blanket?”

“Of course, but we have to keep quiet when it gets late, so your mother won’t hear.”

“I promise.”

“Come after dinner time, all right?”

“Yay!”

Although the dinner was just as tasteless as lunch, and just as harrowing thanks to Queen Aurinda’s unwanted attention, Lirien did his best to distract himself by talking to the children. Sorin was the chattiest, but Sonalie was starting to become more talkative with Lirien, which made him happy.

Nina kept a watchful eye on Lirien and the Queen, and only offered to speak when she could share her opinion on what Ardeth would be like if she were in power. It was clear Lirien usurping her still stung, and even clearer she thought Lirien wasn’t going to be as good of a ruler as she. And Lirien didn’t say anything to that, because it was absolutely true.

When the children were dismissed, and before the Queen could catch him, Lirien stopped Nina in the hallway. “Nina, I’m so sorry about all of this.”

She sighed. “I’m mad, but I’m not mad at you. Not really. Even though I seem like I am.” She frowned. “Mother’s acting funny. She’s so focused on you. I know she made you Prince to try to make right with Father even though he’s not here anymore, but... I don’t like how she acts with you. Something seems wrong. I don’t know.”

But she did know. Not everything, but enough.

Lirien opened his mouth, ready to blurt out the truth to her, but Sorin interrupted them. "I'm just going to get a book and I'll be right over!" he cried, a merry grin on his face.

"Nina, do you want to come too?" Lirien asked.

She looked down at the floor. "I'm not ready to see Father's room yet. All his things, like he's still there. But he's not." This time, Nina touched Lirien's arm. "I'm not mad about that, either. I heard you tried your best. But I'm not ready to see..." she trailed off. Then she gave him a pained half-smile. "I'll talk to you more later. I promise."

Lirien bade her goodnight and headed to his father's room. Sorin arrived shortly afterward, bringing with him a book called *Sir Jonah Sees and Hears*. Lirien took the book and put it on his nightstand, next to the copy of *The Book of Stones* that Kerrick had delivered while Lirien was out. As much as Lirien was happy for Sorin to keep him company, another part of him was desperate to dive into his book to find answers of any kind and a way to break the siren's spell.

Sorin eyed Lirien's book. "You're doing a lot of reading again," he observed.

"All about magic. What's your book about?"

"Well, I want us to read it together, so you'll see. But I'll give you a hint. It's about magic, too. A magic helmet. But first, let's play some games. I don't want to read the book until bedtime."

"Sounds good to me."

"Let me teach you a hand-clap game!"

One game became several, and then handclapping became sword fighting, and the two had a lovely time together, laughing and playing. When the night stretched on and began to draw to a close, they both headed to bed. Lirien placed one of the giant pillows in his lap and Sorin curled around him like a cat as he listened to the stories of *Sir Jonah Sees and Hears*.

The book was about all the things the knight Sir Jonah could see when he wore the Seer's Helm, an enchanted helmet that let you look through the eyes of another person and listen to the things around them when you put it on. It was supposed to be a real relic made by the dwarves and elves together, and it was lost in a dragon's horde of great shining things.

It didn't take long for Sorin to fall deeply asleep. Lirien leaned over and set the book on the nightstand and grabbed *The Book of Stones*. He flipped through the contents until he found the chapter on havoc stones. He read.

Havoc stones are small, bloodred stones made from the hearts of trickster spirits.

Lirien thought about it. Tricksters— that meant creatures who were fae in nature. Not faeries, specifically, but long-living residents of the faerie realm. They were playful and flitted between benevolence and malevolence with their interactions with humans. Beings like phoukas, night sprites, and fae foxes, for example, fit the description.

He immediately remembered the talking fox that helped him out of the forest years ago. That was his first and only encounter with a fae fox, and she didn't trick him at all. She must have been in a benevolent mood the day she helped him. He was glad she didn't try to harm him, as other tricksters were wont to do.

You must kill the trickster and remove the heart. It will shrink down in size and harden into a stone. Make a wish on the stone, but be wary. The heart of the trickster comes from chaos, and chaos it will exact, the price of the wish coming true.

How did one even catch and kill a trickster? They were intelligent creatures and of course, their whole point was tricking humans! And honestly, Lirien didn't want to kill anything or anyone. Maybe havoc stones already existed out in the world, and he could get his hands on one. But of course, there was the whole warning about chaos as the price of the wish. What would happen if he made a wish and things went disastrously?

What if the havoc stone decided to take a life in order to spare his own?

Who knew what the cost would be if he wished on a havoc stone to break the spell on the Queen. Lirien wanted to try something else before relying on a magic so dangerous, but he didn't want to abandon the idea. He filed it under "last resorts" and tried to go to sleep.

His stomach rumbled in the dark, and a great hunger brewed inside of him. He had eaten all of his meals, none of which were small, but it wasn't enough. He craved more. But he couldn't think of any specific food that would satisfy him, not when it all tasted like nothing. He yearned for *something*; he just didn't know what.

Then it hit him: was this the siren part of him further awakening? Did he crave human flesh?

A voice inside of his head that sounded like his own, but *not quite*, said to him, "You can do it. What you were meant to do. Just eat."

Frightened, Lirien shut his eyes and focused on the sound of Sorin's gentle, rhythmic breathing before he nodded off into a light slumber.

Soon he awoke to the sound of a door opening and the brush of curtains. He cracked his eyes open enough to confirm what he expected: the Queen was standing there staring at him. He closed his eyes and feigned sleep as the Queen hovered by his bedside in silence. It felt like ages before she turned and went back to her room, and only when she was gone did Lirien at last surrender to true rest.

The next day, after yet another flavorless dinner, Lirien caught Sorin in the hallway and brought up the prospect of having another sleepover in his room. Sorin heartily agreed. "Let me get on my nightclothes and I'll come right over!" Lirien heard Sorin's feet scamper along the marble floors as he disappeared around the corner.

Then he heard the Queen. "You're a growing boy. You need to sleep in your own room. Leave Lirien be."

Sorin pouted. "But Lirien said he—"

"You've had your time together, and I'm glad, but it's over now."

"But it was fun."

"You can still have fun later," she said. "You have plenty of time during the day to do so. Now, give me a kiss."

The click of shoes on the floor alerted Lirien that the Queen was coming right for him. He hurried away, but she caught up to him and grabbed his arm.

"I know what you're trying to do. You will hide from me no longer." She leaned close to whisper in his ear, her lips almost touching him. "I'll see you later tonight." She let go of him as Corva entered the corridor.

"Corva. Walk with me." The two headed away down the hall.

"Your Majesty, how fared the fox hunt? I heard you went without the hounds this time," Corva said.

"It was not without difficulty, but I got what I needed..." Their voices died down as they disappeared from Lirien's sight.

Lirien's heart thudded in his chest as panic filled him. The Queen was coming for him, and everything within him screamed that something was going to be different about tonight, that the Queen would try something terrible.

He couldn't go to his room because the Queen would come to him there. He wondered where he could flee. The library wasn't safe because no doubt someone would run into him; after all, Kerrick had. He couldn't hide in any of the children's rooms because the Queen had figured out he was using them to stay away from her, and she'd probably look there at some point.

The more the fear grew within him, the less rational he became. He could only think of running. And then he did, his legs carrying him as quickly as they could, his mind not catching up with how fast he was going. The only thoughts were: *I have to get out I have to get out.*

He barreled out of the castle, through the courtyard and barbican, and out to sea. He heard one of the guards call out after him, "Your Highness!" but Lirien ignored her. He just kept going, running and running along the beach.

He sped along the sands past the castle town until he spied the forest of Pinemore atop the rocky cliffs. It was the first time he'd been out this far since he was a boy, and now carved into the rock face where he had once climbed were a set of stone steps leading upward into the forest.

He halted, out of breath. Why had he come out here? There wasn't any place for him to actually go. If he ventured any farther, his body would change, and he would die.

Part of him thought he would rather die than give the Queen any satisfaction, but he didn't want to leave his siblings behind. He loved them too much to leave them in mourning, and even if he somehow survived, he couldn't imagine not being able to see them again; it would hurt him deeply.

The sound quickly came, the thudding along the sands and the clinking of armor as a handful of guards appeared, sprinting toward him. They called his name.

Lirien whirled around to them, then his gaze flicked in all directions. He had the forest or the sea, which meant he had nothing.

"Leave me be!" he shouted at them, trying to summon a princely, commanding voice.

Lirien recognized one of the Queen's top guardsmen,

Richard, leading the group. There would be no reasoning with soldiers under the direct command of his stepmother, and they might hurt him somehow if he resisted them, so, helplessly, he just stood there as they surrounded him.

"The Queen said you were unwell and might take flight," Richard explained. "Please, come back with us. The Queen is worried about you, Your Highness."

"I'm not safe," Lirien said in despair. "I'm not safe as long as I'm in that castle. I'm not safe anywhere."

Zan, another guard Lirien recognized, advanced toward him, though she kept her hand on the hilt of her sword. "We will keep you safe, Your Highness. It is our duty."

Lirien suddenly felt very exhausted, a hollowed husk of himself. His vision blurred with unshed tears, and he surrendered. "Fine. Take me back."

The soldiers tightened their circle around Lirien as the group of them walked along the beach toward the castle. Halfway there, Lirien spotted the Queen making her way down the rocky sands toward them.

The soldiers bowed to her when she drew close.

"I demand privacy. Leave us," the Queen said. Her voice did not come out sharply as Lirien expected it to. The authority was there, but she sounded disappointed, almost sad.

The guards nodded and dispersed, heading up the rocky path back to the battlements.

"Lirien, I am so very tired," the Queen said.

"As am I." Lirien's voice came out bitter.

"You avoid me. You flee from me. I don't understand. There is so much I want to give you. You have no idea the depths of my heart, how much I love and adore you. All I ask is that you love me back." Her voice trembled as she spoke. "Tell me you love me."

"The love you ask of me is *wrong,* Your Majesty. I cannot give you what you want."

She stepped closer to him, and Lirien retreated two steps back. "You needn't be afraid. There is no transgression. We are of no blood—"

"But you are my mother. Stepmother, but mother all the same."

"I will never look on you as my son!" she shouted, her hands balled into fists. Tears streamed down from her face. "Don't torture me anymore, Lirien. I cannot bear it. Please. Tell me you love me. Give yourself to me. With all of your heart and soul, say the words."

Lirien greeted her with silence, and the Queen let out a wavering sigh as she pulled out something glittery, small, and round, a deep color of crimson, like blood.

"Do you know what this is?" she asked, turning it around in her hand. "This takes a wish and makes it come true. That's the most powerful magic there is, the ability to shape the world to one's will. If you will not consent to be mine, then I can force you, Lirien."

Sickness began to build in Lirien's stomach as he recognized the stone she held in her hand— the very magic he had considered using against her. If there were some poetry in that, he found it woeful and bitter. "Your Majesty, don't do this."

She crushed the havoc stone in her palm until it devolved into a shimmery, sparkling dust. Then she blew into it and the grains floated away on the warm summer wind. "Tell me you love me."

A tear fell down Lirien's cheek as a compulsion swarmed over him. He spoke, sounding beautiful and tremulous: "I love you." It seemed to echo around them: "I love you; I love you; I love you." Then Lirien felt something well up inside him, something fluttery and powerful trying to force its way out.

Lirien opened his mouth and a glimmering amber light, like faint tendrils of glowing smoke, escaped, and it repeated again and again, "I love you."

The dusky light took the form of a large, golden bird with long, lustrous plumage trailing behind it, and it circled above the Queen in the sky. "I love you," it called, in Lirien's voice.

The Queen let out a strange sound— something ecstatic, something indecent —and clutched at her heart before sinking to the ground, laughing and sobbing.

"I love you." The bird landed at her feet and cautiously approached her. "I love you."

A glimmering, shimmery gust of wind blew around them, with glistening particles swirling about, and they took the form of three figures in the sand. The children.

Lirien opened his mouth to cry out but nothing came from him. He tried again, and the bird said, "I love you." The Queen embraced it, her body shaking and breath coming out in heaves from laughter and tears.

There was something wrong with the children. They were shining and ghostly, not corporeal, but almost spiritual in form.

Nina stared around her, bewildered. "How did I get here?"

Sorin shouted Lirien's name and Sonalie cried out, "Mother, I'm scared! Why are we here?"

Then the glittery specks circled each of the children, reconstituting their forms. Lirien watched in horror as Nina's spectral figure shrank to that of a ghostly white snake. Sonalie's body rounded and her arms became wings, and she transformed into a swan. Sorin stretched and horns grew from his head, as he changed into a glowing white stag. The animals were not yet solid in form; they were sparkling beings of light that the wind suddenly whipped up into the air, pulling them away from Lirien and the Queen.

The air spirited the animals away, leaving trails of twinkling flecks of gold after them, and they rode the wind toward the forest of Pinemore.

Not the forest! Lirien knew if he entered the woods too long, he would turn to stone, but the Queen was too interested in Lirien's voice declaring its love for her. She didn't summon guards. No one was coming after the children.

Lirien knew he was the only one left to help, and if that meant he would die trying, so be it. The thought frightened him, but what scared him more was the possibility his siblings would be lost forever. Despite his fears, he sprinted across the beach and the Queen screamed his name after him. He ignored her. He ignored everything. He focused only on leaping up the stone stairs two steps, three steps at a time, and rushed into the woods.

There was a flash of light. And now, a solid, flesh-and-blood swan flew into the sky high above. Another light shone in the distance, big enough to suggest it belonged to the stag, and Lirien headed that way.

As Lirien dashed through the woods, the grim truth struck him: the Queen, in her desire to possess him, got what she wanted... just not all of him. She captured the thing that enraptured her the most, the voice that had ensnared her with its curse, and it would sing of its love for her just as she wished.

CHAPTER 6

Lirien continued to sprint through the forest as the sun set, jumping over thick roots and dodging the twisting pine trees. He raced toward where he thought he'd seen the brilliant flash of light, and halted once he thought he'd reached it. Except by then, the light was gone.

Where could the stag— where could Sorin —have run off to? Lirien surveyed his surroundings, and everywhere looked the same. Just lines and lines of trees for miles.

He didn't know how far he was in. It couldn't have been by much; he didn't feel like he'd been in the woods for all that long. He looked behind him, wondering why the guards weren't after him. No, not after him, but after the children.

Lirien clenched his fists as he ran, and his heart thrummed faster in his chest. The Queen didn't care about her children. All she cared about was Lirien's voice declaring its love. And time was running out. Lirien could die before he even found the children. And if Lirien *did* manage to find his siblings, what then? How would such an elaborate spell on them be broken?

His heart continued to beat rapidly, a combination of exertion from sprinting and the fear that threatened to overtake him any moment. The children were nowhere to be seen. He had no idea where they went. He didn't know how much longer he had left before his body would change and he would die. And if no one was coming after his family, they would certainly be lost forever. Would a bird of prey find and catch Nina? Would Sorin be hunted as a trophy stag? Would Sonalie fly away, never to return? Lirien's life wasn't the only one in danger. He had no choice but to keep searching, despite the threat to his life.

Out of the corner of Lirien's eye, he spotted something long, solid, bright, and white, on the forest floor. A snake.

Nina! His mouth made the shape of her name, but nothing came out. He couldn't even push his breath through to make a whisper. All his words had been stolen from him.

Nina slithered toward him, her forked tongue flicking in and out, her ruby-colored eyes staring ahead.

He didn't know what kind of snake she was. From what he'd read in bestiaries, some had bites suffused with venom, and others didn't but killed with the pressure of their own bodies.

Lirien got down on his knees, hoping Nina was neither of the two, and kept still, watching her, mentally pleading she would continue his way.

She did. Her tongue flicked across his fingers, and then she slid upward, seeking warmth underneath his velvet jacket. He twitched as she curled around his forearm and then poked her head out from underneath the cuff of his sleeve.

Lirien couldn't believe his luck: that somehow Nina had kept up with him, that somehow she knew to come to him. Perhaps there was some human cognizance left in her, which gave Lirien hope that if he found the other children, they, too, would know to come to him.

In the distance, a bright, golden light shone through the trees. Lirien realized the sun was setting, but the light took on a different quality, as though there was something magical about it. Could that be Sorin?

Lirien picked up his pace and the light brightened the closer Lirien got to it. He came upon a small clearing surrounded by unfamiliar trees with leaves of varying colors— orange, red, yellow, and brown, all bearing the richness of autumn.

Glistening gilded blooms covered the grassy floor and grew at the bases of the trees. He'd never seen nor could have imagined anything like it. When he walked across the little field, as soon as he brushed against the hundreds of flowers, a glimmering, powdery substance dusted the air, infusing it with a sweet smell. It was dizzying but not unpleasant.

Then the sun started rising. Incredulous, Lirien gaped at it. What was happening here?

Lirien turned around slowly, trying to make sense of what he was seeing. All of the pine trees were gone. In every direction, his surroundings looked different: just rows and rows of colorful trees and gold blooms that gave off glittering dust. The trees were so thick, he couldn't even see where he had entered the clearing.

Everything about this place told him it was a crisp autumn morning, even though he had just left a warm summer evening.

Think, he told himself, *think*. What have you heard; what have you read? How would something like this be possible? He needed to know where he was in case he ended up even farther away from his siblings. He prayed that this new location would somehow be closer to them, that this new development was somehow a gift to help him along the way.

He remembered his childhood atlas of all the realms within and beyond Ardeth. There was a special place that couldn't be mapped, a forest that wandered where it willed. Elythia.

A rustling sound made him jump. Flitting across the clearing from the woods, a strange creature the size of a cat—

or maybe something like a rabbit —ran past him. It had long, pointed ears that flopped behind it, and an even longer tail with a tuft of fur on the end. The strangest thing about it was its coloring, a bright, mossy green with hints of shimmering dust, probably from brushing up against the mysterious flowers.

It was just a green smudge to Lirien as it passed, and then less than a minute later, a shape in brown followed just as fast. What seemed to be a child rode the back of a wild boar with a spear raised, ready to strike. Brown leaves decorated with this-tledown clothed the child's body, and a wreath crowned his head. The boy and the boar disappeared into the forest just as quickly as they came.

Lirien waited, keeping his body perfectly still as he expected something else to follow in pursuit. When nothing happened, he took in a breath, checked on Nina in his sleeve, and advanced into the wood. He chose the direction the child came from. If there were more people that way, perhaps he could get some kind of help from them. Well, if he could figure out how to ask for help, anyway.

As he hurried through the woods, Lirien recalled a child-hood song that Kerrick had taught him:

Sirens are monsters that dwell in the seas.
The fae are the creatures that do as they please.
The giants and tricksters are beings of pride.
While all elves and dwarves live and work side by side.

The fae, the giants, the tricksters— each called Elythia home, and their part of the song felt like a little warning. Lirien was already scared about what would become of his brother and sisters; should he be afraid of this forest, too?

And why wasn't Lirien dead yet? He had taken a moment to slap his booted foot and calf, an obvious test of sensation, and he felt as he always had before. There was no hardening of his body, no loss of feeling in his limbs. Maybe the strangeness, the magic in the forest, was helping him somehow. Maybe it was protecting him from changing? At least for now... Maybe his time was still limited. He wasn't sure. He just knew he needed to continue on.

The sun was halfway up in the sky when Lirien came upon a small rectangle of open land that stretched before him. A single twisted tree with yellow leaves grew in the center of the landscape, and he approached it with curiosity.

Glittering trinkets adorned the tree branches in a careful assemblage. Two small chandeliers hung from each side of the tree. Numerous gold chains, jeweled carcanets, brooches, bracelets, and rings were draped beautifully along the bark and branches.

Lirien stepped closer, admiring the strange combination of natural and manmade beauty, when small brown passerine birds, hidden above him in the branches, started singing. One of them swooped down and fluttered in front of Lirien's face, its little head twisting back and forth, almost in appraisal. It tweeted, and a few more birds joined it, all of them darting around Lirien at different angles.

Nina peeked out of Lirien's sleeve, her tongue flicking rapidly, as the birds came together in a very coordinated formation in the air. Making a perfect circle, they swooped down and seized the thick gold chain Lirien wore around the top of his velvet doublet. Lirien jerked his head to the side and tried to wave them away, but they easily lifted the heavy chain from his neck and then slid it over one of the lower branches in the center of the tree, keeping a deliberate symmetry with all the other shining items.

The birds chirped happily as they flew back up into the branches and settled in their perches. In disbelief, Lirien raised his hand to the branch where his chain rested, and a sharp blow landed across his face.

One of the thinner tree branches had swung back and hit him.

That was a more-than-obvious warning not to touch anything, and feeling shocked and confused as he rubbed his cheek, Lirien bowed before the tree and then hurried across the clearing into the forest behind it.

He trudged on through the woods, unaware of the time. Lirien had regularly been unsure of how quickly or slowly time passed, but in the strange realm of Elythia, time felt thicker and heavier. There was no other way to describe it. And having it be day when it should be night didn't help matters.

Lirien's body pushed for sleep as his mind raced. His stomach growled, and his throat felt parched. He had gone through days of eating food without feeling sated, craving flavor and tasting none. There was something about this forest that made his hunger feel even worse.

After another hour of aimless walking, punctuated by weird visions out of the corner of his eye— tiny figures with dragonfly wings or long, thin humanoid shadows stalking him through the wood —he reached an area of marshland. With a thirst like nothing he ever felt before, he hurried to the marsh's edge and lay on his stomach, his face mere inches from the water.

He didn't know if he should drink it. But something in him commanded his body, twisted it with yearning for a sip of cool water.

He held his arm out to see if Nina wanted a break, and when she didn't move, he dipped his free arm into the water, cupping his hand and bringing it to his lips. He tasted nothing, but the coolness of it felt good.

Then the hairs on the back of his neck stood on end, and a shiver coursed through him.

Something large disturbed the solitude, sending small waves rippling up against the long green grasses and reeds. Then a loud whoosh of cascading water echoed through the trees as something rose up from the marsh.

Lirien's heart beat fast as he slowly brought his face up to look at the source of the sound.

A horse's head hovered just above the water, large and jet black, and stared at him with burning eyes of emerald fire. It whinnied at him, flashing a set of sharp, pointed teeth that chilled Lirien's blood.

Lirien rose to his knees, not daring to look away from the water horse, willing himself not to blink, fearing that if he closed his eyes, the creature would be upon him.

The horse eyed him, unblinking, until at last it huffed air through its nostrils and dipped back under the surface of the water.

A bright voice punctuated by the sound of tiny bells spoke in his ear: "You're lucky he didn't kill you. He respects all children of the water."

Lirien jumped to his feet, searching around him for the owner of the sweet, melodic voice.

"Indeed, is that what you are? I wouldn't have guessed it," the voice said, and let out a pleasant, tinkling laugh.

The spirit's breath tickled him and Lirien couldn't help swatting at it, and more laughter rang around him.

"Oh, such fun! Here I am! Catch me!" The voice darted here and there, in all directions, and Lirien jerked his head about, then started whirling around to find the source.

"Turnabout! Turnabout! Dance for me, dance!" The silvery tinkling in the high-pitched voice devolved into discordant tubular bells, and the more the spirit spoke, the deeper and more distorted its voice became: "Tuurrrrrn aboouut, daaance!" As the voice transformed, something large and invisible clutched Lirien by the shoulders and kept spinning him in circles. The thing pushed him away from the marsh, sending Lirien flying backward, and he stumbled and fell. Somehow, he managed not to squish Nina amid the chaos.

"Ha. Ha. Haaaa."

Lirien lay still, trying to recover from his dizziness and begging his heart to slow its beating. He closed his eyes tight, trying to will away whatever malevolent creature was playing with him.

Moments passed and nothing happened. Lirien opened his eyes cautiously and looked around. The weird voice, the invisible presence, was gone.

Taking in a sharp breath, Lirien got back up and tried to walk with dignity out of that part of the forest. Once it was out of view, he sprinted. *I have to get out of here, I have to get out!* The longer he stayed in Elythia, the more danger, and the farther away from Sonalie and Sorin he felt.

He ventured on regardless, hoping to find friendly faces somewhere, all the while looking for signs of a white stag or swan. He saw nothing of them.

After another hour, maybe longer, of walking, he needed rest. Drowsiness weighed on him heavily, and he knew that back home it was long hours past midnight. He spied no comfortable place for him to lie down. The gold flowers grew in bunches at most of the bases of the trees, which was where he thought it best to lay his head, but he didn't want to kick up any more of the glimmering powder that came off them.

A little farther, he spied a small patch of cleared ground beneath a great oak. Remembering his experience with the other tree, he checked the branches for birds and hidden objects. Finding none, he leaned back against the trunk.

Nina uncoiled herself from his arm and slid onto the ground. She chose a spot next to him, a little crook between his leg and a tree root, and nestled into a spiral of coils, keeping perfectly still. Lirien, seeing she was well enough, closed his eyes.

In the state between wakefulness and slumber, he felt the familiar sensation of being watched as he slept. Confused, Lirien awoke with a start, half-expecting to find the Queen standing there, gazing at him.

For a fraction of a moment, three childlike figures clad in leaves of purplish red, huddled and stacked on each other like tumblers, peered at him curiously.

"What do you suppose it is?" one of them whispered.

Another said, "I don't know, but it's ugly."

In the next second, they were gone, snickering as Lirien blinked them away.

He realized he would get no more rest in this place. And if he thought about it, should he? Sorin and Sonalie felt so far away from him. Slowing down wouldn't help.

With new resolve, he got up and looked to Nina. Was she sleeping? Her eyes weren't closed. The red orbs stared blankly ahead, and Lirien remembered snakes slept with their eyes open. It was a little unnerving.

He extended his finger and held it in front of her nostrils and waited. The snake's tiny tongue whipped out and flicked at him, and Lirien patted Nina's head. He held his arm out to her, and dutifully, she slithered back under the sleeve into her hiding place.

On and on Lirien walked through a forest that seemed never-ending. If only he could yell out the children's names, they could hear his call and come to him. If only he could find help of any kind before it was too late, but no. He was truly alone, even his own voice betraying him in his impossible task to rescue them.

He walked until it was dusk, his stomach growling, his body

beating back the throes of sleep as he journeyed forward. He came across a river with the bluest water he'd ever seen, rushing along large boulders the size of stallions and churning in fierce whirlpools in the deepest parts.

He was so hungry. He eyed the water for fish. Not that he knew how to catch them, let alone clean and cook them, but he was willing to try if it would just quiet his restless stomach.

Then a thudding sounded, and the birds screeched, flying out of the trees, zooming along the sky in a murmuration. The tops of the trees bowed back and forth, the leaves moving like the waves in the ocean, as the sound of heavy steps grew closer and louder.

Something huge approached. Lirien's eyes widened as he tried to think of a place to go, but before he could move, there was a splash and a rumble. One of the river boulders had loosed from under the foot of a woman so tall her head rose above the treetops.

She lurched forward and cried, "Dammit!" as the boulder rolled and landed in a pool.

She lifted her skirts of moss and lichen and held out a sandaled foot, checking the damage. Her big toe had reddened and started to swell. "That hurt!"

Her voice was low and pleasing, and a little husky. She turned to Lirien and, exasperated, let out a sigh. "And you saw it all. At least you didn't laugh."

She dropped her skirt and stepped onto the land, towering over Lirien. Her imposing height startled Lirien, and he wasn't sure if he could count her as friend or foe. But the rest of her appearance didn't seem as menacing, rather, beautiful.

She had skin the color of ivy, and a pair of antlers dipped in gold adorned her head, a strong contrast to her dark, evergreen hair. Her startling, dark purple eyes blinked at him curiously before she knelt down in front of him. "What sort of thing are you, anyway?"

She poked at him with a long, lanky finger, and the force of it knocked him down flat on his back. His hand immediately flew to Nina in his sleeve, trying to see if she was all right.

"Hmm? Answer me. What are you?"

Lirien tapped his throat twice and made an 'x' with his arms.

"Can't talk?"

Lirien shook his head.

"Good. Then you won't tell anyone Bella Morgana made an ass of herself today." She reached for him, clutching the back of his doublet, and hauled him to his feet. Lirien's body hung limply like a ragdoll's as she set him upright.

"Well. See you, strange one." And she continued along her way, thudding through the forest.

Lirien smoothed his hair back from his forehead, sighing. Elythia was equally beautiful and dangerous, and more often than not, just strange. Lirien wanted help from someone so badly but didn't know how many more of these interactions he could take.

Lirien also felt like he didn't want to journey on. It was growing dark and Lirien didn't want to lose his way, and he needed to rest in order to have the strength to keep looking for his family.

What time was it in the world outside of Elythia? Lirien prayed the children found a safe place to stay for the night, and that they weren't hungry or afraid. It would be even better if they found each other somehow, and could stay together until Lirien found them.

Lirien surveyed his surroundings and chose the riverside as his place to settle for the night. He set Nina down, then stepped over to the river and stared at its waters, especially its whirlpools, for any signs of life in them. Satisfied they were devoid of water horses and other such creatures, Lirien took a drink of the cool, blue waters. He drank what he thought would be enough to quench his thirst, without feeling quenched. It was a strange sensation, to feel himself fill up but not be satisfied by it.

His hunger, the hunger of the past few days, had brought about a strange pain that seemed to worsen in Elythia. It was as though his stomach was being wrenched like a screw. He thought again about fishing, but as with drinking water, he knew that his appetite would not be satisfied with anything he caught— if he managed to catch anything at all. Defeated, he pulled off his doublet and set it aside, along with his white shirt underneath, and did a quick, cursory wash of what he could.

A chill had settled in the night. Lirien had planned to sleep in his blouse and use the doublet as a pillow, but he pulled all his clothes back on. He needed as many layers as he could in order to make it through the night. He worried for Nina, wondering what would happen if she got too cold.

He found a spot of smooth grass to lie down on and folded his hands underneath his head. He looked for Nina. She slinked over to him and settled up against his body, and he finally nodded off to an uninterrupted sleep.

He awoke to sunlight streaming through the trees. The sun was high enough in the sky to indicate it was not morning. He hadn't felt any watchful eyes on him or any sort of presence nearby as he slept. It was the same when he woke. It was the first time he truly felt alone in the woods.

He carefully avoided Nina as he rose to his feet and headed over to the river. Crouching down, he dipped his hand in the cold water and rinsed his mouth out, then washed his face. He felt a stronger motivation to try fishing, but he had no idea how to go about it. He stepped along the rocks that crossed the river and peered into the pools and along the rushing water but didn't see any fish.

Now that he was finally out of the castle and out in the world, he regretted his sheltered upbringing. He didn't know how to do anything practical. No singing would summon a meal before him. Playing the lyre would not light a campfire at night. While he had some education, nothing in all his learning prepared him properly to survive on his own.

Frustrated, he headed back to fetch Nina so they could be on their way. She still looked to be sleeping, as she kept perfectly still, red eyes looking straight ahead. He wanted to call her by name but settled on doing what he did before. Holding his hand out to her, he waited to see if she would rouse herself at his scent. She didn't at first, so he ran a finger along the top of her head, a gentle pet, and she stirred.

He gestured for her to come to him and held out his arm, and she took her familiar, comfortable spot underneath his sleeve as they set off.

Soon Lirien came upon a meadow surrounded by more of the dusty, shimmery gold flowers that pervaded the forest. Stretched out lazily on a blanket of moss was a languid, lissome man— no, a fae —with long, dark-red hair the shade of garnets, eyes of the same color, and glistening bronze skin. He wore a cuff with tiny dangling jewels from each pointed ear, rings on every finger, and a suit the color of juniper leaves made from crushed silk.

Next to him lay a stunning fae woman with flowing silver hair and deep ebony skin in a gown of gossamer, its many layers of milky translucence glowing from the sun. The woman wove her fingers through the fae man's hands and kissed them sweetly, her silvery eyes gazing longingly into his. She, too, wore copious amounts of jewelry, and glass beads woven through her hair caught the sunlight like droplets of dew on a spider's web. She closed her eyes then, and nuzzled the man's neck, giving him a soft, silent kiss.

As if from the air, the red-haired fae produced a bunch of green grapes and slid one into his mouth. Then he took the fae woman's chin and pulled her in for a deep kiss. Lirien could see the man pass the grape with his tongue into the woman's mouth. He blushed, knowing he had walked in on a private moment between the two, who were without a doubt the most gorgeous couple he had ever seen.

"You can join us, you know." The fae man kissed the woman one more time, a brief peck, and the two rose to their feet. "We've never seen your like before. Come closer. Let us have a look at you."

Lirien couldn't decide if the fae folk were truly his friends or not. They seemed kind enough, inviting him over to them. He decided to take a chance, hoping that the two fae might be able to help him find Sorin and Sonalie. He stood before the two as they appraised him.

"Yes, you're something else entirely," the man said, a curious smile spreading over his face.

The woman took a lock of Lirien's hair between her fingers. "You have such beautiful hair," she said, "shining with so many colors. What do you think, my Lord?"

The man tilted his head to the side, his gaze piercing Lirien's own. "Yes, it is exquisite, but I'm partial to his eyes. Like persimmons ripened in the fall," he said. He held out his arm to Lirien. "You may sit with us."

"Wait a moment, love." She turned to Lirien. "You should recall your manners and bow before us."

Lirien eyed them one by one, nervous that he suddenly upset her, then bent at his waist.

"Deeper," the woman said. "You wouldn't want to insult us further."

The man kissed the knuckles of her hand. "Now, now, my dear, forgive him. It seems he has no idea who he's come upon, or what we are." He straightened his back into a regal posture and announced with pride, "Lord Iesin and Lady Ariana welcome you to Autumn Wood."

CHAPTER 7

Lord Iesin and Lady Ariana took Lirien by his arms and sat him on the mossy blanket on the ground, right between them. Their attentions fixed on him made him feel uneasy. The two sat quite close to him, their legs touching, and they just kept staring at him.

"What a gorgeous serpent you have there," Lady Ariana said. She held her arm out to Nina, as if she wanted to take her from Lirien, and Nina backed farther up into Lirien's sleeve, completely hidden. Lady Ariana laughed, her voice rich and full.

"We are the rulers of Autumn Wood. There are woods for every season here in Elythia, each with their own Lord and Lady, but of all the fae, we are the most powerful. Our magic is far-reaching in this realm," the Lady explained.

"I can see you are cursed, and that you cannot speak," Lord Iesin said, "but I do not know the depth of it. Give me your hand so that I may read the spell on you."

Lirien thought perhaps Lord Iesin and Lady Ariana could help him, maybe even wanted to help him, so he obeyed. He held out his hand and Lord Iesin, whose palm was warm and soft, took it in his own.

At their connection, a twinge of heat and a current of energy coursed through Lirien's skin for a fraction of a second. Then Lord Iesin let go.

"Prince Lirien," he began, and Lirien was startled at his name. "There are so many layers of magic to this spell. There's the magic you were born with, the magic you unleashed on your Queen, the magic she unleashed on you, and then the magic that took your brother and sisters."

Lady Ariana reached out. "Let me see it, too," she said, and without waiting for Lirien to respond, she wound her long, graceful fingers in his own, and again the warmth hummed through Lirien's hand.

"So that's why we've never seen anything like you before," she said, her voice soft in wonder. "You come from the sea." She removed her hand. "Has *any* sea spirit crossed into Elythia before?"

"Not to my knowledge. That curse on you must have been lifted for the time being."

Lirien shot him a quizzical look.

"The magic you were born with. More than just the song. The siren's curse that has plagued you since birth. Curses, you know, have to latch onto something. It's in their nature to fiercely hold on and not let go. Your curse was attached to your voice and now your voice is gone. That's why you can travel where you wish. But I would caution you to be careful. The body always remembers."

What did that warning even mean? But Lirien was so relieved to confirm that he could go where he pleased, he immediately dismissed the thought. He could save the children. True, this freedom had a limit, but for now, it meant he could search for the children safely.

But what about the other magic? The one that made the Queen obsessed with him?

Lirien formed the shape of the words with his mouth: The other spells?

Lord Iesin raised his hand dismissively. "No, that won't do. Just make your thoughts into a form"— *Like this.*

The last two words entered Lirien's mind directly, echoing there.

Lirien concentrated hard and thought back to Lord Iesin, *Like this?*

But the way Lord Iesin sat there waiting made it clear Lirien wasn't doing it right.

"Hear anything?" Lady Ariana asked.

"No," said Lord Iesin.

"Hmm. I'll give you a boost," Lady Ariana said. "But I won't do everything for you. There are rules. One— you can only speak like this for as long as you are in Autumn Wood. Once you leave it, you lose the ability. And two— you can only speak to creatures touched by magic. You'll just have to improvise with everyone else. Now... what shall you give in return?" She thought about it for a moment. "We request a dance at the Midnight Revel."

Something about the way she said it told Lirien that it wasn't really a request. But Lirien nodded anyway, not seeing any harm in dancing, and Lady Ariana passed her hand over him in a quick motion, and a blast of heat surged through his skin.

Is it working?

"Of course!" Lady Ariana said. She folded her arms across her chest and made a pout, clearly offended. "Why wouldn't it?"

I'm sorry. I'm not used to this. Can both of you hear me?

"Yes," Lord Iesin said. "Anyone who is in your presence will be able to hear you as long as you direct your thoughts to them. If you want to keep your thoughts your own, you must only think to yourself. It sounds complicated, but you'll get used to it quickly."

"Hearing your thoughts," Lady Ariana said, "you have an extraordinary... well, no, I can't quite call it a voice when it's like this, but... Huh. So that's what a siren sounds like."

Lirien folded his hands together, trying to keep from fidgeting as urgent questions came to him. *If my siren curse was attached to my voice, and it's gone now... is my... is my spell on the Queen also?*

"Ah, that magic... it's not anything I've seen before," Lord Iesin said. "That's attached to your heart. And for the spell to stop, your heart must, too."

Once more, Lirien heard it again— he'd have to die to stop the spell on the Queen. He didn't want to think on that any longer. *Do you know how to break the spell on the children?*

"You should really see Kitra about that," Lady Ariana said. She lowered her voice to Lord Iesin. "She needs to know what happened. We can let her decide what to do with him."

Who is Kitra? he asked. *How do I find them?*

"She'll find you," Lord Iesin said.

"We'll see you tonight," Lady Ariana said with a laugh, and when Lirien blinked his eyes, the couple was gone, like spirits of the air.

Lirien searched the forest until twilight, and all the while, creatures in shadow followed him between the trees. They did not reveal themselves except for their whispers, and Lirien swore he heard something say, "Smells sweet," which unsettled him enough that he sped up his pace through the wood.

Then he saw a light, something reddish-gold hovering among the trees, an orb made of flames that wavered and flicked at the air. Lirien stared at it in wonder, then shook his head. Something about the fiery ball told him he should keep away from it, so he turned the other way. He hurried along quickly for a while, checking Nina every now and again, then halted.

Another red ball of light floated in front of him, as if it had always been there.

Did I... did I get turned around somehow? Elythia's games were only making things worse, taking even more time away from his search for Sorin and Sonalie. If they were in Elythia, they could run into as many strange things as Lirien had when he entered the forest. He didn't have time to get lost. He had to keep moving for his family's sake.

Lirien looked to the left and to the right, trying to catch any more of the strange glowing spheres. Another one lingered up just ahead, and again Lirien had the sensation of wanting to avoid them.

He chose another way.

Another circle of flame waited for him.

This time, he stared at it, confused... until the flickering and dancing of the fire drew him in. He looked at it, unblinking, for who knew how many minutes, until something within him changed.

I must— I need to —follow these.

Could some magical force be leading him to Sonalie or Sorin? He broke into a run, searching for more fire, and found they made a pathway through the wood, zigging and zagging among the trees. Another, and another, and another—

He came up behind a fox that easily dwarfed him in size, bigger than one of the Queen's carriages. The vixen turned her head toward him, narrowed her eyes, and opened her jaws. At the back of her throat, a flaming ball formed, grew in size, and escaped her mouth, hovering there in place.

As Lirien witnessed this strange occurrence, he felt no fear but a sense of familiarity there.

The fox let out a funny sound, a gekkering of a laugh, then spoke in a young woman's voice. "Greetings, mortal. I have a riddle for—" And then her eyes widened.

She jumped into the air and dove, pouncing on Lirien and knocking him hard on his back. She crawled on top of him. "Kai! You've seen Kai! I smell him on you! Tell me, where is he?" She started sniffing him more aggressively, and Lirien held his arms across his face and chest, trying to put a barrier between the two of them.

Then, just as quickly as her searching started, it stopped. She hopped off of him and turned her snout up toward the sky, and let out a hair-raising sound, a mix of a howl and a screech. Her paws scraped at a tree, her claws drawing lines in the bark, and she attacked it relentlessly, wailing.

Then she rounded on Lirien, tears streaming down her fox face. Her ears flicked back, and she bared her teeth. "Who did it? Was it you?"

Lirien's heart thudded in his chest, fearful for his life. *I don't know what you mean!*

"Who did it?" she said, and her voice grew sharper, more dangerous. "Who made my brother a havoc stone and wished on his heart?"

It wasn't me; the magic was forced upon me—

"By whom?" She opened her jaws again, and her throat started to glow with the fire that built inside it.

The Queen! The Queen of Ardeth!

The fox's jaws snapped shut. "A... Queen? An actual Queen? If you know this Queen—take me to her!

102

I don't have much time. I'm sorry. I have to save my brother and sisters!

That quieted her for a moment. "So you have a brother, too." She took a step towards him. "I can see there is magic on you, more than just my brother's heart. Let me read the spell." She again pinned him to the ground. Lirien squeezed his eyes shut as she licked his forehead and then placed hers on his.

After a moment, she got up and a transformation began. She rose on her hind legs and her limbs shrunk in size and grew more elongated. Her fox snout also shrunk, moving inward until the shape was more like a human's. She became a young woman, but something more than that. She was clearly fae, but parts of her remained fox-like still. She kept her amber eyes and slit pupils, her fox ears, and her fluffy tail, but the rest of her was humanlike. She had pale skin and shoulder-length orange-red hair, and she wore an outfit that reminded Lirien of the coloring of her fur— a fox-red doublet and cream-colored breeches with thigh-high black boots and matching black gloves.

Lirien stared at her. A strange, fluttery sensation in his stomach made its way up to his heart, and then he shook his head, embarrassed at the improper timing of this reaction. The fox seemed about to kill him, after all.

"If you promise to take me to the Queen, I'll tell you how to break your spell," the fae fox said darkly.

What will you do when you meet her?

"I don't know yet. I don't know what I can do. But she needs to know what she's done." She wiped her eyes with her knuckles, the movement more angry than sad.

All roads will lead back to the Queen anyway. At the end of the spell, I have to go back to her with the children. You can come with me then.

"Maybe I'll come with you now," she said, "and stay with

you until you've fulfilled your part of the bargain. So, do we have a deal or not?"

How do I know you can do as you say?

"You don't believe me? I may be a trickster but I'm no liar. I'll tell you what I know of your curse. I know the wish, the price, and the prize. The wish— that you love your stepmother, and not in a... wholesome way. The prize— your voice, which tells the Queen every waking moment that you love her. The price— your family is no longer human. And I know how to fix it all, but you don't get the rest until we make a pact."

Lirien couldn't wait to decide any longer. He chose to trust her, and hoped it wasn't the wrong decision. He didn't really have a choice, anyway— if he wanted a chance, he had to take it.

Let's do it, then.

The young woman changed back into a fox and opened her jaws wide. *She's going to bite me!* Lirien closed his eyes and with his thought-speak shouted, *My blood is poison!*

That halted her, but only for a moment. "I won't break the skin. Just a little nip to make it binding."

She gave him a spirited but gentle bite, something light to the touch, almost like how a cat would play with its owner. "Poison, eh? That's new." She changed back into her womanly form.

It's my siren blood. All sirens have it.

"I appreciate the warning. Anyway, you've made a pact with a fae, and not just any fae, but a fae fox. There's no walking away from our bargain. If you don't fulfill your half, that bite will burn into your skin and cause you agony for the remainder of your days."

That is definitely something you should have disclosed beforehand!

"If it makes you feel better, if I don't live up to my half, I'll lose control of my foxfire and burn. So there. We both are in danger if we fail each other."

She wiped her eyes and took a deep intake of breath, something shaky and drawn out as she turned her back to Lirien. "I'll be all right, I'll be all right," she told herself in hushed tones. "Kai will wait for me to see it done."

The young woman faced Lirien again, her face rosy from crying, but her eyes now dry. Just like that, she seemed like another person as she sat on the ground, folding her legs underneath her. She gestured to Lirien to sit with her and held out her hand to him. "I'm Kitra, by the way."

Lirien shook her hand, then realized, *Kitra! Lord Iesin and Lady Ariana told me to find you.*

"You've seen the Lord and Lady already? And they didn't... snatch you up?"

They're the ones who helped me speak like this. But I can only do it as long as I'm in Autumn Wood. And I have to dance at some sort of party.

"The Midnight Revel?" Kitra's eyes grew wide. "Oh, you don't want to dance with a fae. You'll never be able to stop. You'll keep at it until your shoes wear down and your toes bleed, and even then, you'll keep going. Why did you even agree to something like that?"

I didn't know. I don't know anything about fae. About any of this.

"Looks like I'm going to have to be your keeper while you're here," she said. "Maybe it's a good thing you met me. What's your name?"

Lirien. Uh... Prince Lirien.

"Prince, huh?"

But you can just call me Lirien.

"I will." She paused to stare at him. "Years ago, when

Elythia placed me in Pinemore. I saw a little boy crying. That had to have been you."

You are the one who helped me? You saved me that day.

"I have a soft spot for people when they cry, that's all." She spoke very nonchalantly. "You've grown up well."

Lirien didn't know how to respond to that. He returned to the most important subject. *Can you tell me more about this spell? Any help you can give me to aid my brother and sisters would be appreciated.*

"Yes. Spells are really like riddles if you think about it. Here you are, and so you can remember it, it rhymes:

"The children who are curséd be
Are only saved by objects three,
Each one woven skillfully.
The glittering stars that shine by and by,
The light of the moon when the tide is high,
Aurora that ribbons across the sky.
You will need each jewel of the night
For the spell to be set aright,
And free each child from their plight."

Lirien stopped and thought about it for some time. Did he have to collect these things? How would that even be possible?

"There's actually more," Kitra said. Her ears were flicked downward, her gaze cast aside. "I don't know how to make it rhyme." She seemed embarrassed for a moment. "Can you think of something that rhymes with 'woven?' And not an eye rhyme like 'proven'...I hate that, when they look like they could rhyme but they actually don't, it messes up the sound so much—"

It doesn't have to rhyme. You can just tell me.

"Where's the fun in that?" But she continued anyway. "Once you find those three things, you have to weave them together into robes. Put the robes on the enchanted children and they'll become human, and you'll speak again. There isn't a firm deadline for completing this task, but you should know that the longer you take, the wilder your family will become, and they may not be able to change back at all."

Then we have to find them immediately. There's no time.

"Well, yes and no. If they're in Elythia, time is something you have plenty of. The gilt flowers, those blooms you see everywhere— they control the flow of time here, with their pollen and powder. Things move differently here."

But what about outside Elythia? If they're not here, what then?

"Then that is a problem. Elythia likes to play with time, releasing you when it sees fit. If you're here for a day, it could be something like two weeks out there. On the other hand, you could be here for two weeks and have only a minute pass out there. It's not exactly consistent. Elythia is strange like that. The forest takes you in and pushes you out completely on its own whims. Unless you're a Lord or Lady, of course. They at least can talk to it and ask it to do their bidding. Although even then, Elythia makes the final decision on its own."

The only way I can get out of the forest is if I ask Lord Iesin and Lady Ariana to let me out?

"You have to ask them so they can ask Elythia, but yes."

Lirien's face fell. *So, I have to go to this revel if I want a chance to leave.*

"You have to go to the revel because you made an agreement with a fae. You don't want to trifle with the Lord and Lady of Autumn Wood. But once you finish up at the Revel, the sooner we can try to leave Elythia, and the sooner we can finish your quest and begin mine."

A tiny humanlike creature flew in on the back of a jeweled hummingbird and flitted around Lirien's head before sailing over to Kitra. Its voice sounded like tinkling glass and Lirien couldn't make out any of the words it shared with Kitra.

What was that about? Lirien asked as it flew off.

"A messenger from the Lord and Lady. They want you to go see Bella Morgana to be outfitted for the revel. We don't have much time with it almost being dark." She rose to her feet, brushing the leaves off the back of her pants. Lirien also stood and dusted himself off.

"Follow me." She turned back into a giant fox and blew out a fireball that hovered next to them, like a floating lamp. It traveled with them as they journeyed through tall and closely spaced trees.

Kitra seemed to be quite well known in Elythia. More forest creatures felt brazen enough to reveal themselves as they passed through the wood, calling out to Kitra to say hello, or to stare at Lirien curiously.

A tall, sticklike being with sharp teeth and pointy, overlong limbs trailed after Lirien. It walked quickly but in an unsettling, twitchy manner. "I can smell your blood," its raspy voice called out, "and it smells sweet. Give us a taste, would you?"

Kitra quickly rounded on the creature. "Don't test me, Berach," she said, baring her teeth. "I'll snap you in half."

"Apologies, milady fox," it mumbled, and stayed back, looking longingly after Lirien as it licked its dry, cracked lips.

Lirien sped up his pace, staying closer to Kitra as they continued on.

"That will probably continue to happen," Kitra explained. "You're different. They'll look on you with wonder, and hunger, too." As she said it, another creature lumbered through the wood just up ahead of them— a large brown bear with a giant paddle-like tail dragging behind it. The creature's most striking feature was its bright yellow eyes.

"Greetings, Adalbern. How goes it?"

"There are whispers about something strange at the fae fox's side. I came to see it for myself."

It trundled over to Lirien, sniffing him curiously. "What a peculiar smell. What are you?"

I am a siren's son, Lirien said, sure to add, *but I am human.*

"I've never seen anything so pretty," Kitra admitted, and Lirien did a double take. Pretty?

"I doubt so. Keep him safe, Kitra. I'm sure something here will see him as a prize."

"I will. We are in a pact together, and our bargain is not concluded. He is mine until then."

Adalbern nodded. "I also came to give you a warning. The Verdant One has awoken. He wanders, disappearing and reappearing much like Elythia itself."

Who is the 'Verdant One?'

"He has many names," Kitra said. "The Verdant One, the Woodwose, and more commonly, the Green Man."

"He was once a guardian of the forest, its protector," the bear explained. "But something corrupted him, and now he feeds. No one has been able to stop him, and not even Elythia has pushed him out. Not a one of us can understand it. And the Lords and Ladies can't do anything, for they are brethren and cannot kill their own kind."

Kitra's ears flicked back. "Do you know where he was last seen?"

"Near Winter Wood. All the gnomes in the hollow are gone. He took all of them."

"We'll be careful. We're heading to the border with Spring Wood, so we should be fine."

"Bella Morgana's?"

"Of course! We need to dress Lirien up for the Revel." Kitra bowed her head to Adalbern. "Your information was helpful."

Thank you, Lirien said.

Kitra's face screwed up and Adalbern shook his head.

"Don't ever say that," Kitra said. "To fae, a 'thank you' suggests you were owed the gift you were given. It offends us. Don't say it again."

Lirien's mouth dropped open in surprise, then he shut it and made a little frown in embarrassment. *I'm sorry.*

"It's clear you didn't know," said the bear. "But now you do. Heed the lesson well."

I will. Lirien paused, fidgeting with his hands. *I feel like because of my mistake I shouldn't demand more of you, but may I ask you a question?*

"I'll allow it."

Have you seen a white stag, or a swan, in the wood? I've been looking for them.

"No, son, I'm afraid not."

I want you to tell me if you see them while I'm here.

"I will do as you request. If that's all, I'll be on my way."

"Farewell, friend." Kitra licked the top of Adalbern's head and something that looked like a smile spread across his face, his sharp teeth poking out between his lips. Then the bear plodded away farther into the forest and Lirien continued to follow Kitra onward.

"Time for another lesson," Kitra said. "You need to be careful when making requests or bargains with fae creatures. You should've told Adalbern to tell you *where* he's seen the animals. Now he can just walk up to you and say, 'I saw them,' and that is all he'll be required to do. And you also said, 'while I'm here.' Well, you're not going to be 'here' anymore. In a few seconds, you'll be 'there,' and now he's released from his agreement to help you. Do you understand what I'm trying to tell you? You have to ask precisely for the thing you need. The fae will find a way around it if you don't."

I understand. I'll try my best not to make any more mistakes.

They walked farther, and Lirien thought to himself about all the things he had to do. Find Sorin and Sonalie. Find a way to get the stars and moonlight... and what was it? The aurora? Aurora was another name for 'dawn,' but the riddle clearly said the aurora in the night sky, which had to be the multicolored northern lights. How would he go about getting such things out of the sky?

And then it hit him— the sword so sharp that it could slice the air to pieces. Alibrandr. Perhaps if it could cut the air, it could cut the moonlight, stars, and aurora from the sky. It was his only hope. And of course, it was under lock and key in the royal treasury back in Ardeth.

All roads lead to the Queen, he thought miserably. But he couldn't go back there yet, or anytime soon. His priority before anything else was finding Sorin and Sonalie.

Can I ask you a question?

"Sure."

Lady Ariana gave me rules for speaking like this. She said that as long as I was in Autumn Wood, I could speak to creatures touched by magic until I leave the forest. I know she meant the fae and other beings who live in Elythia, but I was thinking... my brother and sisters are touched by magic because of the spell they're under. Do you think I could talk to them?

"There's only one way to find out."

Lirien stopped what he was doing and crouched on the ground. *Nina. Slide off my arm, and then circle the trunk of that tree before returning to me. Please.*

He held his breath, waiting to see if Nina could listen and obey.

She did precisely as asked, and Lirien felt something well up in his chest, relief that almost brought him to tears.

Can you talk back to me?

Nina just flicked her tongue at him. She moved her head to

the right and left, swishing part of her body back and forth, and Lirien took it as a 'no.'

Well, as long as you can hear me. Nina, if we ever get separated outside of Elythia, you need to go to...

Lirien had to think of a meeting place. Ardeth would not be safe as long as the Queen remained obsessed with him, and he wasn't going to go there until the end of it all, anyway. He tried to think of an ally, not only for him, but for his brother and sisters. He settled on the neighboring kingdom, Asherin, the home where his aunts, Eira and Idela, ruled.

If we get separated, go to Asherin. Go to the lake. Lake Karda. Lirien remembered from his atlas that the small lake was close to Castle Asherin. It was a noticeable enough landmark that it should work out for all of them as a meeting place. *I know it will take you a long time, but I will come and wait for you there.*

Nina coiled around Lirien's arm a little tighter, which he hoped signaled her understanding.

Lirien repeated his thoughts, calling out to the twins. *Sorin! Sonalie! I'm trying my best to find you, but I don't know where you are. Go to Lake Karda in Asherin. Wait there until I come to you! No matter what, wait there! I love you and I'll see you again.* He prayed that no matter where the twins were, his words reached them.

CHAPTER 8

The giantess Bella Morgana lived on the border of Autumn Wood and Spring Wood, on the side full of colorful trees and fallen leaves. It was like an invisible barrier, a stark line that divided the forest realms. There was no transition between the two as the colors of autumn suddenly switched to green, with a sea of cherry blossoms whose pinkish white petals trickled down like falling bits of snow in the night. The only constant between the two woods was the presence of the gold blooms that controlled the flow of time in Elythia.

Bella Morgana's shop was an abandoned stone keep that dwarfed the ruins of a small castle. The tower maintained its shape and roof well, the only part of the structure still intact. The rest of the castle walls were overgrown with ivy, full of glassless windows and grassy floors on the other side, with small clusters of gilt flowers here and there.

There was an enormous door large enough for a giant to pass through, and a secondary, smaller door carved into the bottom meant for ordinary fae to enter. A single candle in glass illuminated a small sign with a needle and thread painted on it.

It hung just above the smaller door to the keep and read, *Bella Morgana, Master Clothier.*

Kitra extinguished her ball of fire, no trace of smoke left behind, and changed back into her fae form. She grabbed the heavy door knocker with both hands, the beating against the door carrying through the quiet forest.

"Do you have an appointment?" Bella Morgana's lovely, husky voice called out from within the keep.

Lirien recognized it as the voice of the giantess he had run into earlier near the river. He swallowed. Their interaction was more peculiar than anything else, and he wasn't sure if he could handle anything stranger than what he'd been through. But, on the other hand, she seemed friendly enough.

"We don't have one, but Lord Iesin and Lady Ariana sent us. It's Kitra and I'm here with Lirien. He needs clothes for the revel tonight."

"Well, shit, they certainly like to spring things at the last minute. Come on in, then."

Kitra opened the door and held it for Lirien. He nodded his head in appreciation and stepped through. He had to crane his neck to take in everything as Bella Morgana said proudly, "Welcome to the workshop."

The keep's interior was hollow. Multiple torches along the walls revealed square slots in the stone where wooden beams and a floor used to be attached, and these continued up various levels, indicating at least four separate compartments back during the castle's heyday.

Shelves had been built against one side of the round tower walls, and half of them were filled with fabrics of all imaginable colors and kinds. The other half of the shelving contained strange materials. Different types of leaves, flower petals, a shelf filled entirely with cobwebs, a glass jar with fireflies in it, moss, reeds, and rushes— all were stored and ready for use.

Pegs stuck out along the stone walls and numerous outfits hung from the hangers. There was also a section of wall entirely filled with mirrors of varying sizes and lengths.

The keep was one big workroom full of wondrous things. Lirien never cared for clothing but many of the items on display caught his eye: luscious ballgowns, diaphanous skirts, brilliantly colored suits and doublets. He wondered what sort of garment Bella Morgana would have ready for him.

"I remember you," she said to Lirien, and gently patted his head. "Quiet one you are. Much appreciated." She cleared her throat. "So, the Midnight Revel, huh? I've got... oh, what, a few hours to do my magic? That's more than enough time for you to get the whole experience, and be outfitted from head to toe. It's not just clothing from me, but the entire ensemble— hair, accessories, cosmetics, you name it."

"I'm glad you can help. Lirien's invitation was very sudden. You don't have to worry about my clothes, I'll just wear—"

"No!" Bella Morgana practically roared. "You certainly *cannot* wear whatever the hell you have on now. Have you not been to a revel before? What are you thinking?"

"It's been a while. A few years, at least."

Bella Morgana grabbed a long ribbon marked with notches and lines for measurements. "Can you put your magical snake friend aside for a moment? Just until I'm finished."

Lirien bent low and let Nina uncoil from his arm. She slid across the floor and curled up inside one of the empty cubbies along the ground, looking quite comfortable.

"You should leave your snake with me during the festivities," Bella Morgana said. "Too many creatures could try to run off with something so pretty."

"You can trust Bella Morgana," Kitra added. "It's safe here."

...That would be a great help. I'll come back to pick her up once it's over.

"Not a problem." Bella Morgana took her measurement ribbon and noted Lirien's arm length, the broadness of his chest, his inseam, his outseam, and then completely frivolous things like the size of his earlobes and the length of his sideburns. She hummed an off-key tune as she jotted down Lirien's numbers.

"Now, now, what colors?" She looked him over thoughtfully. "Overall, you're sort of bluish, aren't you? And that hair, that sheen that appears when the light hits it, looks like..." she trailed off. "Perhaps I should bring out the orange of your eyes, though. Hmm... What to do, what to do..." She searched her hangers and pulled out a doublet and breeches of dark teal with a subtle gold trim. Lirien couldn't recognize the fabric. It looked like velvet but took on a more liquid quality, and he had to admit it was lovely.

Then Bella Morgana grabbed a capelet that matched the suit, but underneath the cape, it was a gentle burnt orange with a matching sash that crossed over the body. It looked to be made of the same material.

"Here, try these on."

Lirien looked around. There was no place for privacy. He didn't really mind if Bella Morgana saw him, but there was something about Kitra that made him suddenly quite shy.

Bella Morgana picked up on it. "Kitra, can you step outside for a little bit? I'll call you to come back in."

Kitra raised her eyebrow for a moment, then got it. "All right. See you."

As soon as she was gone, Lirien pulled off his doublet and set it aside.

"You feel something when you look at her, don't you?"

Is it that obvious?

"Yes, when you stare at her like that. Looks like more than curiosity to me."

Lirien reddened. *I am curious about her. What's wrong with that?* He pulled the teal doublet over his head and straightened it out, then very quickly stepped out of his breeches and into the new pair.

"Ah, curiosity," she said with a smile. "Sometimes people are just drawn to each other, and then it grows from there. I wish you the best of luck with Kitra. She's a darling girl."

She spun her finger in the air. "Let's turn you around, let me get a look at you to see the fit of those clothes."

There wasn't anything she had to worry about. The doublet and breeches were perfect. "Now put on the capelet and sash... yes, that's good. Brings out your eyes, just as I thought it would. You can go ahead and take them off now. I'll work on the embellishments."

Lirien slipped on his other clothes and watched Bella Morgana take a jar of live butterflies colored the same orange as the sash, and she proceeded to sew them to it. Something like sewing, anyway. She stitched a line down the middle of the sash with her giant needle, making the seams enormous. Then she ran her finger over them, and they shrank to the point they couldn't even be seen. The butterflies all latched onto where the stitches were, and with the tip of the needle she tapped the abdomens of each one. She didn't pierce them; she didn't draw the needle through them, but she connected them with faint gold threads all the same.

She hung the capelet and sash back up, and the butterflies slowly flapped their wings in a calming rhythm. "I've protected them with my stitches. You won't have to worry about crushing them or doing them any harm while you dance. They're just a living decoration."

Incredible. What will you do for Kitra?

"Let's see. Kitra!" she called out, "He's done changing. You can come back inside."

"Oh, wow, butterflies!" Kitra cried when she saw Lirien's clothes.

Bella Morgana smiled. "Does that mean you're more amenable to letting me dress you now?"

"Yes, all right. Just... don't put me in a gown, please. That's not my style."

"Fair enough." She looked Kitra over. "Teal would look great on you, too, with your hair and fur color." She gestured to Lirien's ensemble. "Would you dislike matching?"

To Lirien's surprise, Kitra's cheeks turned rosy. "No... that won't be a problem."

"Of course, the clothes themselves will be different," Bella Morgana said, and she grabbed her measurement ribbon once more. She noted Kitra's sizes with the standards as well as taking more bizarre notations, such as the length of the tuft of black fur that grew from the tops of Kitra's ears, and the size of the center of the widow's peak on her forehead.

"All right, I have just the thing, but I'm going to have to take it in." She grabbed a suit of shimmering satin that glimmered with an underlay of gold when the light hit it. The jacket was unlike any Lirien had ever seen, a fashion where the length of the coat went all the way down mid-calf and fanned out into an 'A' line. Bella Morgana paired it with a white blouse with copious ruffles and lace at the neck and sleeves.

"If you can try this on for me," she said.

Lirien hurried to the door as soon as Kitra started unbuttoning.

As he waited outside the keep, he couldn't stop thinking about her. It was true, he'd felt something immediately when he saw Kitra. He thought it was simple curiosity, or— all right, he admitted, an attraction to her unusual beauty. He'd decided quickly that he liked her. She was strong, being able to put her thoughts of her brother aside so she could continue on. She was funny, coming up with her ridiculous rhymes and riddles. And she was playful and exciting, with the way she flitted from fox to fae and back again with a jumpy sort of energy.

He especially wondered what Kitra would be doing at the revel, if she would be his keeper like she'd mentioned earlier. He knew one thing for certain— he wanted to spend more time with her.

"Lirien, we're all finished."

He stepped back inside, and Bella Morgana was busy laying the clothes on a worktable. She had applied pins all over the place, where the jacket, shirt, and breeches needed to be taken in. She threaded a new needle.

"This will take me a little while. Maybe an hour, maybe less. You can watch me in the meantime or find some way to amuse yourselves."

"Let's amuse ourselves," Kitra said to Lirien. "I need your help with something. Come back outside with me?"

Lirien followed her out.

For a brief moment she switched back to a giant fox, long enough to blow three different fireballs into the air to provide light in the darkness. Then she was in her fae form once more. The fire hovered in place, their flames licking the air and casting a gentle orange glow over everything.

What did you need help with?

"Guess." The corner of her mouth turned up.

"On the ground and in the air,
In a one, or in a pair,
Or ensemble if you please.
It's difficult or quite with ease.

"What am I?"

Lirien was convinced she was talking about fireflies until she got to the last line of her riddle. *I had somewhat of an idea, but now I'm lost.*

"Dance. I need help with dancing. It's been forever since I've attended the Midnight Revel. I remember what happens, but..." She folded her hands and rubbed her thumbs together. "I need some practice. And I could use the distraction, to be honest. When we aren't busy, my mind wanders..."

She must be thinking of her brother, Lirien thought. A twinge of guilt felt like a tremor in his heart. Here, Lirien had found a way to restore his brother and sisters, but Kitra's brother was never coming back.

"Anyway, I want you to dance with me." Kitra's voice had brightened once again.

Lirien's face warmed, and he was grateful for the firelight to hide his blushing. *All right. To be honest, I'm worried about my dancing, too.*

He had to quickly learn a few formal dances before his naming ceremony in order to not make a fool of himself at the fete, but because he'd left early, he'd never had a chance to try anything out. His dancing master was judicious and sparing in his praise, making Lirien worry he just wasn't good enough.

"Let's be terrible together, then." Kitra took Lirien's hand. "Stand beside me and follow my lead. This is usually the very first dance of the night."

Kitra started out with something similar to the pavane, but with extra steps. At the end of each interval, the partners bowed deeply, then they'd clap three times. One partner circled the other, their hands linked above their heads, then the second partner would repeat the step in the other direction. Then it would all start again, each couple doing the dance in four directions until the music stopped.

It was simple enough for Lirien to grasp without shaming himself, but the next dance Lirien botched easily. He recognized something like the galliard, but a more complicated version that went beyond the hops and kicking out of the feet. Lirien knew how to keep time, but his body didn't.

Is this really something they like to do? I'm in trouble.

Kitra chuckled at him. "No, no, you look marvelous! Don't change a thing about it."

Lirien grinned sheepishly. *Let's try something else.*

They continued with dances like the almaine, complete with skipping and spinning, and then something just as intimate as the volta, where Lirien had to turn and lift Kitra by her waist. Lirien felt something tremble in his chest as he raised her in the air.

"Wow, you're tall," Kitra said, and she let out another warm, delightful laugh.

When he finally set her down, Lirien asked, *Do you think we'll be ready for tonight?*

"I do wonder what the Lord and Lady will ask of you," Kitra admitted. "We've done the most popular dances but that's not always their style. They're both elegant. As long as you can strut like you're graceful, you should be fine."

Is it a big event?

"They have it every midnight, so you'd think it would lose its sheen, but it's still popular. Many of Elythia attend, all sorts of people and creatures. But some nights Lord Iesin and Lady Ariana want more intimate proceedings, so I've seen the revel have as few as eight people or so."

I hope we have one of the nights with less guests. I don't want so many witnesses to my failure.

Kitra smiled at him. "You can be funny."

Lirien hadn't tried to be, but he appreciated her approval all the same.

"You can come now," Bella Morgana called. "I'm done stitching. Kitra, it might be a good idea to feed Lirien before the party."

"Oh, that's a very good point."

It's as though you've read my mind. I am terribly hungry. But he knew the dinner would bring him no pleasure. He bit his lip. It was another thing he should have asked the Lord and Lady about, but he was so focused on other things, he'd forgotten to.

Lirien and Kitra went back inside, and while Lirien checked on Nina, Kitra explained, "You're a mortal. There are way too many risks for you at the Midnight Revel. The biggest one being food and drink. Stay especially away from the fruit."

"You'll be sorely tempted to dine on everything you see," Bella Morgana said, "and it will all look marvelous, but you have to resist. Just tell them I fed you and you didn't want to be rude to me. They can deal with it. I have some rabbit stew from my own dinner I can reheat for you."

Lirien wasn't sure he should mention his current affliction with food. He didn't want to tell Bella Morgana her food was flavorless, so he opted to keep his mouth shut and eat whatever she put in front of him. It was probably best he fill his body anyway, though the cravings hadn't really gone away.

Bella Morgana heated up his food and handed him a decent amount in a very large bowl that made his serving look small. "Sorry, out of respect for my fae friends, no salt. But I've seasoned it with herbs, so it should be fine."

Lirien reviewed the rules of the fae he'd learned so far: no "thanks," no food, no fruit, no salt, be wary of bargains, and always speak precisely what you mean to get what you want.

"Do you want to eat anything, Kitra?" Bella Morgana asked.

"I'm saving my appetite for the party. Food and drink are safe for me. But maybe I won't drink. It's probably better if I don't. I have to keep my wits about me to make sure nobody slips you some lavenderberry wine."

You'll really be my keeper, then?

"I said I would mind you, yes."

"So," Bella Morgana said as she took away Lirien's bowl once he finished, "Let's discuss payment."

"I thought Lord Iesin and Lady Ariana were taking care of this one," Kitra said. "Since they're the ones who requested we come here."

"They have an account with me, it's true, but it's been a while since they... Oops, I don't think I can say that. Well, uh... payment *now* would be nice as opposed to later. I'll just leave it at that. I promise it will be something affordable that you won't miss."

What do you want?

She looked at him dreamily. "A piece of your hair, please. The way the colors change when the lights hit it, from darkest blue to green and aquamarine— it would make a remarkable silk."

Silk?

Her eyes lit up. "My spinning wheel can work any material into thread or yarn, and that's how I make my fabrics. I'd make your hair into a fine fiber, then weave it on the loom. And I only need just a snip. You won't miss it."

May I watch?

"Oh, you want to see! Of course! I love showing off." She hummed cheerfully as she grabbed a set of scissors. She found a spot on Lirien's head that would be subtle and cut a small piece off.

Kitra gave Lirien a curious look, something he couldn't read; her eyebrows furrowed slightly at him, the corner of her mouth turning up into a half-smile.

Bella Morgana came over to the worktable, carrying a sizeable spinning wheel, and carefully set it on the floor so Lirien and Kitra could see what she was doing easily.

She pointed out the parts of the spinning wheel such as the bobbin and the whorl and set up a small string of already-spun, silvery silk into the bobbin. "This is the starter, to help with winding the unspun pieces into yarn." She held the clump of Lirien's hair in between her fingertips.

"Spindles have long been associated with magic," Bella Morgana said. "My spindle helps in a special way." She touched the hair to its point. "I'm able to do *this*." A shimmer coursed through the clipping from his hair when it hit the spindle, and immediately she ran her fingers over it. The hair stretched out easily into long, thick strands that went down to the floor.

She layered a piece of the unspun hair over the premade string and started the wheel, pumping her feet on the treadle rhythmically. "Feed it in small pieces. One hand holds the material, and the other passes it in as it spins. You keep going, section by section, pulling it apart, stretching it out, and giving it to the wheel. The newly made yarn will fill up the bobbin and you work it until you have a skein of it. Once you have as many skeins as you need, that's when you can put it on the loom and weave it into fabric."

As she worked through Lirien's hair, a dazzling multicolored fiber of blues and greens filled up the bobbin. It was shiny and fluid. Lirien wondered what Bella Morgana would make with it, but he thought of a more important question. *What sort materials have you used on the wheel? The strangest ones.*

"I've spun the light from fireflies, the powder from a moth's wings—"

Firefly light? Excitement shot through him. If she could make a yarn or thread from that kind of material, moonlight and stars should be no problem.

Bella Morgana. I need your help. Lirien explained the curse he and the children were under, and what he needed to do to break it.

Bella Morgana listened to him intently. "I think you're right, that the only way you can break the spell is to use my spinning wheel. And if you're to make robes, you'll need my loom, too. I can show you how to make these magical materials, but I can't do any of the work for you, as you're the spell-breaker. The task is yours."

You're letting me use your wheel and loom?

"For a price."

Lirien wasn't surprised. He was asking a big favor of her, so of course Bella Morgana would want something in return. He just hoped it was something he could give.

What do you want?

"That fish-scale mole."

Lirien paused. It was a mark that connected him to his father, something inherited despite being more magical than just a simple mole. He would look less like his father without it, and he wasn't sure if he felt comfortable losing it. *You want the whole thing?*

"Are you going to miss it? Just a little stab should do the trick. It won't hurt. My magic will see to that. There might be a little scar, the slightest indentation where it used to be, but no discoloration." She tilted her head, looking at the mark under his right eye. "I want it. It has an iridescence to it, like a rainbow on a pearl. You give me that so I can use it now, and when the time comes, you can borrow my things."

Lirien didn't give much thought to it. True, his mole had always been there, and sometimes he thought it was pretty, but more so, weird. And if it meant he could get his siblings back, he'd trade anything.

That's fine. Can I— can I thank giants?

Bella Morgana laughed. "So many rules to remember here.

Yes, you can thank me. I am no fae though I live in the fae's world. I appreciate a humble thanks now and again."

Lirien gave her a bow. *Thank you so much.*

She inclined her head in return. "Are we set, then?"

Yes.

"Let me grab my special needle." She went to her stores and pulled out something that looked more like the blade of a rapier. "Just tilt your head back up toward the ceiling and you'll feel a poke. Like I said, it won't hurt."

Lirien did as she said, but he swallowed, his throat suddenly dry. He didn't like having something sharp shoved in his face. He closed his eyes.

It happened quickly, just as Bella Morgana had said. He could feel the point of the needle touch his mark, but it wasn't anything like being stabbed. Nothing hurt.

"Done now."

He opened his eyes. At the end of the needle was his mole, stuck to the tip, but not impaled by it. He touched his face where the scale used to be, and felt a little dip there, but otherwise his skin was smooth.

Bella Morgana quickly put his fish-scale mole in a jar and set it with her other stores. "We have our deal. When you have the items you need, my wheel and loom are welcome to you."

"Well done, Lirien," Kitra said. "You've figured out part of the spell already. Now it's just a matter of finding a way to get those things from the sky."

I've figured that out, too. Well, sort of. I need the sword Alibrandr.

"I haven't heard that name in a long time. I know the elves have never forgiven Ardeth for taking it."

And somehow, I have to take it back from Ardeth. It will be the most difficult task. The sword had to be awakened, and once it was, it could be dangerous. Everything about the spell required a huge risk.

"I don't doubt it will be difficult," Kitra said.

"But one difficult task at a time," Bella Morgana said. "Next up—the revel."

CHAPTER 9

The Midnight Revel was held on a giant lawn in front of a grand house built up in the air on the trunks and boughs of enormous trees with leaves the color of deep mulberry. Wooden steps with handrails of branches cut and twisted into different shapes descended from a great entrance in the center of the house. The forest mansion was open and airy, with large windows, thin columns, and curving roofs.

There were faeries and creatures of all kinds, at least fifty. *So much for a small, intimate gathering*, Lirien thought. There were a variety of fae with pointed ears and wings like butterflies and moths; small pixies darting to and fro in the air, their translucent wings catching the firelight; a satyr with dark curling hair playing a lute; a youth with the face of a hedgehog accompanying him on the flute; and what Lirien knew to be a couple of Glynnan elves, though it was the first time he'd ever seen some in person.

The elves from the mountains of Glynna were known for their gray skin, steely eyes that glinted like metal, and hair in varying colors of black, gray, and white. They blended into the stone of the mountains, and were metalsmiths who peacefully worked alongside the dwarves.

At least, they were until the sacred sword Alibrandr was stolen for the royal treasury. Since then, Lirien had heard, they'd learned how to fight, how to spy, how to hunt. But even so, they'd never recovered Alibrandr.

Lirien eyed the two elves, a man and woman both with hair the color of charcoal and figures long and lithe. While they were both dressed for the revel in suits of dark gray velvet with tiny glittering specks of silver throughout, they each wore a quiver of arrows and bows on their backs, which they removed and handed to a fairy in livery.

Maybe I should avoid them, Lirien thought. *If they realize I'm from Ardeth, there might be trouble.*

Lirien scooted closer to Kitra as he surveyed his surroundings. Everyone was costumed in a dizzying array of finery that far exceeded the royal court of Ardeth. There were gowns of materials from charmeuse and chiffon to bark and berries, and suits with lacy collars and slashed sleeves. Real flowers, leaves, and branches, along with gold and silver chainwork, decorated the clothing. It was a marvel of fashion Lirien knew he would not see again.

He himself felt awkward in his clothes, and although his suit could be described as gorgeous, he was unaccustomed to being called such. When he'd put the finished garments on, their embellishments added and last-minute embroidery sewn on, Bella Morgana had let out a satisfied sigh and told him how beautiful he was.

She'd gelled his hair back from his face and brushed miniscule golden sparkles through it, making his hair glittery and more textured. She'd clipped on hanging chandelier earrings of gold and iridescent blue feldspar, and she'd lined his upper eyelids with a stick of gold. He noticed in the mirror the faint fleck where his scale used to be, and saw that it wasn't a big deal that it was missing. No doubt people wouldn't be staring at that mark anyway, not with all the cosmetics and jewelry he was wearing.

As for Kitra, when Lirien saw her fully dressed, the breath left his body for a moment. Bella Morgana had styled her hair and pinned it in an updo with several strands of freshly curled hair cascading downwards, and real teal blooms to match the flower trimmings she had added to Kitra's suit. As for jewelry, Kitra wore gold filigree ear cuffs and a variety of rings on her fingers.

Lirien couldn't stop sneaking looks at Kitra, and he hoped upon hope she didn't notice. Then he heard someone call him.

Lord Iesin and Lady Ariana were garbed in paired outfits of various shades of red wine and gray dripping and mingling together like watercolors. Lady Ariana beckoned him over to them. A large rug covered in a variety of beautiful, colorful pillows stretched across the ground and the Lord and Lady lay upon it. Four posts held up a transparent fabric curtain over their heads, forming a canopy, and glittering lights in different-colored glass balls hung from it.

"I see we're not the only matching couple tonight," Lady Ariana said, looking Kitra over. "You both look good. Bella Morgana's done wondrous work as usual."

"You're standing so close to the Prince, dear Kitra," Lord Iesin said with a smile.

"I'm not letting him out of my sight, my Lord," Kitra answered.

"Because he is a friend or because he is a foe?"

"We have a pact."

"Ah, I see. Well, you're perfectly welcome here. No need to mind each other so closely. I suggest both of you relax and enjoy yourselves tonight." He waved his hand nonchalantly and a current of warmth passed over Lirien, and for the first time since he entered Elythia, the tension melted from his body. Something like a pleasant haze hung over him, dulling his senses, and a lazy, playful smile erupted on his face.

Kitra's eyes seemed clouded, and her shoulders relaxed as she, too, grinned languidly back.

Lord Iesin waved his hands again, and the warmth came to Lirien once more. "Both of you will dance at the revel with whomever asks you until I decide otherwise."

Kitra turned to Lirien and started with, "May I—" but Lady Ariana's voice overlapped hers.

"The first dance is mine," she said, holding her hand out to Lirien. He accepted it and helped her off the heavily pillowed carpet, then she took the lead and pulled him onto the lawn where various couples were assembled to dance.

Her left hand rested on Lirien's lower back. She tugged at his right hand and placed it at the small of her own back, their arms crossing. "Keep your hand there, just like I've done with you."

Lirien recognized the rhythm of the music as a variation of the volta. The first step was a promenade of sorts in a circle, which was simple enough, then he and Lady Ariana had to move their hands in order for him to spin her once. Then, when she faced him again, he lifted her by her waist in the air, turning her once, setting her down, then lifting and whirling her once more. They repeated these steps two more times until they made one large circle, then the dance restarted from the beginning, but in the opposite direction. After going to the left and right, the tempo would speed up slightly and the dance would restart.

After several repetitions, Lord Iesin gently grabbed Lady Ariana's shoulder. "May I intercede?" The Lady nodded and

Lord Iesin placed his hand on Lirien's lower back for the promenade.

"Same steps. I lead."

Lirien nodded obediently, letting the music pull him along until Lord Iesin was the one doing so. He barely registered anything as he was being lifted and spun by his waist in the air.

When the song ended, Lord Iesin bowed deeply to Lirien, who politely returned it.

Lady Ariana found her way to Lord Iesin's side and embraced him low around the waist. "What do you think, my love?" she purred at him.

"Absolutely delightful."

Had Lirien full control of his senses, he would have noticed the way they looked at him, spiders spinning webs behind their eyes.

The two of them gave each other a quick kiss and Lady Ariana said to Lirien, "Have fun. We'll invite you to our canopy once more soon."

They left Lirien alone on the lawn and a shy tap on his lower back signaled him to turn around. A faun who nervously kept looking aside as he tucked his hair behind his ears asked him for the next dance, and Lirien dreamily complied. After that, he partnered with a beautiful sylph who glided toward him and matched his height only because she stepped on the air to dance with him. Then he paired with the elven woman he saw earlier, and soon after with a ram-headed man and a slew of other dancers in the night, but at no point did Kitra make her way to him. She was busy being crowded and surrounded by fae requesting her to dance.

And strangely enough, Lirien found he didn't seem to care. He felt fine, just fine, the movements of his body flowing and continuous as a river cutting through rock, constant and beyond his control.

Soon he felt himself pulled by a different current, all the way to Lord Iesin and Lady Ariana's canopy.

Then he was lying down, and Lady Ariana gently placed her hand on his chest and a comfortable heat seeped into him. With her other hand, she brushed along his fingertips with her thumb in a soothing, almost hypnotic pattern.

If he had any cares or worries left within him, they were gone. Everything seeped out of him.

Lady Ariana nestled up against him comfortably and Lord Iesin leaned over him, his long, dark red hair grazing Lirien's cheek. But all Lirien seemed to take note of were the lights in the colored glass hanging above his head.

I could stay like this forever, he thought to himself dizzily.

Soft lips pressed against his and lingered in a gentle kiss. Garnet eyes peered down at him. There was a vague hint of a smile before the second kiss came, strong and heated.

At the same time, the hand that was on his heart slid underneath his clothes, warm skin against his bare chest, and another set of lips caressed his ear.

His heart thudded rapidly, and a wave of panic overtook him. He felt no pleasure; only thoughts of the Queen.

No. Stop!

Lirien was on his feet, his breathing changed, a feeling of dread and disgust as memories came back to him. The Lord and Lady quickly rose to their feet, staring him down in anger.

"Bravery and folly," Lord Iesin said, "to refuse a gift from the Lord and Lady of Autumn Wood."

"Our kiss is not without worth," the Lady spoke, "yet you would treat it thus."

Lirien felt more and more of himself returning as his thoughts cleared. *It's because a kiss has worth that I cannot accept or give it so freely.*

Lord Iesin's expression and tone changed. He looked at Lirien in amusement. "What a noble thing to say, of a kiss."

"An innocent creature you are, indeed." Lady Ariana laughed. "Blessed be the one who earns your lips." Then she was very serious. "You were blessed to earn ours, yet you insulted us. It cannot be overlooked. You will be punished for this."

A mix of fear and anger flooded Lirien. *It is not a gift when it is forced upon you. You didn't ask me.*

"Enough." Lady Ariana raised her hand to stop his thoughts. "Have you designed something suitable, my love?"

Lord Iesin nodded. He leaned in close to her and whispered something that Lirien couldn't catch, and the Lady's hand flew to her mouth as she tried to stifle more laughter. "Brilliant," she said.

Lord Iesin waved his hand over Lirien, and a heat overwhelmed his body, though it only lasted a few seconds. "I have placed a compulsion on you. It begins now."

Lirien's limbs moved of their own accord and he started walking out of the revel. In truth it was what he wanted to do, but the pressure to keep moving overwhelmed him and the fact that he had lost his will frightened him. What was he compelled to do?

"Best of luck to you, Prince," Lord Iesin called after him. "May we see you again soon."

Lirien took one look back toward the crowd to spot Kitra in a languid dance with a rabbit-like, dark-furred phouka. Lirien reached out to her with his mind, calling desperately, *Kitra! Help me, please!*

She didn't respond, and he continued his forced strides into the forest.

In complete darkness, Lirien hurried through Autumn Wood, not knowing where his legs were carrying him. He thought he would continue straight forever, but then he veered sharply left, going off the trail and kicking up the gold dust of the gilt flowers as he traversed the forest. Things in the night wordlessly whispered at him as he passed the tall, lush trees of the wood.

He walked and walked until dawn, and though he was exhausted, his body kept moving. He had no idea where he was; all his surroundings were unfamiliar to him. He barreled through the sea of trees and then jerked suddenly to the left yet again. He grabbed onto a trunk, locking his arms around it, physically trying to stop himself from moving, but even his struggling couldn't curb the compulsion to keep going. The fae's spell won out.

As he journeyed, his thoughts flew to Nina— back at Bella Morgana's, waiting for his return. He'd veered so far off track that he had no idea how far away he was from the giantess's keep, and the more he wandered, the more nervous he became. He thought of Sorin and Sonalie, and then rebuked himself for angering the Lord and Lady when they were his chance to get out of Elythia.

Then he thought of Kitra, stuck back at the revel, forced to honor every request made of her to dance. He was able to break out of the Lord and Lady's initial hold, but why wasn't Kitra able to? He felt a pang of guilt, leaving her there alone with all of them, stuck under the spell. He hoped upon hope she'd be free of the enchantment once daylight hit, and that she'd be able to find him and help him out of whatever spell was placed upon him.

The colorful trees started thinning out and the land became stonier, then there was a clear line where the trees switched to gigantic pines, taller and thicker than those of Pinemore. Snow dusted the branches and stuck to the pinecones that dotted the trees and the forest floor, and the land was coated in tiny gold flecks from the gilt flowers that popped up through the snow. The temperature had immediately dropped, and in the distance, Lirien saw that the snow grew heavier and thicker on the ground.

This must be Winter Wood. And I'm about to cross right into it.

He rushed through the boundary between Woods and felt something pull away from him, a sensation around his head, like a loosening, and he knew that Lord Iesin and Lady Ariana's gift of thought-speak had disappeared.

Not long into the forest, strange, leafy green vines with thorns started to appear, weaving through the trees like strands on a web. Something inside him wanted to turn back, to flee from these plants that seemed so out of place, but the pressure inside of him pushed him forward.

He jumped when a midnight-colored deer with striking sky-blue eyes landed in front of him, running desperately away from wherever Lirien seemed to be travelling. There was a bloody red hole on its backside, glistening and fresh, as it darted past him.

As Lirien continued his march, he made out strange shapes in the vines that had thickened into clusters. First, he saw something that looked like a bird of prey. Then a larger creature, with gory thorns circling it— a boar. The figures increased the more he journeyed on, and the vines enveloped the bodies, creating a nightmarish topiary of creatures whose corpses were barely visible underneath, save for the thin streams of blood that colored the sharp barbs.

The vines moved and pulsed in a strange rhythm, and with a sucking sound, something disgusting and wet, the crimson rivulets dripped upward and disappeared inside the tips of the spines.

Before he could process what he was looking at, he finally halted in front of one of the trees where a large shape was cocooned inside the net of vines and thorns. He could see long, blond hair through cracks in the vines, and a face contorted in pain, with dull, lifeless eyes and gnarled hands with scraped fingers— a fae man. At his feet laid a sword, and Lirien grabbed it as he careened ahead into the wood.

What am I doing? As if in answer, beyond his control he swung the sword and hacked at one of the vines, cutting through it in one fell swoop. Brilliant red blood gushed out.

A horrendous groan echoed through the forest, and birds cawed and flew from the trees at the sound.

Lirien's throat tightened, and his heart felt like it would explode out of his chest. He was afraid of the thing that had made such a sound, and even more afraid that he seemed to be heading right toward it.

And then he saw it: standing in the center of a maze of criss-crossing spikes, the towering figure of a bearded man crowned with leaves, with curling hair the color of pines and robes of moss and ferns. He was no giant, but still much bigger than Lirien, and he vomited spiked vines from his mouth and from the tear ducts of his eyes. The thorns scraped at his own skin the color and texture of thin bark, and blood spilled from him but he didn't seem to care. The creeping plants rushed out of his body and created a wall of lush, green briars that looped around and wove together the trees.

The Green Man.

And Lirien was all but running right toward him now, his arms raising the sword high above his head. His body screamed *attack* while his mind screamed *run,* and Lirien brought the blade down on another vine, cleaving it in two. Blood poured out of the plant, but only for a moment, and then with that same disgusting sucking sound, the red liquid retreated inward, back into the thorns.

The Green Man let out a laugh that sounded like tree branches snapping. "A new champion," he said in a knobby, deep voice. He tilted his head back, closing his eyes, and took in a drag of air. "Smells sweet. I will relish your taste, young man." And as soon as he opened his eyes, a thorny vine shot from somewhere on his back, straight toward Lirien.

Lirien did a sort of tumble-roll— at least, that's what he thought it was. He was no fighter, but his body seemed to know what to do as he somehow got out of the way of the Green Man's attack, flew to his feet, and hacked another piece away.

A spiked rope of green flew past him, nearly swiping the side of his face, and Lirien sliced it off. Then he broke into a run, his hands tightening around the sword's hilt, and he made to thrust it into the Green Man's stomach, but he couldn't get close enough without more vines shooting out at him. He ducked, he rolled, he jumped back, and he carved up what he could, but he saw that he wasn't making much progress. Every time he cut off a leafy limb, another one exploded out of the Green Man's body, aiming right for him. And Lirien's every impulse pushed him to swing the fae knight's sword in what was turning out to be a never-ending battle.

A huge fireball soared through the air and collided with the Green Man's upper body, small flames spreading across his chest. The Green Man bellowed and smothered the flames with countless vines until it was out. He aimed his vines at the source, and they wrapped around the giant fox's snout and wired her mouth shut.

Kitra!

She made terrible, high-pitched whimpering sounds as she fled from the attacking briars, unable to open her jaws to release more fire. She circled behind the Green Man and launched herself at him, claws bared, trying to tear at his head with her paws.

It was no use. One of the thorny branches from the Green Man's eyes circled around and struck her across her shoulder blade. It impaled her deeply, and the Green Man lifted Kitra high off the ground. He flung her against the thorny web as if she were nothing, and she stuck there, her arms and legs splayed out in different directions.

Lirien opened his mouth, forming Kitra's name to shout it, but no sound came out. Then he snapped to attention as the Green Man advanced toward her. His back was open, and Lirien, summoning strength he didn't know he had, launched his sword with impeccable, otherworldly aim, straight for his lower back to impale him through the stomach.

The Green Man's head whipped around and instantly his skin hardened into the thick bark of a tree. The sword ricocheted off him and landed far out of Lirien's reach.

As the Green Man turned to face Lirien, his thorns cocooned Kitra, and she bled everywhere the spikes had punctured her, leaving red droplets in the snow. The thorns drank their fill.

Lirien ran for the sword, but the Green Man vomited a new set of vines his way, and they wrapped around his waist, stabbing his back and stomach as the Green Man lifted him up in the air. Lirien's body jerked and struggled beyond his control, while his mind tried to calm itself. As terrified as he was to be caught, he remembered what he was, who he was. He didn't have to do anything at all.

The Green Man brought Lirien inches away from his face. "A taste like never before," he said, as his thorns quenched their thirst. Then the Green Man's eyes rolled back in his head, and he spit out a great clot of blood. The vines that poured from his mouth and tear ducts retreated inward. All of the briars that wove through the pines turned a darker shade of green and their texture changed to a thick and slimy mass, freeing the blood-drained animal corpses and other victims. Kitra dropped to the ground, and she lost her fox form, changing back into a fae woman as she fainted.

Lirien fell onto his back. The puncture wounds from where the Green Man's spikes had stabbed him burned, and he felt the blood ooze out of him as he lay on the wet ground.

The Green Man continued to turn into a thick jelly, until he dissolved into a glob vaguely in the shape of a human.

Lirien waited until the Green Man's form was completely lifeless and then, with difficulty, crawled to his feet. He staggered over to Kitra and knelt at her side, cradling her.

She looked awful. She was covered in crimson marks and had puncture wounds all over her body, her arms, her legs, and her face... It looked incredibly painful. Lirien gently shook her, trying to see if she would wake, and when she didn't, he resolved to carry her. One of his arms reached under the crook of her legs and another arm supported her back, then he lifted her up off the ground.

As soon as the Green Man was dead, Lirien had regained control over his body. The feeling of automation had disappeared, and he moved with complete purpose as he retraced his steps out of that part of the forest. The trees thickened, the land grew less sparse and rocky, and the snow dissipated. Once he was out of Winter Wood and back into Autumn, he quickened his pace, breaking into a run. He didn't know where he was heading; he just hoped he would find help along the way.

He hurried with Kitra in his arms as fast as he could go, and then he stopped when he heard the sound of heavy footfalls moving at a fast pace through the wood. Was it another giant?

Nothing like it. A cottage with a thatched roof and welcoming plume of smoke coming from the chimney galloped toward him. *Galloped.* The house had six brown equine legs, larger and thicker than an actual horse's, and its hooves made a rapid, audible rhythm on the forest floor.

Lirien retreated and stumbled over a large tree root, almost losing his grip on Kitra, before the house abruptly halted. The legs lowered the cottage to the ground and disappeared beneath the foundation, as if they were never there at all.

The door to the house flew open and a fae-like creature stood there; his eyes widened when he saw Kitra and Lirien. The man looked to be in his late twenties or early thirties. He had solid black eyes, even where the whites should have been, and pale green skin. Two obsidian horns escaped the long locks of white hair that cascaded down to his shoulders. "Hurry up, get inside!"

Lirien hesitated, unsure whether or not to trust another being of Elythia, but the man assured him, "I'm a friend. My house only greets those who are in need of saving. No bargains or payment required. I'm in service to Elythia and its peoples— it's my purpose. Please, come inside. I can help you."

Lirien bowed his head in appreciation and rushed in after the man, who pointed to a bed. "You can set her there."

Lirien laid Kitra down as gently as he could, wincing. The wounds in his stomach and lower back stung whenever he moved, and he felt blood once again trickle down his skin.

"What happened to you? From the looks of you both, I'd guess the Green Man, but he rarely leaves survivors."

Lirien tried to think at him— *You're right, and I killed him* — but the blank look on the man's face indicated that Lirien's ability truly was gone; returning to Autumn Wood was not enough to bring it back. Lirien touched his hand to his throat and shook his head.

"Can't speak. All right. Well, I'll help you both as best as I can. At the very least, I'll treat your wounds." He washed his hands, then went to a cupboard filled with supplies, pulling out rolls of bandages and jars with herbs inside of them. "I'm Jerrad. People call me the Gentle Goblin of the Wood. Much like Elythia, my cottage wanders about of its own accord. I travel through the four seasonal forests, seeking out those in immediate need— people who require food, water, shelter, healing— but only in the direst circumstances. And my house only comes to those who can be saved... and unfortunately, not everyone can be." He set his items on a small table and brought it over next to the bed. "Let me get to you first. Take off your jacket and shirt, please."

Lirien complied, gritting his teeth when Jerrad pulled the fabric away from his punctured skin and took his clothes from him, laying them gently on his dining table.

Lirien reached out to touch Jerrad's shoulder. *Blood,* he mouthed. *Poison.*

Jerrad looked at him with a raised eyebrow, as though he was trying to work out Lirien's words. "Poison?"

Lirien nodded. He pointed to his mouth, then made an 'x' with his hands. Then he shook his head.

"I understand. I'll be careful." Jerrad grabbed a large bowl and filled it with water, then took one of the jars he had brought over, containing what looked like tiny, crumbled leaves. He dumped the contents into the water and they dissolved, turning the liquid a dark brown. He took a cloth and dipped it in the bowl. "Let me clean you." He brought the cloth close to Lirien's stomach, then added, "This is going to hurt."

Jerrad didn't lie. The burning sensation from the liquid

stung even more than when the thorns first broke Lirien's skin, and he squeezed his eyes shut from the pain.

"Two more of those big wounds and we're finished, all right?" Jerrad finished tending to the holes in Lirien's skin and then wrapped his stomach and back in fresh bandages.

"Now, let's see about your friend. She seems to have gotten the worst of whatever happened to you." He wet a new cloth in the medicinal water and started to wipe down Kitra's face.

She opened her eyes.

CHAPTER 10

Kitra let out a soft "nngh" when the medicine hit her skin. "Oh, that feels awful."

"It'll help keep infection away," Jerrad explained. He introduced himself once more before adding gently, "I'll need you to remove your clothes. But here, you can tie these around you so you may keep your modesty." He grabbed two long, thick scarves as Kitra sat up, a little groan escaping her lips. He handed her the fabric as Kitra painfully slid out of her jacket and reached for the bottom of her blouse. Lirien turned around to give her privacy.

"I will need your help when she's ready," Jerrad said to him. "The wounds are numerous."

Lirien could hear Kitra's clothing drop onto the floor, and a few moments later, she said, "You can turn around." She let out a pained laugh. "I look like I have the blight."

Lirien furrowed his brow in sympathy. His own wounds burned in his bandages; he couldn't imagine the pain Kitra must feel being completely covered with wounds where the thorns had stabbed her.

Jerrad handed Lirien a fresh cloth and gestured to soak it in the medicinal water. The two of them, with gentle movements, wiped Kitra down, and her entire body tensed with every contact.

"Almost done," Jerrad said.

"Lirien," Kitra said, wincing. "How did you get us out of there?"

Lirien tapped his forehead, then his throat, and shook his head.

Jerrad rose from Kitra's bedside to his feet and got more bandages from the cupboard, then a sheet of paper and stick of charcoal. "Here. I'm interested in your explanation, too. You said your blood was poison— was that the thing that helped you?"

Jerrad started wrapping Kitra's numerous wounds as Lirien scribbled on the paper. He held it up to them: *Yes. As siren-born, my blood is poison. It was nothing special on my part. He drank my blood, and it killed him.*

Jerrad's jaw dropped. "He's dead?"

Lirien nodded, and a smile erupted across Jerrad's face.

"I'm so glad. You may think you've done nothing heroic— Lirien, was it? —but this is no small thing. The Green Man has plagued us for ages. He was once called Gildaran, ruler of Summer Wood, but something in him changed, and no one knows what or why. He would wander, devour, then sleep, then eat again. And because he was a Lord, the Lords and Ladies could not kill him. It was part of a geas, you see, not to destroy their brethren. And Elythia, venerable and benevolent realm as it is, would not, could not, push him out. Word of this will travel fast. You've saved countless of us."

"And you saved me," Kitra added, her voice growing quiet. "You took me out of Winter Wood and brought me here."

Lirien dismissed her with a wave, meant to convey that it

was no trouble. And he didn't think he'd actually saved Kitra—Jerrad seemed to be doing a fine enough job of that.

"Of course, you'll be rewarded for your service to Elythia," Jerrad said.

Lord Iesin and Lady Ariana compelled me to fight, Lirien wrote. *It was a punishment. I doubt they will reward me.*

"They owe you for the significant task they gave you. And the fae don't take obligation lightly."

Kitra gritted her teeth for a moment as she leaned forward and touched Lirien's hand. "That's how it works. I owe you, too."

Lirien added to his paper. *What if I say it was a gift?*

"Then I give you a gift in return. I know we are bound to each other for the duration of our pact, but if you accept me, Lirien, I will follow you beyond it, until you have what you wish, until it is impossible to be with one another."

I don't want you to feel obligated to me. His face grew warm. *You have to want to be with me on your own.*

"Then I want to be with you."

"Good. You can keep an eye on each other's recovery," Jerrad said. "You can get dressed again. Let me pack up some supplies for you and tell you how to care for your wounds as you heal."

As Jerrad did so, Lirien once again turned away while Kitra put her bloody clothes back on, and Lirien carefully put back on his own shirt and doublet. All of Bella Morgana's beautiful work for the revel was ruined. He wondered what she would say, then immediately went to his paper and charcoal. When Jerrad was done talking, Lirien held up his note to him. *Can your house take us to Bella Morgana's?*

"My house can travel anywhere in Elythia. And, unless someone is in pressing need, it usually listens to me." Jerrad tapped the floor with his foot. "Take us to Bella Morgana's, old friend."

The house tilted and Lirien and Kitra braced themselves, Kitra clutching the bedpost and him latching onto a table that had been nailed to the floor. Jerrad held onto nothing— he seemed completely used to it and stayed effortlessly balanced as the house trotted, then galloped, through Autumn Wood.

It knew exactly where to go. Once it had stopped in front of Bella Morgana's keep, the house stooped to the ground.

Jerrad opened the door and handed Lirien a bag filled with bandages and medicine. "You'll need to keep an eye on those wounds and redress them."

Lirien nodded. He held his hand out to shake Jerrad's in appreciation, and Jerrad accepted. "Happy to be of service," he said.

Kitra slowly and mechanically got out of Jerrad's bed and followed Lirien to the door. She gave the tiniest of bows, a quick dip of her body, to Jerrad. "Farewell."

Once the two stepped out of Jerrad's house, the horse legs reappeared and the home lifted off the grassy floor. It broke into a gallop, then passed through a doorway, or something like it, that Lirien couldn't see. The house was there, and then it wasn't.

Lirien moved to Bella Morgana's door and gave it a knock. She poked her head out, looking down at them, and her mouth opened in a gasp. "What the hell happened to you?"

"The Green Man," Kitra said. "And Lirien killed him."

There was a squawk from one of the trees across the way into Spring Wood, echoed by several other calls of birds. The branches of the trees waved back and forth as the birds flew from them and off in different directions.

"Well, now that news will spread," Bella Morgana said. "It won't be long before Lord Iesin and Lady Ariana learn of this." She opened her door wider to them. "Please, come inside. Let's get you out of those bloody clothes."

As Lirien and Kitra entered the keep, Kitra said, "I'm sorry we ruined your costumes."

"I'm sorry too, but you killed the Green Man, and you lived — that's far more important. And I still have some materials left, so if I want, I can make them again."

She handed them their clothes from before the Revel, and Lirien once again gave Kitra privacy as the two changed back into their own clothes. He couldn't help wincing as he slipped into his pants, pulling them up to the wound in his stomach and lower back, which created a burning, tugging sensation, and then the fabric rubbed against his bandages. He couldn't imagine what Kitra must have been feeling as she stepped back into her own outfit.

Out of the corner of his eye, he spotted movement at his feet and he jumped back— Nina. He awkwardly bent his body to grab her, trying not to put too much stress on his injuries, but it still hurt. Nina coiled around his wrist, eyeing him intently, her tongue flicking in and out.

Was she expecting him to think at her? He wasn't sure. He tapped his forehead and shook his head, then tapped his throat, shaking his head again. As far as he knew, shaking his head and nodding were probably going to be his main ways of communication from there on out.

Nina's head tilted to the side, and then she slinked up his sleeve, taking her favorite spot on his arm, all the while poking her head out to see everything.

Bella Morgana took Lirien's bloody suit away from him. "I saw you tap your forehead and throat," she said. "So, no more talking for you?"

Kitra slowly advanced to them. "Once he left the boundaries of Autumn Wood, he lost the power of thought-speak."

Lirien reached into the bag from Jerrad and pulled out a book of blank pages and the charcoal stick. He noticed more writing tools and paper had been added, including some chalk.

He wrote: *It will be all right. I need to learn to speak without it, anyway.*

"True. When you're finally able to leave Elythia, you'll have to fare without it in the world outside."

A banging on the door interrupted their conversation and Bella Morgana opened it. Lord Iesin and Lady Ariana stood there, gorgeous smiles spread across their faces, in completely different spirits from when Lirien last left them.

"Lirien! I knew you could do it!" Lord Iesin exclaimed, barging into the keep with Lady Ariana at his side.

"We had every faith in you," the Lady added.

Lirien was furious. *You forced me to fight,* he scribbled, *and Kitra nearly died.*

"Well, yes," said Lord Iesin, "a punishment is a punishment. But even so, we knew it would all work out."

"When we read your curses, we read your blood and saw the potential there," Lady Ariana said. "We understand your fury, but everything has worked out as it should. And we will reward you for the great work you've done."

"First, we will heal you. Make your wounds as if they were never there. And then, Lirien, you may request one thing from us, and we will grant it, as long as it is within our power," said Lord Iesin.

Lady Ariana went to Kitra, who muttered, "Well, the clothes come off again." Kitra started pulling her doublet off and Lirien turned around. Lord Iesin faced him.

"Where are you hurt?" he asked.

Lirien lifted his shirt, showing the bandages around his stomach and lower back. Lord Iesin gently unwrapped him and set the fabric on the table. His hands hovered just above the puncture in Lirien's stomach, and as heat poured into Lirien's body, Lirien watched his skin knit itself together, the redness disappearing. It was as the fae had said: there was no trace that anything had happened to him.

Lord Iesin moved to Lirien's back. "You have an older wound here," he said. "And the one on your hand. Though they are not from the Green Man, I shall heal them, too." Lord Iesin used his magic on every mark on Lirien's body, and Lirien couldn't help but feel grateful for his power. It would make travel much easier, and save time, as Lirien wouldn't have to stop and redress the bandages and reapply medicine. But he took care to offer no thanks, so as not to again offend the fae.

Lady Ariana rejoined Lord Iesin's side when she had finished healing Kitra. "Have you thought about it? What you want?"

Lirien once again wrote on his paper. *Give me the ability to talk to Elythia.*

The Lord and Lady looked at each other, then Lord Iesin spoke. "We can try, but we cannot promise that Elythia will allow it. The forest decides for itself what it will allow."

The Lord and Lady flanked Lirien, holding their palms out to him, bowing their heads and shutting their eyes as if in deep concentration. A humming sensation bloomed from Lirien's throat, up his face, and settled in his forehead. But it felt deeper than that, as though it was permeating the inside of his skull. Then it quickly disappeared.

"Well," Lady Ariana said, brushing her arms off as if they were dirty, "I didn't expect that to work so well, and quickly, too. Since you cannot vocalize at present, just use thought-speak to talk to Elythia. It will hear you, though it may not always give you what you want."

I'll try it in a moment, Lirien wrote.

"We'll be on our way, then." The Lord and Lady linked their

arms together and headed out the door, and as soon as they passed through it, they were gone.

Kitra turned to Lirien. "What will you do now? Call on Elythia?"

Lirien nodded. *We need to leave as soon as possible.*

Bella Morgana squinted at his writing. "Before you do that," she said, "I have something for you, too, Lirien, for your service to us." She searched through her hangers of outfits until she came across something tucked behind numerous gowns. She pulled it out and revealed a hooded cloak made with many different furs, of animals Lirien did and did not recognize. They were all sewn together in a patchwork pattern, making a unique, if somewhat ugly, cloak.

Bella Morgana handed him the furs. "It's quite valuable, so you can only borrow it. When you put this on, you will be unrecognizable to any human you may come across. They'll still see you— it won't make you invisible —but no one will know you, not even your closest kin. When you return out into the world, you may need it— a prince on his own is usually a prince in danger." She slipped it over his shoulders, and he tied the strings at his collar.

"He's not going to be on his own," Kitra said. "He'll have me."

Lirien's cheeks warmed as she said those words, and he lowered his head to her.

"That's good. Now, as with all magical things, there are rules to the cloak," Bella Morgana explained. "The first is the obvious one— the magic stops working once you take it off. And the next rule— if this tears or rips in any way, the cloak will never work again."

Lirien bowed to her in appreciation. It made him feel far more at ease knowing he had something that could keep the

Queen off his trail for the time being, and that he would be safe from anyone who'd cross their path.

Lirien tucked his paper and charcoal stick inside Jerrad's bag, patted Nina's head, and gestured to Kitra to head out the door. "This is farewell," Bella Morgana said. Lirien nodded and Kitra waved goodbye as the two left the keep.

He wasn't sure if there was anything special he needed to do to talk to Elythia. Should he be reverent? Should he bow his head as if in prayer? He wanted to be respectful, so he lowered his gaze to the ground, then closed his eyes in thought. *Elythia. Let me out. Please. I need to save my family.* If Elythia didn't answer him, he didn't know what he would do.

Lirien opened his eyes to find that the cherry blossom forest that made up Spring Wood had completely changed. The woods were darker, filled with cedars and twisting black limbs of trees that he couldn't name. Moss and ferns covered everything, and a gray mist permeated the air, giving the woods a haunted look. Green-covered stones dotted the trail that cut through rocky land. The mountains of Glynna appeared in the sky in the distance, covered in thick snow-powdered greenery, except toward the tops of the crags, where dark gray stone peeked through.

Lirien's breath left his body at the beauty of the mountains in the distance. It was so much more than what pictures in books rendered. And he thought of his atlas, trying to place where he and Kitra must be. It was most likely Yanna.

Yanna was a sizeable wood that spread across the two countries Ardeth bordered, Léandor and Asherin. A primordial cedar forest with narrow pathways cut through it, the amount of moss and greenery told which kingdom you were in. The greener and more mysterious the wood, you were on the Léandor side— an ancient forest in an ancient kingdom. If you headed east, the more spread out the trees and the lighter the forest became, which meant you were in Asherin.

Judging by the look of the forest that stretched out in front of them, they were probably about to enter Léandor. It was impossible to tell where they were going to be once they entered, though as long as they headed east, Asherin was theirs. But whether or not the twins would be at Lake Karda remained to be seen. Lirien took a moment to pray for their safe arrival in Asherin and hoped that he would meet them there.

Thank you, Elythia, Lirien thought to the forest.

Kitra stood beside him, suddenly giving him a mischievous grin.

"What we're on will take us far
To places new and lands unseen
That test and show us who we are
As we pursue our goal and dream.

"What am I?"

Lirien got it. *Quest,* he mouthed.

Kitra was able to read his lips, and smiled. "Perfect. Let's begin."

THEY'D BEEN WALKING EASTWARD for a few hours when the sun began to set. The path through the wood was a little trickier than Lirien expected, and he had to be more careful with his footing because the mist that hung in the air coated the rocks and fallen leaves with moisture, making everything a bit slippery.

To his surprise, Kitra did not return to her fox form. In fact, she changed her appearance once more— to that of a human. She tapped her fox ears and they disappeared; swiped her hand along her tail until it turned invisible; and blinked her eyes so the pupils rounded and the color changed to a soft brown.

"Glamour is one of the few magicks the fae can use outside of Elythia," she explained. "Disguising appearances. It's safer for me if the world doesn't know what I am. They might seek my heart." Her voice grew quiet at the end of her sentence, and Lirien assumed she must be thinking of her brother.

They walked along the ever-rising path, which was wide enough only for two people to pass through. "I honestly don't know how it happened. How Kai could've been taken. Elythia lets him out, but rarely. He must have seized the moment to venture outside. Usually he kept his fox form in the mortal world; it protects you when you're hungry and cold. Someone must've gotten him then."

Lirien nodded to show he was listening. He had some trouble coming up with gestures that weren't repetitive, finding difficulty doing more beyond nodding 'yes' and shaking his head 'no,' and lots of shrugging for when he didn't know, and bowing his head to show appreciation.

He adjusted the fur cloak, grateful for the added warmth it provided. It was quite soft and comfortable to wear in Yanna, where the gray mist added a chill to everything. He wasn't sure if the forest and elevation made it so much cooler or if they were in a different season altogether. When he first came to Elythia, he left summer for autumn. He guessed it was now early spring, and that meant at least seven months had passed on the outside while he was in the wandering realm. Feeling a sense of urgency, he quickened his pace.

A strange pressure came from behind his eyes, and he winced. Just as soon as it started, it stopped. He had no idea what it was. He rubbed his eyes for good measure, although it was a meaningless gesture.

Kitra was staring at him with a raised eyebrow. "Are you alright?"

Lirien raised his hand dismissively with a nod. Kitra still eyed him carefully but said nothing.

With the sun going down, she suggested they prepare to spend the night in the forest. They found a place that was a little more open and the ground clearer. Her gaze circled around their space, and seeing no one, she changed quickly into a giant fox. She dug a pit into the ground, then said to him, "You can get sticks for the fire, and I'll catch dinner. I'll be quick about it. I don't feel comfortable being like this for too long." She darted off.

Lirien let Nina slide off his arm. He wondered if she was hungry, too, and hoped she would know how to hunt as a snake. Within a few minutes, he had his answer. He turned around to see a large bulge in Nina's belly that wasn't there moments before. *Good for you.*

He found plenty of dried, fallen branches for kindling as Kitra hunted. He tried to remember what he saw the soldiers in the castle courtyard do for their fire. He eyed Kitra's pit and placed some stones round the edges of it in a circle, then arranged the sticks inside the way he'd seen before.

Lighting the fire was another story. He had no idea how to go about it. He struggled with striking some rocks together, then tossed them aside in frustration when nothing happened.

Kitra returned and dropped several fish at his feet, took one look at the readied pit, and blew a ball of foxfire into it, lighting the wood with ease.

"I found a stream near here," she said. "I'll show you after supper." She changed back into her human disguise, then kindly showed him how to prepare and cook his fish. He ate it, almost feverish with hunger, but it was tasteless. He nearly cried over it. He looked up at Kitra, who was busy with her own food, and he was grateful she didn't notice his eyes mist up.

After eating, Kitra led him to the stream she had found. He caught his reflection in the water and his jaw dropped. He must've been human enough to see the spell that the fur cloak cast on him. His hair had changed to a golden-brown color; his orange eyes now matched his new hair; and his pale skin had darkened and warmed to a faint peachy tan. He looked unrecognizable as Lirien, but he could see all the more clearly the parts of King Neven that were in him all along. It must've been what he would've looked like if he were fully human. And for the first time, he felt the loss of the fish scale mole that he had given up to Bella Morgana. It had been inherited from his father; it had been something they shared in common. Now it was gone, like his father.

He took the cloak off and watched his colors change from golds back to blues. *Incredible.* He carefully folded up the cloak and set it aside. He started to unbutton his top, then realized Kitra was still there. He circled his finger in the air: *turn around.*

"Oh! Sorry!" She did as he asked, and when he felt he wasn't being watched, he pulled his doublet and white undershirt off, standing in the cold air bare-chested and freezing.

He thought about his breeches and decided to hold off removing them. He wasn't going to wash everything, not with Kitra right there. He dipped his hands in the icy stream and cleaned his upper body and face, smoothed some water through his hair, and used his doublet to dab himself off before sliding his blouse over his head again.

Kitra dutifully still stood with her back turned to him. He approached her cautiously and placed his hand on her shoulder, ever so gently. He wasn't sure why he was so nervous to touch her— it wasn't like she was fragile and about to blow away in the wind. But all the same, he kept his hand light.

She faced him. "All clean?"

He shrugged, then with his hand flat and palm facedown, rocked it back and forth: *so-so.*

"Maybe tomorrow we'll find a proper river or pool for bathing," she said. "In the meantime, should we call it a night?"

He nodded— *again* with the nodding —and followed her back to their camp. He eyed Nina curled up into coils underneath the arch of a rock, staying perfectly still. He assumed she understood they were turning in for the night, and just to make sure, he crept over to her and mouthed the word, *goodnight.*

He eyed the fur cloak he still carried in his hands. What should he do about it? He could sleep in it, but he wondered if it was worth the risk of damaging the cloak. He settled on the safer choice and put it back in his satchel, then found a spot a cautious distance from the fire to stretch out. He puffed up the satchel with a few smacks and used it as a pillow for his head.

Kitra fidgeted with her fingers. She looked at the forest floor, then at Lirien, then at the forest floor again. She sprawled down on the ground and lay on her side, resting her head on folded arms. Then after a while, she switched positions, rolling onto her other side. Within a few minutes, she turned onto her back, staring up at the sky.

It wasn't long before she groaned. "I can't stand it. I can't sleep like this."

She took on her fox form and curled her body into a giant circle, her limbs completely covered by her big fluffy tail, which she tucked underneath her chin. She was a giant ball of fur, and she looked so cute he couldn't help but smile.

"What are you grinning at? I can't help it; it's comfortable like this." She stared at him for a while. "Come here," she said. "When the fire dwindles in the night, you're going to be freezing. I understand you want to keep the cloak safe, but what are you going to do to stay warm? You might as well come here."

Lirien stood and draped the strap of the satchel over his body before cautiously stepping closer to Kitra.

She raised her tail. "Lie down here. Right up against me."

He crawled toward her and nestled himself into her side. She smelled of the sweetness of the gilt flowers from Elythia, and the woody mustiness of dried fall leaves mixed with the wetness of the greenery around them. It was a strange scent, an amalgam of nature that Lirien was happy to sink into.

Nina stirred from her place under the rock, and she slinked over to him and Kitra. She found a hollow between them, what looked to be the warmest spot, and made herself comfortable. Once she was in a good place, Lirien nodded off easily, and when he woke, it was before Kitra had opened her eyes. He spotted tears beneath her closed lashes, and he wondered if she dreamed of her brother when she slept. While she spoke of him a little, she, for the most part, seemed to shelve her feelings of Kai in order to move forward with Lirien's quest. He wondered what sort of toll that was taking on her, that her melancholy only came out at night during slumber.

Seven days and nights continued this way. Eight hours of walking with breaks during the day, with Kitra revealing more and more about herself to him, and Lirien enjoying her all the more. Sometimes he felt guilty over the happy moments he shared with her, feeling that all of his time and concentration should be spent on getting to the children. But they had bright moments together, and that helped relieve the tension of his plight to save his family.

On the other hand, Kitra had her own bouts of melancholy, though she did well enough to hide it. But not when she was sleeping. He felt sad for her whenever he spotted the trace of tears on her face in the mornings before she woke. Maybe that's why she wanted him to sleep by her side, to not be alone in her sorrow. But he chose not to address it with her, unsure if she wanted to talk about it. He felt like she would if she wanted to.

In the meantime, he learned from her that fae foxes were more like foxes and less like the fae. Foxes were solitary creatures, only living in a pack when parents had to raise their young. They hunted alone, they wandered alone, and they lived alone, so she had been on her own for most of her life. She visited her parents from time to time, but never really ran into her brothers or sisters except for Kai, who was her favorite. She'd checked up on him periodically because he was the most wild and mischievous fae fox in the family. That was all she said about him on their journey together.

When they were sitting down on the mossy stones to take a break, Kitra asked, "What about your family? I know you have a brother and sisters. What are they like?"

Lirien, at this point, took to writing. *Sorin is the friendliest. Sonalie is cute and shy. Nina is smart and good with people.*

"I would ask you about your parents, but maybe that's a little painful."

He shrugged. *Until my mother showed up on my twentieth birthday, I had never seen her before. She said she loved me. I don't know.*

He thought about why she had allowed him to live, since he couldn't fully be a creature of the sea. That must have been what she thought love was, that it was enough to let him survive. Maybe she had waited until Lirien came of age, until he was an "adult," before taking King Neven's life— making sure he was fine on his own before he lost his father.

His father. Lirien wrote, *I think Father loved me. At least as best as he could. He was kind but he always looked at me a certain way, like he was in pain. Maybe I reminded him of my mother. Every night he'd go to the sea, looking for her. He was obsessed from the siren song in his own way. Nothing like my stepmother.*

"I am so sorry things turned out the way that they did," Kitra said, placing her hand on his. "I still hold out hope for another way to break the spell on her. Spells are meant to be broken, after all."

They continued traveling that way. It was mostly Kitra speaking, and she tried to ask simple questions of him, but it was a little bit trickier for them to get to know each other when he couldn't answer in much detail. He was grateful for his booklet of paper, but he tried to use it sparingly, worried he'd go through the pages. He wanted to talk to Kitra as much as possible but felt like he needed to use some restraint.

Every night Kitra invited him to sleep by her side, and his mind would wander. Sometimes he would imagine what it would be like if Kitra was in her human or fae form, how she would look sleeping up against him. Would she be just as soft as when she was a fox? He wondered if Kitra would ever want to sleep beside him as a woman, and when the thought crossed his mind, he'd push it away just as fast.

Then he remembered Kitra's promise to him; that she would be with him, a life for a life. After first calling it a debt, she later said it wasn't obligation that made her decision. But sometimes, when he remembered that she was still a fae, he couldn't help but worry that Kitra felt she owed him. And a relationship shouldn't be built on something like that.

There were so many things passing through Lirien's mind as the eighth day of travelling came— Kitra, Sorin, Sonalie, Queen Aurinda —that he stopped watching where they were going, walking mindlessly, one step after another.

An arrow shot out of nowhere and landed in front of him just when he was about to take his next step— he nearly kicked right into it.

By reflex, he turned to see where it had come from, and another whizzed passed him.

Kitra grabbed him by the arm and yanked him behind a thick tree. She narrowed her eyes. "It's a Glynnan elf. Hurry up, he's about to fire another one—"

Shoom. The arrow pierced the tree, close to Lirien's head. If the elf had meant to kill him, he clearly could have. These seemed like deliberate misses, an extreme way to draw his attention.

"Prince Lirien of Ardeth," a young male voice called out, "I've come to take you to Queen Aurinda."

Lirien whirled around when Kitra nipped him lightly on the shoulder. She was a fox again, and she lowered herself to the ground. "Get on. Hold tight."

Lirien clambered on with some awkwardness, pulling himself up as fast as he could. In the absence of reins or anything easy to hold onto, he gripped Kitra's fur, his hands curled into fists, and Kitra ran off into the wood.

A youthful voice shouted after them, "It will do no good to run! I'll find you!"

Kitra sprinted, with Lirien bobbling gracelessly on her back, well past the point where they lost sight of the mountain elf who pursued them. He assumed she wanted to put as much distance between them as possible, which he didn't mind in the least.

What was that all about, anyway? He thought the Glynnan elves hated Ardeth's royal family, so why would one of them be in service to the Queen?

His heart sank. He shouldn't have been surprised the Queen would send someone after him. Of course his voice wasn't enough for her; of course she wanted more. But if they were in

Elythia for at least seven months, how could the elf have known where to find them?

Kitra stopped when she felt it was safe and lowered herself to the ground. "Here, get off." She didn't say it gruffly, but it sounded a little abrupt. She transformed back into a young woman. "I don't want to make a habit out of that. I'm not a form of transportation."

Lirien couldn't help smiling at how she said it, and he nodded before lowering his head to her in gratitude. He didn't actually say, "thank you," so he assumed he didn't violate any rules of fae decorum.

Kitra said nothing about it. "Could you see who that was at all?"

Lirien shook his head.

"He was younger. Maybe seventeen? He wasn't one of the elves at the revel. I have no idea how he found us. Elythia may not always do as you wish, but it does have a habit of dropping you off right where it thinks you need to be. I didn't expect danger to come so soon, let alone from an elf. He must've been tracking us for a while." She cocked her head to the side and raised her shoulders in a shrug. "All this time I thought your fellow humans would be the ones to give us trouble. The elf was a surprise. Just in case we have any more surprises waiting for us..."

She switched back into a giant fox once more and opened her jaws, letting out a ball of orange flame. It hovered there, a glowing circle with tendrils of fire dancing around it, and then several feet away from that small globe, Kitra blew out another one. "Just going to create a path of them and lead people off our trail." She disappeared, leaving flaming orbs behind her. After a few moments, they all turned hazy, like a trick in the mist.

That was the thing about foxfire— or "will-o'-the-wisp," as it was also called —it was a mysterious light that led you away from where you needed to go. Once it caught your eye, it was hard not to follow it along until you got completely lost. Yet when he had followed it in Elythia, it brought him right to Kitra. Was that really him being led astray? She had turned out to be quite the ally, and the more time they shared together, the more he wanted to count her as a close friend. It was almost as though he was meant to find her.

Kitra came back to him as a human. They continued their journey, with Lirien puzzling over the Glynnan elf while Kitra kept looking around, stopping and listening from time to time.

They didn't encounter anyone else on the way. They were alone, and Kitra didn't pick up on anything. After another day of uneventful walking, the path through Yanna started widening out, enough that a horse and wagon could make it through. The forest was still thick, but here and there downed trees and severed stumps dotted the landscape, until finally the woods gave way to a clearing with a faded wooden sign that welcomed travelers to the village of Pocket.

It was more of a settlement than anything else. Lirien counted ten different buildings in total, most of the structures made of cedar with thick daubing between the beams that held them together. The same path through the wood, now the size of a narrow road, cut through the center of the village. At the end of it, a large barn stood with a paddock for horses, a small vegetable farm, and a coop for chickens. On the other side, the only other two-story building, was a tavern called The Cedar King. A makeshift coat of arms decorated the sign: a crown with two handsaws crossing each other below to form an 'X' and a tree flanking each side.

"It's going to be dark soon. I'm hesitant to spend much time here, knowing the elf is after us, but we also have a chance to get information."

Lirien paused. She had a point. They needed to know when and where they were.

He held an invisible spoon in his hand and mimed eating, giving her a questioning look.

"I want to. Definitely. Do you have any money?"

Lirien shook his head.

"You must be sick of fish and rabbits, though, right?"

It didn't really matter to him. During all this time, he still didn't have a taste for food, despite being perpetually hungry. He ate and ate, but no solace came from it. But he didn't know how to tell Kitra about it, and whether or not he should.

Kitra didn't notice he was lost in thought. "Time for a little bit of glamour."

She picked up some pebbles from the path and waved her hands over them. They changed to several coins. "It'll wear off by morning."

Lirien looked at her incredulously.

"What? I'm a trickster." And with a little grin and a skip in her step, she headed to The Cedar King.

Lirien followed her into the tavern, and it looked like the whole of the settlement was crowded inside of it. Every table was filled with people laughing, talking, eating, and drinking, and the only seats available were directly at the bar.

Kitra pulled out a stool for Lirien to sit on, and he looked down at Nina. She was far too noticeable, even under the sleeve, because whenever he shifted or moved his arm, her little head and flickering tongue poked out from underneath. He decided to keep his arm in his lap and not use it if he could help it.

The barkeep, a tall man in his fifties with brown hair, pinkish skin, and a graying beard, turned around to face them. He gaped at Lirien. "Well, I'll be, if it isn't the King of Ardeth himself!" And with a hard chuckle, he slapped Lirien's back.

Lirien froze. The fur cloak was meant to make him unrecognizable. Sure, he looked like his father, but he never expected this kind of reaction to his appearance. He now thought the cloak made more trouble than it was worth...

Until he saw the proclamations hanging up at the corner of the bar. His face, plastered on one of the larger ones, stared back at him, with words in large black typeface: "Prince Lirien, wanted for the murder of the royal children of Ardeth. Bring him LIVING to Castle Ardeth and you can name your reward, which will be granted by the full powers of the Queen." A description of his appearance was written below.

He tapped Kitra's shoulder and pointed at the sign. She looked at him, her eyes wide. "Oh, wow."

The barkeep grinned at her. "'Name your reward.' Crazy, isn't it? But I suppose anyone would go mad at the death of their children. I'm sure there's a catch to it. 'Full powers of the Queen,' right? I bet the Queen would tell you there's all sorts of things outside her power to give. Not two million gold pieces or anything like that. What would you ask for if you brought him in?"

"Don't know," Kitra said, "Haven't thought about it."

"You probably don't need to, not when you have the King by your side." He laughed again. "It's uncanny, son. I used to live in Ardeth. Had my own pub, The Drunken Sow, but I came back here to take care of my sick father, so I took over his business. And I tell you what, one time, during the Longsol Festival, the King and his Queen paraded through the crowd, and the King was *this* close to me." The barkeep gestured, making a width of about two feet with his arms. "He was young then. Just married. And you look just like him!" He sighed. "It's a shame what happened to him, those things taking him below. Such a shame. I'm Hamish, by the way. Nice to meet you. What are your names, strangers?"

"I'm Klara and this is... Lucius." Kitra ignored Lirien's sidelong glance as she continued, "He's my older brother."

"What's with that outfit, if I may ask? Is that some sort of hunter's trophy? Showing off the goods? It looks a little, ah…"

Kitra could barely suppress a smile as Hamish struggled to find the rest of his sentence. "It's strange, I know," she said, "but it's a gift, and Lucius feels bound to wear it."

"Dutiful fellow, aren't you?" He cleared his throat. "So, where are you travelling to? Nobody ever stops in Pocket unless they're taking a breath before going someplace else. Before they stopped logging, it used to be a more popular stop along the lumberers' route, but now we rarely get visitors. Still, we like to be here, just in case, for any weary traveler passing through."

"We're just on the way to Asherin," Kitra said. "You wouldn't have a map by any chance, would you? We got a little lost in the woods."

Hamish headed over to where Lirien's face hung on the wall and opened a small drawer beneath it. He gave the paper to Kitra, who unfolded it and placed it on the counter. She found Pocket marked on the map, and Lirien's eyes wandered to Lake Karda. He pointed at it three times for emphasis.

"That's where you're going?" Hamish asked.

Lirien nodded.

"What do you think, Hamish?" Kitra asked. "Two more days of walking? Three?"

"I'd budget for four. There's still snow up in those mountains."

"You mean the flowers won't be out?"

"It's spring, true, but it's a little too early for the dragon blossoms to come out. Here, the best time to see them—" He pulled out a small book with a calendar from his pocket and opened it.

Lirien gaped at the calendar. It was the start of spring, yes—

but over a year and a half had passed. Nineteen months, to be exact.

Lirien pointed to it frantically and stared at Kitra, hoping she could get what he wanted.

Kitra blurted out, "Uh, what day is it?"

Hamish laughed but raised an eyebrow at them. "You must've gotten good and lost if you couldn't keep track of your days."

"That's exactly what happened."

"It's the seventh."

Lirien almost knocked over his glass. Specifically, it was the twins' birthday, and the passage of time meant Sorin and Sonalie just turned nine. Nina was twelve, and he himself was now twenty-one. Except that didn't seem right, because only a day had passed while in Elythia. Was he still twenty, then?

"Oh, be careful there, son! Anyway, the best time to see the dragon blossoms on the shore is the end of the month, when they're in their fullest bloom."

"It's too bad we'll miss them," Kitra said, "as we're in a bit of a hurry."

"Not spending the night, then?"

"Just a drink and a nibble if you please. I'll have some black-thorn wine. And my brother here— what do you want?"

Lirien was hungry for *something,* and had been for the longest time, but he couldn't put a name to what he craved. He'd given up completely on finding something with taste. He held his hands above the bar counter and moved them up and down in intervals, trying to make the shape of waves with them.

Thank goodness Kitra understood. "He'll just have water."

"Oh," Hamish said, looking at Lirien as if he just realized something. "I'LL GET YOUR DRINKS SHORTLY." He disappeared behind the bar.

Kitra's eyes started to roll, but Lirien reached out and touched her arm. "Yes?"

He pointed his thumb toward the door.

"I understand. We lost a lot of time. We can leave right after we drink, then."

Hamish came back with two glasses. "HERE YOU ARE."

"Thank you," Kitra said. "My brother can hear you. He just can't speak."

Hamish apologized, a sheepish look spreading across his face.

The two had their drinks and Kitra paid for them with her bewitched pebbles. Lirien had turned his back to Hamish as he accepted Kitra's money, feeling guilty that in truth they had stolen from him.

"You look troubled," Kitra said as they headed out the door.

Lirien picked up one of the pebbles from the ground and shook his head before tossing it aside.

"Fine. I won't do it again. Will that make you feel better?"

He nodded.

"What an upstanding gentleman you are." She spoke with mirth in her voice. "Let's go. We've got maybe two hours of walking 'til sunset."

The path stayed wide, and Lirien worried they would run into more people, so he signaled to Kitra to go off the trail into the woods. The land rose gradually, and he didn't realize how high they had ascended until there was a marked change in temperature. A chill had settled as they walked and the clouds had melded together, graying the sky.

"Tonight's going to be rough," Kitra said. "I can smell the ice in the air."

Maybe they should have stayed in the inn after all, and gotten food to eat there, but Lirien wanted to increase the distance between them and the elf who hunted them. True, Kitra had sprinted quite a way off, and maybe he should have trusted that, but he couldn't shake the uneasy feeling of being tracked.

The sky dimmed and the scent of snow tickled their nostrils, and then the sleet came— thick droplets of rain mixed with white flakes. He pulled his hood up and waved at Kitra to catch her attention. He held his arms wide, trying to indicate a large size. Then he pointed to her, gesturing to where her ears and tail used to be. *Change,* he mouthed.

Kitra listened, and she was a giant fox once more. "Might as well climb on," she said, a hint of annoyance in her voice.

He clambered onto her back, and she darted off, leaping over large rocks and carefully sidestepping gnarled tree roots. She hadn't journeyed far when she abruptly stopped.

They'd come across an old hunter's shelter built partway up in the trees, meant more for observation than comfort. A small ladder led upward to the door, and the structure looked large enough to fit only one person. But at least it had a roof.

"We'll make it work somehow," Kitra said as he slid off her and she changed. "I suppose I could make a burrow, but that would..."

He didn't really hear what she was saying. His eyes lingered on her. Her thick red hair was wild and dotted with clumps of snowflakes caught amid the strands, and a vivid rose had crept into her cheeks and at the tip of her nose, where the cold had settled in.

She noticed him staring, and her eyes met his. The corner of her mouth had turned up slightly, and she gazed at him evenly until he turned his head from her.

"Let's get inside," she said after a moment.

Lirien collected himself and gestured for Kitra to climb up the ladder first. She opened the door to the shelter easily and stepped inside, then poked her head back out to look down at him.

"You'll definitely have to duck when you come in."

He nodded and lowered his head, the door frame barely brushing along the top of his hair. Head still bowed, he eyed the tiny space.

A stool was placed in front of a shuttered window, and right up against the wall was a single pallet with a small pillow and heavy fur blanket folded at the end of it. There wasn't enough room for a separate bed to be made on the floor. Lirien and Kitra nearly stood on the bedding as it was, the shelter was so narrow.

Lirien scratched the back of his head nervously. Well, maybe he could sleep upright on the stool somehow...

"Want to get out of that damp cloak?" Kitra held her hand out to him. He pulled it off and gave it to her, and she hung it on a single hook on the wall.

Kitra slid off her gloves and unfastened her doublet, pulling it off to reveal the thin white blouse she wore underneath. She draped the doublet over the chair to dry— *so much for sleeping there*, Lirien thought —and then she climbed onto the pallet. She stretched out on the mattress, facing the wall, scooting against it as close as possible to give Lirien room.

He just watched.

Kitra looked back at him and pulled the cover aside. "Don't you want to get warm?"

He fidgeted with his hands, then hesitantly took his place next to her on the makeshift bed, his back toward hers. Kitra fixed the blanket to cover them both, and his booted feet poked out from underneath the fur.

After some silence, Kitra observed, "You're trying very hard not to touch me."

Something tickled in Lirien's stomach, and he let out a breath.

Kitra rolled over onto her side, and she was so close to him he could feel her talking to his back. "The closer we are together, the warmer we'll be. You don't have to be shy. Every night you've been sleeping up against me. Or would you rather I sleep against you this time?"

He swallowed. If he nestled up to her, he'd want to embrace her tightly and not let go. That would be too much.

He bungled his response, somehow nodding and shrugging at the same time. So much for being nonchalant about it.

"Is that a 'yes?'"

He gave her a single nod. She scooted up to him, resting her head against his back, her legs right up behind his, her knees an inch away from the crooks of his own. "Is this all right?"

Surely Kitra would notice his heart beating faster, but she said nothing. He exhaled again, then nodded slightly, barely moving his head. Nina squirmed on his arm, repositioning herself underneath his sleeve, as Kitra yawned.

"Goodnight."

She fell asleep like that. He didn't move, afraid of disrupting her slumber. After a while his eyelids fluttered, then closed. He assumed his thoughts would be only for Kitra, but as he measured the course of their day, his attention turned to what he'd learned about the twins— the twins, now nine years old.

He couldn't believe it. Something in his heart ached when he realized how long they'd been alone, away from him. Well, he hoped not alone. He hoped at some point during his time in Elythia they'd found each other and made it to Lake Karda, and all he had to do was meet them there.

He fell asleep with images of Sorin and Sonalie running through the castle courtyard, playing tag with each other. When he opened his eyes again, they were standing before him, back in the southwest watchtower, wearing the same bedclothes from the night they had transformed.

Lirien was lucid enough to know it was a dream, but he didn't care. He rushed to the twins and opened his arms to them.

"Brother!" Sorin shouted, and he started sobbing, running to Lirien for a hug. Sonalie, who was always a little bit shy and not one for contact, came at him too, surprising Lirien by wrapping her arms around him.

They had changed in the time that had passed. Both had gotten taller, their bodies wiry and long, but Sonalie had an inch on Sorin. Sorin's cheeks looked a little less chubby, and Sonalie's face less babyish.

Lirien felt something well up inside him, and he choked out, "Sorin. Sonalie." Then his eyes widened. *I have a voice here!* "I've missed you, so, so much." He squeezed them tightly.

"Is this real?" Sorin asked, wiping his eyes.

"It's got to be magic," Sonalie said. "I wished and wished with all my might for our birthday that we could see you again, Lirien, and here we are. It has to be a gift of magic, a gift from the spell, somehow."

He patted Sonalie's head, and she grabbed onto his hand, weaving her fingers through his.

"Your fish scale is gone!" she said, more curious than upset.

"I gave it up, for a very good reason. Don't you worry about it."

"Brother, why is it taking so long for you to find us?" she asked. Her small voice was stronger, more assured, than it had been from over a year ago.

"I was in Elythia. I was only there a couple days, but the time there flows differently. I had no idea we'd lose over a year and a half from being there. My friend Kitra said the forest drops you off where you need to be, but I don't understand why we ended up where and when we did. There must be a reason, but I haven't figured it out yet. Anyway, please tell me, how are you doing? Are you safe?"

"I'm with a flock of swans and we've made our home on the lake in Asherin. They know I'm different from them, but they let me stay with them all the same. They keep me safe."

"I'm... I'm alone," Sorin said. "I don't have anyone. The other deer have stayed away. They don't trust me because they can still smell human on me. And I'm in danger all the time. Once there was a wolf, and then a bear... and now, I'm being hunted. I wish I weren't a white stag, just an ordinary one, so I could just blend in. I can't believe I haven't been caught yet. I hide a lot of places, lots of strange places. But I hate it. I hate this, all of this. I just want to go home."

Lirien's eyes watered, but no tears fell. He was glad Sonalie seemed safe, but terrified for Sorin. He needed to get to him as soon as possible.

"I'm trying to get to you as quick as I can. I'm maybe only three days away from you, if you can both stay near the lake. When I find you, we'll all travel together and I'll keep you safe. My friend will keep us safe, too. She's a fae fox, and she gets really big. I'm sure she could keep other things away from you."

"How's Nina?" Sonalie asked.

"She's—" Lirien looked down to his arm, surprised to find Nina had not accompanied him into the dream. "She's asleep beside me. She's been with me the whole time. I know she loves and misses you. You'll see her curled up on my arm when we finally meet up. It's her favorite place to stay with me."

"And Mother?" Sorin added.

Lirien hesitated. *I have to tell them, and I have to do it as delicately as possible.* So, he told them. He told them how he tried to rescue Father, that his use of the siren song bewitched the Queen and caused her to act strangely. He couldn't bring himself to specify the Queen's behavior— not how she threatened him with death, used a knife on him, or her multiple advances toward him. He simply said the Queen was driven mad with grief, and that madness led her to use the havoc stone, and that's how the children changed and he lost his voice.

"There is something else that's happened," Lirien said carefully. "Right now, the Queen has offered a reward for my capture. She's accused me of your murder and I'm supposed to be taken back to the castle."

"What?" Sorin practically shouted. "Why would she say that?"

Lirien knew why. She not only needed to explain away the children's disappearance but she was also going to try anything to get him back to her. Apparently, saying they were all missing wasn't going to do the trick in her eyes. If she would only be patient and wait, though, he would come willingly.

"I think it's just another part of the madness of the siren song," Lirien told them. "It changed her. I didn't mean for it to. She... she wanted me to sing it, and it sort of came out of me." He swallowed. "There's this feeling inside me, something that pushes me to sing the song again. Every day since it happened, I've asked myself if I'm no longer human, if I'm truly meant to be a siren and nothing else, if I'm doomed to sing. I never thought this would happen. Please, please forgive me."

"It's all right, brother," Sonalie said. "You couldn't help what happened. And please don't think you aren't a... you aren't a person. You have a heart—"

"You love us, and sirens don't love anything," Sorin added. "No matter how it happened, it's not your fault." His voice grew quiet. "Can you save us?"

"Yes. Once we're all together and I know you're safe, I'm going to break the spell. We need Alibrandr— I have to use it to cut different things from the sky and weave them into robes for you to wear. When you put them on, you'll change back and I'll be restored, too. In the meantime, do your best to stay safe for three or four more days, and we'll be—"

Pain shot through Lirien, shocking him awake. A hard blow landed against his side from an immensely powerful kick, and his body curled up in response.

Kitra was nowhere to be seen.

Between gasps he glanced up at the Glynnan elf who stood over him, a youth with striking steel eyes, pale gray skin, and waist-long dark silver hair woven into a herringbone braid. He pointed a sizeable dagger at Lirien. "You'll come with me now."

Without waiting for Lirien to get up, the elf seized him roughly by his arm and dragged him to his feet. Lirien forgot to lower his head and the ceiling scraped the top of it. He winced and reflexively rubbed his scalp.

Nina shot out from Lirien's sleeve and bit down hard on the elf's hand, drawing blood. He jerked back in surprise, then yanked the snake off Lirien and tossed her against the wall, her body hitting with a loud thud. She didn't stir.

Lirien moved to run to her, but the elf slammed him against the wall and wrenched his arms behind him, pinning him there.

The youth's strength was nothing Lirien expected or experienced before. He had always restrained himself with the Queen, but he knew he was strong and could fight back. Yet he struggled against the elf's grip and could not free himself.

"The Queen of Ardeth said to bring you back alive, but nothing about unharmed. If you try to run from me, don't think I won't use this," the elven boy said, jabbing the tip of the dagger into his back.

Lirien continued to struggle as the Glynnan elf tied his arms behind him. Then he was whirled around and pulled by the shoulder toward the door.

The elf paused a split-second at the cloak hanging on the hook. "Could be useful," he said, as if he knew what the cloak was about. He hurriedly tied the furs around Lirien's neck, and as the boy knotted the cords, Lirien gestured with his body to Nina, his expression frantic. He couldn't be separated from her.

"No. There's no need for it," he said, eyeing the snake. Nina slowly started to come to, but before she could make her way to him, the elf kicked the door to the shelter open and pushed him, hard. He toppled down the ladder and landed with his legs tangled up in each other, his bottom sore from the landing.

Before him, sprawled out on the ground, was Kitra. She was in her fox form, her eyes closed and her body completely still in the thin layer of snow. A sizeable dart stuck out of her back near her shoulder blade.

No, no, no— is she dead?

As if the elf could hear his thoughts, he responded, "She's just asleep. I'm not a killer. Not like you."

Lirien shook his head frantically as the elf hauled him up. That's what this was about— the elf believed he had murdered the children. He glimpsed Nina trying to make her way down the ladder, coiling around the side of it and slowly working her way down. But he couldn't get to her, nor communicate to the elf who the snake truly was.

It dawned on him that he'd forgotten the most important thing he could do in this situation. Quickly bowing his head, his thoughts screamed, *Elythia! Please come to me!*

But Elythia did not answer him, as many times as he called it. He couldn't understand it— he had heard so many times that Elythia was benevolent —so why would the forest let him be taken away?

As the elf pushed Lirien along through the wood, he said, "I've waited to find you for a long time. Almost two years. I thought you might be in Elythia, but the forest wouldn't come to me or give you up. I just waited until at last it let you out, and for some reason, the forest let you out right where I needed you to be. Almost as if it knew I needed you."

As they continued onward, the trees darkened and the pathway narrowed. They passed a pair of elves around a small fire in the wood, although he thought them to be Yannan elves. He'd read about them before. Just as the Glynnan elves blended into the mountains, the Yannan elves blended into the forest. They had skin the color of smooth, cut cedar wood, and green hair and eyes that matched the leaves on the trees. They eyed him curiously, then one of them pointed at him. "Is that the Prince?"

Again with the cloak! What was the point of hiding himself with it if everyone he ran into could see him anyway?

The Glynnan elf pointed his dagger at the others. "He is mine. I found him. I'm taking him to the Queen myself. Got it?"

The Yannan elf raised his hands, palms open. "No trouble from us. You can keep on your way."

Lirien took that brief moment while his captor held the dagger away from him to break into a run. He didn't look where he was going, exactly, but kept moving as fast as possible. He slipped on a rock underneath a coating of snow and landed on his back, the stones on the forest floor digging into him. He was mortified, his escape an instant failure.

The Glynnan elf laughed as he hauled him back up to his feet. "What was that?" He turned Lirien around and pushed the cloak aside to check his bonds. "Do you want me to carry you like a maiden all the way there? Then walk. Don't try that again."

They continued on until the elf found a large stone turned on its side and held his hand over it. The air between his hand and the surface of the rock rippled until the surface of the stone seemed to waver. The elven youth grabbed Lirien's shoulder and marched him into the quivering currents of air that rose above the stone.

He passed through a surge of air and found himself in Yanna still, but in a completely different location. The elf waved his hand over the stone they had come out of, and the rippling above it stopped. He had opened a portal for them to pass through, then took care to close it.

This pattern continued. The youth would find a giant stone amid all the other rocks that dotted the forest, change the air above it, and the two would walk through. Every step took them farther away from Asherin and Lake Karda, and Lirien felt more and more a sense of despair for all the time he'd lost.

He shook his arms in his bonds, trying to catch the elf's attention.

"What?" The youth said. "We're not stopping."

The route they took brought them near the mountains of Glynna and finally led them over the foothills and up the peaks themselves, until they reached the face of an enormous cliff. Lirien's terror grew with every step. The dizzying heights, the precarious footholds in the snow— he felt like any second he would fall to his death. Even though the Glynnan elf kept a solid grip on him, Lirien didn't trust the boy's strength to prevent him from tumbling down the mountainside. He trembled more with fear than cold as they made their way to a small village of gray stone huts connected to and formed by the rocks of the mountainside.

There was a large cave in the cliff just beyond the village, and he could vaguely make out something inside, like the silhouette of a giant person or a statue of some kind. Before he could discern further details, he was forced ahead to one of the huts. The elf knocked on the door with his free hand and a little elven girl, who looked like a smaller version of his captor, poked her head out. Her face lit up.

"Brand! Everyone, Brandegil's back!" she cried, and went to hug him— but then she noticed him and took a quick step back. "Whoa, who's that?"

"This is Prince Lirien of Ardeth."

The child raised an eyebrow, looking at him quizzically. "He doesn't look like a prince to me. He's weird. I mean, look at his eyes! And why's he wearing all those raggedy furs?"

"It's some sort of enchanted disguise. Doesn't work on elves, though."

"Hey, MOTHER! I said BRAND IS BACK!" the little girl shouted.

An elven woman with darker gray skin and shockingly white hair decorated into three thick braids stepped into the doorframe. She must be the boy's mother, Lirien thought, for the two had similar faces. She smiled but folded her arms across her chest. "The Queen would not appreciate you bringing him back in such a state, Brand, all soaked from the snow, looking worse for wear."

"The paper said 'living' and nothing else," he replied.

"Come on, son," the woman said, and pulled the boy into a hug, "I've missed you. And I'm so proud of you for fulfilling your vow to find the Prince. You're well on your way to bring Alibrandr back to us." She opened the door wider. "Bring him inside. The Queen may not care about the condition of her captive, but we're civilized people up here on the mountain. We'll get him warm and fed."

CHAPTER 12

"Mother, this is serious," Brandegil said once they were inside the stone hut. "The Prince is wanted for murder. This is not a dinner guest."

Lirien started shaking his head "no" furiously, then he jerked his arms, fighting against his bonds.

"It looks like he wants to say something," Brandegil's mother said.

"He can't talk, the papers said. Some sort of bewitchment."

Lirien squirmed against the ropes again, and the older elf woman raised an expectant eyebrow toward her son.

"Fine, I'll untie you," Brandegil sighed. "I think you know what you're up against. You won't be able to run."

Lirien nodded and held his wrists out to the elven boy, who slashed the ropes away. For a moment he stretched his fingers and wrists to restore circulation, then pointed to the front pocket of his bag, which he'd worn at his side all night and throughout their journey.

Brandegil opened the bag up and found the paper booklet and charcoal inside. Lirien made a scribbling motion in the air, as if he were writing. Brandegil shoved the paper and charcoal into his hands.

"Explain yourself, then."

None of what the Queen claims is true, Lirien wrote. *I did not kill anyone. The children are alive and cursed, and I'm working to break that spell. It was from a havoc stone.*

"You used a havoc stone? That's only one of the most dangerous forms of magic!"

No, it's the Queen. She used it. There's far too much to explain. Can you do magic? Can I show you somehow?

"And what good would it do for me to see your story? I'll still take you to the Queen, and she'll give me Alibrandr, and our business will be done."

If you could see, then you'll know the Queen can't be trusted.

That halted Brandegil. He thought for a moment. "I *do* know that. After your people stole the sacred sword from us, we were given empty promises that one day it would be returned. Instead, your family has kept it locked up. And for what purpose? To keep it out of harm's way? No one else can use it but us! It's just another sword until my people awaken it, and that can only be done once it's in our hands." Brandegil clenched and unclenched his fists. "It was ours. We kept it safe. We honored it. It belongs to us. So, I know not to trust the word of a royal of Ardeth. But we've tried to get it back and failed. This is an opportunity without bloodshed, and I want to take it. The Queen is desperate. She has the power to grant us the sword."

I doubt she'll just give you the sword. Then, he wrote with a heavy emphasis, the charcoal lines thicker and blacker, *Please. I beg you not to take me to her now. I need to save my family first.*

"I have to admit I'm curious," Brandegil's mother said. "He doesn't seem like a killer to me."

"Mother…" the sister said, staring up at him and taking in his height. "He's huge. He could totally do it."

"Cindra is right," Brandegil said. "He is completely capable. He could be lying to us about all of this. I said I don't trust any royal of Ardeth, and that starts with him."

Lirien looked to Brandegil's mother and clasped his hands together in a pleading motion. She noticed his gaze and gave a little nod.

"Let's scry the stones, then," she said, "We'll see if he's telling the truth."

Will you see everything?

"I'll see enough. Come back outside."

As soon as they were out, Brandegil's mother knocked the ground with her foot, two hard stomps. Under the layer of snow, a hatch opened in the ground and a stout dwarf poked his head out. He had rosy skin, a long brown beard, and long brown hair that framed his face. He had a soft hat on his head that looked more like a gray sock, and he wore a thick green jacket.

"Gregorach," she said, "may I borrow your hammer? I want to scry the stones."

"Ah, not a problem! Just a minute."

Lirien leaned over, trying to look down the hole. He saw a ladder and a lantern and not much else before the dwarf shut the door. After a moment, the door popped back open and the dwarf climbed out of the ground. With both hands and a bit of difficulty, he passed to Brandegil's mother a large hammer that resembled a mallet more than a weapon. She took it from him easily, as if it weighed no more than a feather.

"Thank you for your help! I'll give it back once I'm done."

The dwarf cheerfully bobbed his head and ducked back underground.

"Come along," she said to him and Brandegil. Cindra

followed a few steps behind, shooting glances at Lirien. When Brandegil saw her following, he secured his grip on his arm, walking him through the village and into the giant cave.

Hundreds of small stones were piled upon each other in cairns, decorating a pathway through the cavern toward what Lirien could now tell was an enormous statue, the figure of an elven woman whose face was chipped away and mostly missing. She had one foot raised on an anvil, a hammer in one hand, and her other hand lifted high into the sky, her fingers wrapped around something invisible.

No, not invisible— something missing. He knew this must have been where the sword was kept. He gaped up at the statue in awe and felt the sense of something ancient, something holy there in the cave, not unlike the feeling of something powerful and unnamable in the sea.

"This is Terinelle. She's the one who forged and named Alibrandr, the greatest sword to ever exist," Brandegil's mother said. "It had its uses in the age it was made. Killing dragons. Felling ogres. Slicing through the underworld, piercing the heavens. It protected us from all sorts of calamity. The 'Brand' in my son's name comes from the sword, did you know that?"

Lirien shook his head reverently.

"Now, it is only a beautiful relic," she continued. "When it was taken from us, we tried to make a new one. We've made many wondrous swords, but nothing with the power Alibrandr was given. It was something that came from Terinelle alone. So Alibrandr is absolutely priceless. Brandegil is right in that we must have it back. It's been far too long away from us." She looked to him with scrutiny. "I wonder what part you have to play in all of this."

Farther off against the wall, some distance away from the statue of Terinelle, lay a large misshapen stone. Pockmarks covered it in some places, while other parts were oddly flat, and then there were jagged sections and corners where pieces of the stone had broken off.

Brandegil's mother raised the hammer and brought it down hard on the stone. A part of it splintered off and shot forward, skipping along the ground and nearly toppling one of the cairns.

She stared at where the stone had broken. "I read the past. An unforeseen outcome and strong consequences."

Then she walked up to the fractured piece of stone and smashed the hammer against it, crumbling it to smaller bits of rock. "I read the present. Allies divided. A sense of loss."

She leaned over the fragments and stayed silent for a moment. Then she smashed the pieces one more time, and they resembled nothing more than pebbles of sand. She peered into them. "I read the future. Failure and success."

One last crash of the hammer, and the final bits looked like chalk powder. "The signs point to truth, and there's a final message: the possible is within the impossible." She wiped the end of the hammer with the hem of her tunic. "I think you should trust what he says, Brand."

"So what if he speaks the truth, then? I told you— nothing is going to change my plans. You said so yourself, Mother, that you know I'm going to bring Alibrandr back to us, that we must have it back, so why don't you just trust *me?*"

You're better off stealing it than asking for it, Lirien wrote.

"Steal it. As if we haven't tried before. People have died for that sword already. I'm not going to die. The Queen is desperate for you. I'll give her what she wants, and she'll grant me my reward."

Or else? Lirien scribbled.

Brandegil pointed a threatening finger at Lirien. "I'm tired of this. Mother, if you want to have him cleaned and fed for the

Queen, fine. But no one can convince me to change my plans. After you eat, we're done."

DOWN THE MOUNTAINS OF GLYNNA. Into the forests of Yanna. Onward to Pinemore. Snow melted and the ground changed to mud, then grass, as they trekked on.

Brandegil reached the final rock on what Lirien began to think of as the "stone highway," the magical path that only the Glynnan elves knew how to take from one place to another. It didn't work with all stones; if that were the case, the Glynnan elves could have made it inside the castle and the treasury with no problem, simply passing through the walls. No, it only worked with giant rocks unhewn and untouched by tools— natural stones that seemed to stand on their own.

On the way from the mountains to the castle, another strange pain visited him. The same pressure behind his eyes built up, and he wanted to rub at them, but his hands were bound once more. He wondered if he should worry that the headache was worse this time. If he suddenly became sensitive to light, he knew he was in trouble and would have to lie down until it passed. But once again, the sensation came and went quickly.

They reached the border of Ardeth by late afternoon, whereas it would've taken them at least two weeks to go by foot any other way, other than through Elythia.

Elythia. Why wouldn't it come? Lirien had begged for it all through their journey, without answer. He couldn't help but feel bitterness, doubting that the ability to talk to the forest was a gift at all when Elythia could simply ignore him.

The final rock of the stone highway left them at the edge of

Pinemore, no more than twenty paces from the gate to the castle town. Brandegil untied Lirien's cloak and took his satchel from him, tucking the furs inside. "I thought maybe I should keep you hidden right up until we made it to the castle, but... I want them to see you. I want them to know a Glynnan elf succeeded where they failed."

Brandegil, gripping Lirien's shoulder tightly, marched him right toward the two guards who stood at the gate, but it was one of the guards who manned the top of the town walls that recognized him first. Lirien looked up when he heard a voice shout, "The Prince!"

The guards at the gate pointed their halberds at Lirien and Brandegil. One of them, a woman with deep brown skin and jet-black eyes, cleared her throat. "I know Prince Lirien, but you — identify yourself!"

Brandegil lowered the hood of his cloak and revealed himself. "You don't need to know my name. Just know that I'm the one who brought the Prince to you."

The other guard, a tan man with a ruddy goatee and thick mustache, shoved his halberd closer to Brandegil. "A Glynnan elf. You know you're not welcome here."

"I'm sure an exception will be made given the precious cargo I have with me. Or, if you won't take me to the Queen, we'll be on our way."

Lirien didn't know how Brandegil could manage such bravado, not with the number of armed and armored guards who watched them, but for some reason, the two who pointed their weapons at them relented.

"We will accompany you to the castle," the woman said.

They opened the gate and led Brandegil and him into the castle town. It was the first time he had actually set foot there; he'd only ever seen its thatched rooftops from the highest castle windows. The main street leading to the castle was wide and cobbled, with smaller streets breaking off to the sides, leading back into narrow alleys and curious nooks. It was crowded with people hawking their wares, making trades, and having conversations.

But all of that stopped when he passed them by. Slack-jawed looks and angry stares greeted him before the people broke out into open jeering. "Killer," they whispered— and then, more brazen, shouted it. "Killer!"

Something whizzed past Lirien's head. An apple rolled along the ground, and then another one hit him in the jaw. A young boy had a basket full of them and lobbed them at Lirien with an ugly look on his face. The boy's mother pulled him back from the crowd and yanked the basket out of his hands, but not before spitting in Lirien's direction.

The hatred bored into him as the guards marched them to the barbican that dominated the entryway to the castle. His body stung, not only from the bristling loathing the people felt toward him, but from the stones that struck him on the last leg of their walk. The townsfolk had quickly grown tired of launching fruit at him and moved on to heavier, sharper, and more dangerous things they'd found in the streets. It had gotten so bad at one point that the guard with the ruddy goatee whirled around and waved his halberd at the crowd, shouting, "Justice belongs to the Queen, not you!" Only then did they stop throwing things.

His eyes had misted up by the time they reached the barbican. It took everything in him not to let tears fall. The walk to the castle was a humiliation unlike any he had ever felt. He swallowed and looked at Brandegil, who had wanted this, who had wanted the people to see him. He thought maybe the elf would be gloating, but to his surprise, Brandegil wore a thoughtful look on his face, his mouth a straight line. His eyes met Lirien's, and the corners of his mouth turned down into the slightest of frowns.

"Richard! Zan!" the goateed guard cried out, "I bet you never thought you'd see this day come."

Lirien recognized the two armored soldiers by the gate as the ones who were there on the night the Queen used the havoc stone. Zan was the first to break formation, practically running up to them. "You've brought the Prince!"

"*I* brought the Prince," Brandegil said.

"Is this true? A Glynnan elf did a service to the Queen?" Richard asked.

The female guard from the town gate nodded. "He came right up to us with him, plain as day. He's got the Prince tied up and everything, ready to go."

"I'll not leave until I'm rewarded," Brandegil said.

"Aye, you will be," Richard said. "Our Queen is fair and will honor her word."

"I should hope so. I wish to speak to her directly."

"Can you two take our post for the time being?" Zan said to a pair of castle guards. "I'll alert the Queen, and Richard will take the elf and the Prince inside."

"Certainly."

Zan dashed into the castle while Richard gestured to Brandegil. "Surrender your weapons and bags to the guards. I promise you'll get them back when you leave."

Brandegil raised an eyebrow, but obeyed Richard. He handed both his and Lirien's bags to the guards, removed his quiver of arrows and bow, and nodded to Richard once he was emptyhanded. The three of them passed through the barbican and into the castle courtyard, then veered sharply away from the castle's main entrance.

Lirien recognized he was being taken to the dungeons. It was worse than being paraded through town because now it was real, it was happening— he was walking to his doom. It was over for him. He only hoped the Queen would somehow give him the chance to explain how the children could be saved. But what state would she be in when she saw him at last?

He looked over to Brandegil, whose eyes had narrowed sharply, but he couldn't make out what emotions were behind them.

Lirien wasn't angry with Brandegil for turning him in. The situation itself terrified him, but Brandegil wasn't to blame for any of it. In fact, he understood even better than before just how important Alibrandr was to his people, how its theft was a wrong that needed to be righted. At least some good would come from his imprisonment and possibly his death. The Glynnan elves deserved the sword.

It was a grim comfort, but a real one nonetheless.

Down they went into the dank, dusky cellars that housed prisoners in iron cells. Richard called out to one of the jailors, "Milla," and a tall, well-muscled woman with broad shoulders and short blonde hair came their direction.

"Oh, it's the Prince," she said in astonishment, then quickly tucked that expression away, replacing it with a stern, serious look. "I'll take it from here. Him, too?" She gestured to Brandegil.

"Yes."

"Now, wait a minute!" Rage stretched across Brandegil's face as a knife, one he'd kept secret, flashed into his hand.

Milla reacted quickly, lunging at Brandegil and locking his arm between both of her own before smashing him hard against the bars of one of the cells. Richard slammed Brandegil's wrist against an iron bar until he dropped his dagger.

Milla and Richard didn't stop— they smashed Brandegil face-first into the ground, and then Richard pinned him there while Milla grabbed a set of manacles from her belt and slapped them on him. Brandegil let out a garbled noise as the cuffs squeezed his injured wrist.

Milla let out a laugh. "I thought Glynnan elves were supposed to be unnaturally strong." Then she manacled Lirien as well.

Into adjacent cells they went, and both were chained to the wall, their arms pinned high above their heads and their ankles shackled.

"You can't do this to me," Brandegil hissed at them. "I brought the Prince to you. I'm entitled to my reward."

"The Queen will honor her word and reward you, elf, but until then, this is for Her Majesty's safety," Richard said. "We know how much your kind hates the royals. Who knows what else you might try to do?"

As Brandegil cursed under his breath, Lirien looked around his dungeon cell. On the opposite wall, sharp instruments hung on hooks, clearly meant for questioning or torture. He never knew that the guards were allowed to do something so horrible, and it shocked him. Was this something Ardeth had always done to its prisoners, or was this new?

He continued to survey the room, the fear rising in him. No one was meant to stay in this place for long. There were no signs of lengthy imprisonment— no bed, no place to relieve yourself —just the restraints and a fresh layer of sand on the floor. Sand to soak up blood.

He couldn't move except to twist in his bonds. He knew it was fruitless to struggle, but it was the only thing he could think to do to keep himself from trembling. What would the Queen do to him? How would she hurt him?

The answer came quickly. Queen Aurinda came gliding down the dungeon hallway as if she were a ghost, her long white-blonde hair trailing loose and wild behind her, her shimmery gown fluttering as she moved. Only Zan accompanied her as guard.

She looked pale and wan, her cheeks hollow but cheekbones sharp, her eyes wide open but with shadows underneath. As soon as she saw him, her gaze fixed on him, her focus piercing him to the very core. Tears came streaming down her face.

Her voice came out flimsy and shaking: "At last. You're here."

She raised her hand to the jailer Milla, who opened the door, and the Queen rushed inside the cell. She buried her face in his chest and wept while he squirmed in his chains.

At last, the Queen looked up at him, reaching up to cup his face with one hand, brushing his cheek for a moment before her fingers slid down his face and stopped at his neck. Her thumb slowly traced the hollow between his collarbones. "Now you've returned to me. After you left."

Her features darkened. "You left." Her voice grew sturdier, more menacing. "You left me." Both hands were at his throat, squeezing, squeezing with a terrible fury. "How dare you!"

He thrashed against the wall, the cuffs of his chains rubbing at his wrists, his arms suspended above him. He tried to twist his head away from her, but she slammed the back of his head against the wall and kept strangling him until he sank lifelessly beneath her grasp. Then she let go of him, and tears fell from his eyes.

The Queen came at him again, only this time she placed her head on his chest and wrapped her arms around his waist in an embrace. She listened to his racing heartbeat, to his desperately gasping breaths, and when he finally stilled, she spoke.

"Every night you tell me you love me," she said, her voice hardly above a whisper. "Every night your voice trembles, quaking with emotion, faltering under the weight of its beauty as you confess your feelings for me. It is a haunting refrain." She rose to her feet, gripping his shoulders, and she leaned in close to his ear as she always had before. "You will prove that love to me, Lirien. I will come back tonight with a priest. We will be wed. Then we will consummate our love."

He shook his head, his eyes wide in absolute horror. His skin went clammy, and a wave of nausea overcame him. He swallowed back the bile and shut his eyes, trying to will away this nightmare. *Oh, God, please no—*

The Queen stopped his thoughts with a kiss, her teeth dragging across his lip.

She didn't care anymore. She didn't care who saw. She didn't care who knew. She revealed her lust openly and without shame, while he burned with humiliation.

He bit down on her lip, hard, until he drew blood. The Queen let out a cry, half-enraged, half-devastated, and she pulled away from him.

The Queen's blood had gotten inside Lirien's mouth... and he closed his eyes, elated.

The taste. The taste of her blood. It was savory in a way that couldn't be described, something full and hearty, the *perfect* answer to his voracious cravings. He gnawed his own lip, trying to quash his desire to come at her again, to bite her again, to go beyond her blood and taste her flesh.

The horror of it all quickly overcame his joy as he realized these were the thoughts of a monster, and that he was surrendering to his siren side.

A slap across his face brought him out of those thoughts, and the Queen stared at him, a sob escaping her. "After all this time," she said, her voice wavering, "you still choose to hurt me."

He wanted to scream at her, *You've hurt me time and again,* but he couldn't. He just glared at her through his tears.

"Once we are married, you will know the depths of my love

for you, and you will never hurt me again," she said. She wiped her eyes and stepped away from him to the bars that separated his cell from Brandegil's.

"Glynnan elf." She looked at him with curiosity. "You're a young one, aren't you? Yet you've accomplished what no one else has been able to. You brought him to me. Well done. Name your reward. If it is within my power, I shall grant it."

"It is, Your Majesty. Please honor the promise of old and return Alibrandr to my people. We will not use it in violence. We will enshrine it and honor it throughout our days."

"I'm afraid I cannot give you the sword," Queen Aurinda said, "as it no longer belongs to me."

Brandegil's face would not have betrayed any emotion if it weren't for the way his jaw tightened, the muscles in his face twitching. "What do you mean?"

"Queen Eira of Asherin possesses it now. And in exchange, she has given me the Seer's Helm."

Lirien remembered the stories he'd heard of the Seer's Helm. When you put it on, you could look through the eyes of another person, and hear everything around them, just as if you were there in their place. Maybe that was why he kept feeling the ache behind his eyes— the Queen was looking through them.

She peered at him. "For a long time, it showed me nothing, which meant you were either dead or within Elythia. I knew in my heart you couldn't be dead, so that left only one other option. But my soldiers could not find the boundaries to enter, so we bided our time." She gestured to Brandegil. "Then this one found you first, and as soon as I heard him vow to return you to me, I knew I no longer had to worry about you."

"Then you already knew I've been after the sword this whole time." Brandegil tried to measure his words and speak carefully, but he couldn't hide the anger in his voice.

"The trade of relics between Ardeth and Asherin happened long before I discovered what you were after."

"You have no idea how hard I've worked to find him, to get him to you. You've got to get the sword back from Asherin as soon as possible!"

"You must not command a queen if you value your life." She gave him a dark look, her brows narrowed. Then she calmed. "I'll tell you what I'll do. I will grant you your freedom." She gestured to Milla and the other guards. "Take him out." Then she turned back to Brandegil. "I'm feeling generous, so I won't send you home empty-handed. I'll give you two hundred gold pieces for bringing Lirien to me."

Brandegil's steely eyes glinted with hatred. "Keep your money."

"Very well."

Milla entered Brandegil's cell and removed him from his bonds, then she manacled his wrists once more for Zan to take him on the long walk out of the dungeons.

Before they left, Queen Aurinda cupped Lirien's face with her hand, her thumb running across his lower lip. "I'll see you tonight."

CHAPTER 13

Lirien trembled as he awaited the Queen's return. He couldn't stop the shaking. This was it. He knew she meant every word of her threats, and he grew ill at the thought that his stepmother would soon be his wife.

Minutes became hours, until Lirien made out a figure in the shadowy corridor moving toward his cell in silence. He thought it was the Queen until he realized the person was covered in a bizarre array of furs.

It was a young man he didn't recognize, a teenaged boy with short brown hair, tanned skin, and vivid green eyes— but the cloak was unmistakable. It had to be Brandegil. Then he noticed the boy's wrist was swollen and purple, a remnant from the fight he'd had with the guards. But there was a new injury, too— an enlarged bloody lip.

Brandegil's good hand clutched a set of keys and he wondered how on earth Brandegil got past Milla or the other guards, but he instantly stopped caring when Brandegil got the cell door open after a few attempts.

Brandegil rushed to him and tried the other keys on his manacles with some difficulty, as his wrist was clearly in agony with every twist. Then at last he found the right one to free him from the wall.

"It's me, Brandegil." Even his voice had changed with his appearance, sounding a half-step higher than normal. "If the Queen thinks she can keep you after how she treated me, she's wrong. I'm not giving you up until I have the sword." He winced once more in pain. "Come on. I don't know how much more time I've got to get you out of here."

Lirien followed him and noticed Brandegil was taking him on a completely different route than the way they'd come in. They avoided all of the occupied prison cells by climbing down into the tunnels that carried waste out through the sewer system. He was grateful they didn't actually have to walk through the sludge, that there was enough space on the walkway alongside the dirty water to make it out unscathed.

Whenever there was a divergence in the tunnels, Brandegil would pause and scan the wall. There were tiny marks on the walls in chalk, a white circle that indicated the way to go. And if there was a way they shouldn't go, a small slash cut the circle in half. Who knew how long Brandegil had wandered down there to map the way through, how many wrong turns he had taken until he found the right way? As Brandegil retraced his steps, he wiped off each mark to try and keep any guards attempting to follow off their tracks.

"Your things came in handy for this," Brandegil said as he stopped at a fork in the tunnels, then hurried down the left one. "Your Queen... something is wrong with her," he said, his voice somber. "I saw everything. Heard everything. You're her son. Stepson, but son all the same. Is that what you were wanting to tell us back there on the mountain?"

He didn't *want* to tell them the degree that the Queen was after him, but he nodded anyway.

"Maybe I should trust you, then," Brandegil said.

At the end of the tunnel was a latched door with bars that revealed the open sea.

Brandegil unlocked the door with a key from his pocket and led him outside. On the ground lay two guards, unconscious. One, lying face-up, had a dart sticking out of his shoulder. The other, facedown, had one in his back. He recognized the darts as the same Brandegil had used on Kitra. Brandegil dropped the ring of keys he'd stolen on the ground by one of the guards.

"It's offensive at how easy that was," he said, suddenly sounding angry. "Did your Queen send all of her best guards to find you and leave only the incompetent ones behind to watch the castle? I had no idea it would be so insecure. It's an insult to the memory of all the elves who lost their lives trying to get Alibrandr back."

He pulled the fur cloak off and tied it around Lirien, who at last saw Brandegil as he knew him. "It's so hot under that fur." Brandegil was still wearing his own cloak from earlier, and he drew his hood up to hide his elf ears.

"We'll need to slide along the side of the castle wall until we're well away from this door so no one watching from above can tell where we left from. When we get close to those rocks over there, walk quickly away from the wall— don't run but move fast —until we're hidden behind the first one. You lead the way."

He nodded. He leaned back against the castle wall, sidestepping along it until he got closer to the standing rocks. He glanced upward and, not seeing or hearing soldiers above him, walked briskly to the first rock and ducked behind it. Brandegil followed behind but was spotted from above, a voice calling out: "Hey, you, what are you doing?"

But it didn't matter. As soon as Brandegil made it behind the craggy black rock, he held his palm over the stone and the air above it wavered. Brandegil roughly grabbed Lirien and pulled him through the gateway.

They were back in Pinemore.

THEY DIDN'T STOP MOVING, racing from one stone to the other, passing through each gateway until Lirien started to feel dizzy from the rippling air and the change in temperature as they dashed along their route. When Lirien recognized they were in Yanna, he knew they were weeks ahead of any soldiers who might pursue them once they found he had escaped.

And still they plunged on from stone to stone. At last, they ended up next to a stream coursing through the forest, filled with plenty of rocks and pebbles. "Now that we're in Asherin," Brandegil said, "we'll camp here for the night and then I'll take you to their Queens when we reach the castle. Maybe they won't be as unreasonable as your stepmother."

Before Lirien could respond, the familiar pain behind his eyes struck, and he winced. *No!* Queen Aurinda must have discovered his escape, and now she was using the Seer's Helm to learn where he was hiding. Would she recognize the forests of Asherin? Or maybe she'd already heard Brandegil say where they were. He wasn't sure if the pain behind his eyes came as soon as the Helm was put on, or if it came slightly after. There was no telling how much the Queen was able to hear.

Lirien surveyed the area as Brandegil stood at the stream. He scooped some water and tried to clean his injured mouth, wincing as he did so. Then he stood and looked around, eyeing the grasses near them.

"Don't... don't try to run away." He suddenly sounded tired.

Lirien dug through the satchel Brandegil had returned to

him and found some paper and his charcoal stick. *I won't. I want us to go to Asherin together. I'll vouch for you.*

"What? After all that I did to you?"

I want you to have the sword. Lirien paused, unsure if he should ask the next question. *Can we find someone first?*

Brandegil paused for a second, thinking. "Oh. Your friend? The fae? If she knows what's good for her, she should stop changing into a fox. It makes her easy to track—"

"Yeah, I figured that out." Kitra stepped into the clearing in her human form, wearing an oval basket on her back, aiming a crossbow at Brandegil. "Looky what I got."

Both he and Brandegil stared at her, stunned. Lirien recovered first and ran toward her, but Kitra shook her head. "Lirien! Don't get in my way."

Brandegil frowned with some difficulty, his swollen lip stretched and misshapen. "How did you find us?"

"Elythia dropped me off just a little way back. And then I could smell you." She tapped her nose. "It still works like a fox's, even when I'm like this." She grinned, and to Lirien's horror, all her teeth were sharpened into points, her fangs glinting. "Teeth still work, too. But, no, I'll just play with this." She raised her crossbow higher. "You shot me, so I shoot you."

"I didn't kill you."

"And I won't kill you. I'll just, I don't know, get you in your kneecap or something."

He ran in front of Brandegil, arms out to the sides.

"What are you doing?" Kitra nearly growled. "Step aside."

He shook his head frantically. *Ally*, he mouthed.

Kitra raised an eyebrow. "What?"

He made fists with his hands, as if he were gripping a sword, and swung it.

"Ah. You need him."

Brandegil blinked. "You need me?" He scowled at Lirien. "I

thought you wanted me to have the sword. Are you trying to take advantage of me?"

He shook his head. Then he tapped his throat, pointed to Kitra, and placed his hands together, pleading.

"You want me to speak for you?" she asked.

He nodded.

Kitra lowered her crossbow. "Fine. Truce."

Brandegil folded his arms across his chest, looking doubtful. "Just like that, truce?"

"Well, for *now*, yes. Unless you'd rather I shoot you. You're pretty defenseless at the moment and look worse for wear—"

"All right, all right. Truce. Just let me... take care of this." Brandegil wandered off for a moment, and as soon as he did, Kitra dropped her weapon and ran to Lirien, wrapping her arms around him tightly.

"I was so, so worried about you. I begged Elythia to help me, and I thought you'd be there, too, but I couldn't find you. Thank goodness the forest let me out when it did."

He went rigid when she touched him, but just for a moment. He exhaled— *this is Kitra* —and then returned her hug. After a second, he pulled back and squeezed her arms, bowing his head to her. Then he let go.

Brandegil was chewing on a small piece of moss when he walked up on them again but said nothing. He grabbed a sliver of the slimy moss, and then proceeded to apply it to the slice on his lip.

Kitra took off the basket she'd been wearing. She opened the lid and out slithered Nina, who immediately wriggled up to Lirien's extended arm. Her ruby snake eyes stared at him for a few moments, not moving, until at last she took her place under his sleeve, her coils feeling tighter than usual, as though she didn't want to let go of him. She poked her head out, and he gently ran his finger along the top of it, relieved to see her well.

Brandegil sat down, reaching into his bag for something to wrap his wrist with. As he wound strips of fabric around it, he gestured for Lirien and Kitra to also sit. "You have your truce, so tell me what you want me to hear."

And Kitra told him everything, in straightforward terms with little delicacy.

"I saw the Queen," Brandegil said. "I saw how... *twisted* ...she was. How she treated him." He looked at him with an expression of pity. "It made me sick to see it." He shifted in his seat. "So, you need me to help you use the sword to cut all the things from the sky. Well, you do need an elf to awaken it, true. And it does look like I'm your only hope. But we need the sword first. The Queens of Asherin have to give it to me. I won't accept anything less. Then I'll help you."

I'll make sure you get it. Lirien offered his hand to Brandegil, who took it and gave a single shake.

"And you have to promise not to shoot me," Brandegil added, eyeing Kitra.

"You have to promise not to shoot me," she said. "And I'll forget what you did as long as you help Lirien."

"I said I'd help." A hint of annoyance tinged Brandegil's voice.

"Good. That's settled, then." Kitra took the weapon she'd set on the ground and proceeded to dismantle it, unsnapping pieces here and there, folding up the limbs, and pushing the weapon into an elongated block.

"I've never seen a faery bow do that before," Brandegil said.

"There's a little bit of magic in it, of course," she said. "I borrowed it from the Lord of Autumn Wood."

"I don't know who that is. I've never been to Elythia before."

"Well, Elythia had its reasons to keep you out, didn't it?"

"I see that now." Brandegil yawned and stretched himself

out on the grass. "I'm going to sleep. I suggest you do the same."

Lirien tucked his fur cloak into his bag and puffed it up into a pillow. He folded his hands underneath it when he laid down and sighed. His eyes were half-closed when he caught Kitra standing over him. She sank to her knees and leaned toward him.

"Lirien," she whispered. "I shouldn't sleep like a fox anymore. But I'm going to get cold. And you're... it's comfortable next to you. So... may I join you?"

He nodded, but this time, he wanted to feel... he didn't know how to describe it. Safe? Protected? Maybe *wanted* was the word, and not in a cruel and loathsome way. He opened his arms to Kitra, beckoning her to him. And instead of sleeping against his back, Kitra nestled into his chest, and Lirien wrapped his arms around her. It was the warmest he'd ever been with her, and at last, feeling comfort, he drifted off to sleep with her up against him.

He woke up in the night and stared at his companion, still nestled up against him, and saw for once Kitra's eyes no longer filled with tears as they had before when she slept.

THE THREE OF them woke at sunrise. Even though Lirien was disguised in his cloak of furs, they agreed to stay off the main paths as a precaution. There were no giant stones along the way to the lake, so they had to resort to a long three days of walking through Asherin's side of the forests of Yanna.

"Hey, Brandegil, I have a riddle for you," Kitra said as the trees had started to thin out before them.

"The one who dares shoot someone's back
Is not in truth brave in attack
But rather, fool and coward be
And all the lesser one is he.

"Who am I?"

Brandegil rolled his eyes at her. "You just won't let it go, will you?"

"You shot me from behind! I was just trying to get some food for us!"

"It was a sleeping dart, not an arrow. Of course you weren't going to die!"

"I want to hear you say you're sorry. Sorry for shooting me and sorry for taking Lirien from me."

"Fine. I'm sorry." But his voice came out gruff.

"You have to mean it!"

On and on they bickered as they journeyed toward Lake Karda. For a little while it distracted Lirien from his growing worry about finding the children. They were getting closer and closer to them, but Sorin could still be hunted and, for all he knew, the Queen could have guards intercept all of them at any point in the journey, even if they were ahead of them for the time being.

As Kitra and Brandegil sniped at each other, Lirien started to get annoyed by it and wrote in bold letters, *QUIET*. And they actually listened to him, Kitra giving him a sheepish apology.

By noon the following day, the trees were scattered and scarce, and he could see in the distance the cleared land leading to the lake. A horn sounded nearby, followed by the rumbling of hooves and movement along the trees to their east.

A white stag rushed in front of them. Lirien gasped in shock. Something in his gut told him it was Sorin— how many other pure-white stags could there be?

Sorin didn't notice them. He ran as fast as he could until an arrow tore through his front right kneecap, shattering it. The stag cried out, a horrible sound like wailing, and bucked—thrusting his leg outward, but it dangled at an odd angle. Then the animal went down.

He ran to Sorin, whose eyes were wide until their whites could be seen and whose breathing was rapid from what seemed like panic.

A group of four hunters on horseback made their way to them. He recognized the leader as Aunt Eira, the Queen. Though it had been years since he'd last seen her, he knew her by the way her wavy red hair cascaded from the top over the cropped left side, and by the same golden-brown eyes as her brother, King Neven. She wore a breastplate of bluish silver armor and had her arrow poised to shoot one more time.

He threw his body over the stag, trying to shield Sorin.

The Queen raised her hand to her entourage and motioned for them to stop.

"Young man," she called out, "why do you care what happens to the Queen's animal, so much that you would risk your life for it?"

He turned to face Aunt Eira, but never relented in his shielding of the stag with his body. He pulled his fur cloak off and tossed it to the ground.

"My God," she said, lowering her bow, looking bewildered. "Lirien. Is that you? What are you doing here? You *never* come here!"

She put her arrow in its quiver and returned the bow to its case on her back, then she practically jumped off her horse. Her fellow hunters dismounted as well, their hands at their sides to reach for their swords if needed.

"Your Majesty," Kitra said, giving Aunt Eira a humble bow,

"that stag is Lirien's brother. He's been enchanted." She elbowed Brandegil, who bowed quickly.

"Your Majesty, we have come so far to see you," Brandegil added. "I have a great need for—"

"Not now," Kitra practically hissed at him.

Aunt Eira looked at the two of them and gave them a dismissive wave as she approached Lirien. "Nephew. It's said you cannot speak, that you lost your voice after you... after the children..." She shook her head. "Is it true, what they say you have done? I couldn't believe it when I heard it, but Queen Aurinda swore that you... We even had their funerals! Now the young woman says this stag is Sorin? Help me to understand!"

Lirien rose to his feet, still blocking Sorin with his body. He touched his throat and sighed. He looked to Kitra to explain, and she understood.

"It's true that his voice is gone, but the children are all alive. You've got the stag and we have the snake here with us. We need only to find the swan—"

"What is this you speak of?"

Lirien raised his sleeve and Nina peeked out of it.

"That's Nina," Kitra said.

"They're all animals?"

"It's a complicated spell. Lirien, how much do you want me to say?"

He waved his palms in the air, shaking his head— *we don't have time to talk about this* —and pointed to Sorin.

Save him, he mouthed.

One of the Queen's hunters approached, inspecting Sorin's ruined leg. "Animals usually don't survive on their own for long with this kind of damage. He's prey to so many different things. We'd usually put the animal out of his misery since he'd likely be killed anyway."

Lirien shook his head frantically.

"Can you understand me?" Aunt Eira asked, facing the stag. "Can you get up?"

Sorin struggled with a cry to shift his legs underneath him. At first stumbling, but then with a clumsy hop, he made it to his feet. His wounded leg hung there, and he moved with a sort of jerking jump as he tried to rebalance himself with only three legs. He hobbled forward, rubbing his face against Lirien's arm. Then, with caution, he approached Eira and nuzzled her.

Aunt Eira brought her hand to the bridge of the animal's nose. "It's true. It must be. No deer would react this way, especially to his hunter." Her face crinkled. "I shot him." She palmed her forehead for a second, then her face returned to the expression she had worn before— one of stern authority. "I'll have my surgeon see to the stag. He's going to lose that leg. And then we have to worry about possible infection while he heals. It's not going to be easy. We've just got to hope he makes it through this ordeal."

She moved to her horse, and her hunting party followed suit. But then she raised her hand to one of the hunters and he halted. "Sir Gregory. Stay behind and accompany my nephew to the castle. Lirien, you are still a wanted criminal. I cannot let you go, not when there is a bounty on your head. Not when my sister-in-law demands your return. You are in my custody now. I will have you write an account of what has happened, and I will consider it carefully before I decide what I will do with you."

Brandegil stepped forward. "Your Majesty, I must tell you, I already brought Lirien to Queen Aurinda."

"Then why is he here now?"

Brandegil's jaw tightened for a moment. "There's much to explain, but I'll tell you plainly that the Queen did not give me my reward because you have it."

"What is it that you seek?"

"Alibrandr. It belongs to my people."

"Ah." She mounted her horse. "We'll talk about that. We'll talk about everything when we get back to the castle. Sir Gregory, once again. Keep an eye on them. Keep an eye on the stag. If the animal can't make it the full way back, then you must resort to carrying him. Lirien, I expect your statement at once. I'll see you all soon."

The group had to pass Lake Karda in order to reach the castle. Although Lirien knew the utmost urgency lay with helping Sorin, he couldn't keep himself from staring out at the bevy of swans that had taken home on the water. In his dream of the twins on the night of their birthday, Sonalie said that she had made it to the lake. Was it true?

He immediately had his answer. A large, beautiful swan whooped and honked, extending her massive wings, and then she took flight across the lake. She skimmed the water's edge before coming up to the shore and walked right up to him.

Lirien couldn't help falling to his knees. He held his arms open and Sonalie allowed him to pick her up, and she wrapped her long neck around his in a swan's embrace. He stroked her smooth downy feathers and then set her back on the ground. His heart welled up with relief and joy that he finally could see her.

Sorin limped over to the two of them, and in alarm, Sonalie extended her wings one more time and flapped them, honking several times. Lirien thought he could sense fear in her cries when she saw Sorin's injury.

He wished he could speak, but Kitra spoke for him. "We're getting him help."

Sonalie looked at Sorin, then him, and honked once more before flying back to her flock across the lake.

When they came to a steep hill, Sorin struggled with great difficulty to go up the slope.

"Maybe it would be better for me to carry him," Kitra said. Without waiting for an answer, she transformed and lowered herself to the ground.

"A fae fox!" Sir Gregory's mouth dropped open, but only for a second. "It's dangerous for you to be outside Elythia."

"Please ensure my safety while I'm here, then. It's the least you can do."

"Very well, miss. I'll notify the Queens once we get to the castle. They'll make sure you're protected."

Lirien pointed to Brandegil and Sir Gregory, then to Sorin. With open palms he brought his hands upward, to show lifting. He wasn't exactly sure how they were going to do it. He knew Sorin as a stag would be heavy, but he hoped three people could handle his weight.

Sorin limped over to Kitra, getting as close to her as he could, and with effort the three men helped Sorin onto her back. He looked strange, dangling helplessly there, but at least he was stable enough on her back for Kitra to move, albeit slow and with caution.

They made it up the hill and across a great field leading to a castle with slate blue roofing and thin white towers of dizzying heights. The heraldic animals of Asherin, the lion, the horse, and the bull, decorated the castle walls along the great gates, as well as above the castle's inner keep.

Several of the guards greeted Lirien and the others, and Sir Gregory double-checked to see if they were aware of what was happening. The Queen and her men had filled them in. With great care they helped Sorin off of Kitra's back before she transformed into her human form. "I will take him to the surgeon now," Sir Gregory told him, and Sorin hobbled his way into the castle.

Lirien tried to go after him, but two of the guards blocked the way. "Your Highness, you will come with us to give your account in writing. As for you, Glynnan elf, the Queens will hear your case now." One of the guards gestured for Brandegil to follow him inside, and they disappeared into the castle.

The other guard turned to Kitra. "Fae fox, you are not needed."

"I'm not leaving Lirien's side," she said. "And if he needs me to speak for him, I will."

"Is this your will, Prince?"

Lirien nodded.

"Very well." And the guards led the two of them in.

"This is… I don't know what else to say but 'disturbing.'" Aunt Eira sat at her throne, with her wife Idela at her side. Idela wore her long jet-black hair in a thick braid that went down almost to her knees, and her brown, curving hooded eyes looked at Lirien with sympathy.

They were alone in the giant chamber. Even the guards had been dismissed from the room. Nonetheless, Lirien knelt before them just as if he were a royal subject in the presence of the court. Kitra stood off to the side to give him his moment with them.

He had told his aunts everything, and decided not to leave anything out, including the Queen's assaults. He made it clear exactly what it was Queen Aurinda wanted from him and what she'd done, and his role in all of it. He needed someone to know the full truth of what had happened, and if he was going to find an ally in his aunts, it was better to not withhold anything from them.

Aunt Eira descended the platform to approach him. "Rise," she said, and opened her arms to him once he was on his feet.

She pulled him in for an embrace. "You poor boy," she said softly, and patted his back. "I'm so sorry this happened to you."

Aunt Idela also stepped down from her throne and came to them, and she clutched his shoulder. "We are on your side."

He couldn't help tearing up at their words. He didn't have to fight to be believed.

Aunt Eira let him go, and she lowered her eyes to the ground. "It was in my hands. The way for me to see the truth. And I just let it go without even trying."

Aunt Idela took Eira's hand in her own, giving her a quick kiss, looking concerned. "What do you mean, my love?"

"The Seer's Helm." She turned to Lirien. "Queen Aurinda bade me to retrieve it. The old stories said that a dragon hoarded it, and we hunted every one we could find. That's why she gave me Alibrandr, so I could slay the dragon. I told her that the Helm wasn't working. When I put it on to look through your eyes, nothing came of it, but she demanded it anyway. I didn't even think of trying it to see the children because I believed her lies. You have to understand, Lirien, we all thought they were dead. Queen Aurinda insisted the children were dead. She was distraught, distressed. When we had the funerals, she could barely keep her composure. Why would she orchestrate this elaborate deception? There are so many other ways she could have gotten you back, could have gotten the children back. Is this all truly the work of the siren's curse?"

Lirien sighed and shrugged his shoulders. Sometimes he wasn't so sure. Sometimes, a nagging voice in his mind wondered how much of the Queen's behavior was under her control. He didn't dare think on it more, though, because if there was some part of her that knew what she was doing, he didn't think he could ever forgive her.

"You have to go to Ardeth, Eira, without delay," Aunt Idela said. "You must talk some sense into Aurinda, to keep her from him. No doubt she knows he's here and has already sent people to return him to Ardeth. And with the Seer's Helm in her hands, she'll easily know Lirien's movements."

"Then she should know that Lirien's been trying to break the curse this whole time. And she doesn't seem to care. It's like an illness has taken hold of her and is changing her. If she were well, if she had full faculty of her senses, there is no way she would forbid Lirien from saving those she loves."

"Lirien. You know how to break the curse on the children," Aunt Idela said. "Do you know how to break the siren's spell?"

Lirien looked at each of his aunts, then swallowed nervously. He dragged two fingers across the base of his throat in a slashing motion.

"No. Don't tell me you have to die!"

"If I may speak, Your Majesties," Kitra said, stepping out of her corner. "I can read curses and spells, and it's true. The only way to end the siren's curse is to end the siren."

Aunt Eira gripped Lirien's shoulder. "Then what can we do?"

Children, he mouthed.

"His priority has always been with saving his family, not himself," Kitra said.

"Queen Aurinda has to know of your plan. I have to stop her from doing anything rash, from trying to hurt you further. I'll ride straightaway for Ardeth and try to talk some sense into her. Meanwhile, Idela will teach you to sign while I'm gone."

Between the two warrior Queens, he knew Aunt Idela served a slightly more diplomatic role due to her knowledge of languages. She was often a visitor to other countries to represent Asherin. But Lirien had no idea she knew sign language.

"I know we won't have a lot of time between us for me to teach you much, but I can show you the alphabet and some important words and gestures. It should make things easier for you while you try to break the spell. I could have my old tutor work with you, but... Lirien, it's such a gift to have you with us, despite the terrible circumstances. It would bring me pleasure to spend more time with you."

"Idela is a good teacher," Aunt Eira said. "You will do well. Now, I must hurry and get to Queen Aurinda as soon as possible. It'll take a few weeks at best. I can only hope she won't try anything desperate while you are here."

He dug out his paper and wrote, *Brandegil has a way to help.*

Aunt Eira pulled on a velvet rope hanging near her throne. Within moments a servant entered, and Aunt Eira called for him to fetch Brandegil.

He arrived fairly quickly. "Your Majesties," he said with a bow.

"Lirien says you may be able to assist us with our problem."

"Per our agreement, I said I would help him with his task if you grant me full ownership of the sword. Was there something else you wanted?"

Can you take my aunt on the stone highway? He wrote.

"What is that?" Aunt Idela asked.

"It's a way the Glynnan elves get from one place to another quickly. It's part of our magic, as creatures of mountain and rock. It saves a lot of time."

"As it is, it'll take weeks for me to get to Ardeth. If you can get me there faster, please, help me," Aunt Eira said.

He clasped his hands together and lowered his head to Brandegil.

"It'll take three days until we reach the first stone, though faster if we have horses, and after that we can get to the castle same day. You can't— this can't be something that others can learn about. It's special to my people, and only Glynnan elves can open the stones for travel."

"Meaning this isn't something we can regularly rely on,"

Aunt Eira said. "Of course. I understand. But the sooner you can get me to Queen Aurinda, the sooner I can protect Lirien."

Brandegil looked to Lirien. "After I saw how she treated you in the dungeon... I know if I was in your place, I couldn't bear it. You have my sympathy. Really. I'll take Queen Eira through the stones."

Lirien lowered his head to Brandegil once more, this time to express gratitude.

"Can I borrow your cloak? There will doubtless be a price on my head for aiding in your escape, so I need to disguise myself in case we run into anyone."

He pulled his furs from his bag, and Brandegil put the cloak on. His appearance changed once more to the tanned boy with green eyes and short brown hair.

"Remarkable," Aunt Idela said.

"Elythian magic," Kitra responded.

"So much magic in one day," Aunt Eira said. "I can hardly fathom it." She turned to Brandegil. "I'll have the horses readied, and we'll leave at once. Idela, my love, I'll see you as soon as I'm able." She gave her wife a sweet kiss on the lips and motioned for Brandegil to follow behind her.

"Lirien." Brandegil stopped right before the door. He gave him a little smile from the corner of his mouth. "I leave Alibrandr in your hands. Keep it safe."

CHAPTER 14

In the days that followed, Lirien learned more details from Aunt Idela about Brandegil's deal with the Queens of Asherin. After centuries of Alibrandr being kept under lock and key in Ardeth, it would be returned to the Glynnan elves on the condition that he be allowed to finish his quest with it. And the other condition was that if Asherin had need of Alibrandr, the Glynnan elves would consider loaning it to them when the time came. Brandegil agreed, and the plan was made official, written and stamped with the royal seal.

The Queens of Asherin gave up the sword so easily. If only Alibrandr had come to Asherin sooner, then the Glynnan elves would've had their relic without years of failed attempts and bloodshed. He wondered how Brandegil felt, knowing that soon the sword would be his to take back. Would he be proud that it was accomplished at long last with nothing more than kind words and kind deeds, or would he feel he was somehow betraying the people who had sacrificed so much, even their lives, in the attempt?

In an odd way, this injustice had only been righted because of Queen Aurinda's desperation for Lirien. Had it not been for the siren spell, she would never have given up the sword, even to family, even in exchange for something like the Seer's Helm. In fact, Lirien was sure the Queen would've found a way to take both of them.

Each night, Lirien slept in a large chamber in Castle Asherin as an honored guest and member of the family, and Kitra was allowed to stay in a room next to his. With assurances from the Queens that Kitra would be safe within the castle, she reverted to her true form, her fae form: her fox ears returned to the top of her head, popping out of her copious red hair, and her impish amber eyes returned with their slit pupils. Her tail materialized, thick and fluffy, and he had to exercise restraint whenever he saw it, because he sometimes had the childlike impulse to give it a little tug.

While he and Kitra made a home in the castle, spending almost all their time together, he figured Sonalie would want to stay on the lake with the other swans, given how attached she seemed to them. Meanwhile, he had a glass container heated by warm stones to serve as a little house for Nina, and he kept her in his room. He even took charge of feeding Nina, although he felt guilty about sacrificing live mice to her.

After spending time with Nina, he would head to the stable where Sorin was kept, to spend time with him and check how his amputated leg was healing. He had heard it needed to be cauterized to stop the bleeding, and he could hardly imagine the pain. With assurances from the surgeon, however, he learned with great relief that Sorin was healing well. Sometimes he would venture down to Lake Karda with Kitra to fetch Sonalie, and he would bring her to Sorin's stable so she could see how he was healing.

Other times, he and Kitra stayed at Lake Karda to spend time with Sonalie alone. He liked to feed her, too, and Sonalie let him stroke the downy feathers on her back whenever she'd come up to him on the shore.

Every afternoon, Aunt Idela gave him language lessons. To his surprise, Kitra accompanied him there as well. "I want to learn, too. I want to be able to have conversations with you," she said. "I figure this was the best way for me to understand you."

He couldn't keep from smiling at her, appreciative that she wanted to be with him, that she genuinely wanted to find a better way to converse with him. He didn't know how long they would spend together or when their paths in life would diverge, but the fact that she wanted to enrich their communication for as long as they were together made him happy.

Aunt Idela taught him and Kitra the alphabet first, then common nouns and verbs for them to use. For whatever words he didn't know, he simply spelled them out or used his own gesture of choice.

He finally felt like he had a voice again.

After lessons with Kitra and Aunt Idela, he would head to the castle courtyard and practice using Alibrandr with some of the Queens' knights. He knew the sword wouldn't reach its full potential without Brandegil, but he felt like he needed to get used to using it all the same, to learn how to hold it, and how swipe and slice.

When he first glimpsed Alibrandr, it was nothing like what he expected. He remembered the giant statue in the cave in the mountains, and he expected the sword to likewise be huge. And yet, Alibrandr, once he got a hold of it, was a blade that Lirien could grip easily, no different than a broadsword. Maybe the sword changed sizes depending on who or what held it? There had to be *some* kind of magic with the sword though, because, just like in his memory of the treasury, the air around the sword grew clean and crisp when he beheld it.

He wondered if the other knights noticed this change in the air when they handled it.

Every knight who saw the sword marveled at its sharpness, and Sir Gregory declared it was the only thing Queen Eira could use to cut through dragon scales.

Lirien wondered what would happen if Brandegil were here to swing the sword. Could he really slice stars from the sky? Would the blade simply obliterate everything in its path? Of course, nothing like that happened with him. Certainly, the sword was beautiful and well made, but there seemed to be nothing else extraordinary about it. When it clashed with other swords, it never chipped or dulled... but was that magic or craftsmanship? Lirien began to wonder if all the stories about it were true, or if he had made a terrible mistake trusting in myth and legend. Then again, perhaps he just needed to be patient and wait for Brandegil.

During sword training Sir Gregory obliged in showing him the proper posture for wielding the weapon, teaching him how to swing and move with it. Sir Gregory seemed eager to teach him, though he wondered if perhaps the knight was more inter-ested in seeing Alibrandr in action. Nonetheless, practice took up Lirien's afternoons from sign language lessons until dinner.

Kitra would often watch him and cheer him on, and some-times offer instruction. "That's it! Swing left! Now dodge it! Excellent!" He concentrated so hard, though, that often her voice dwindled into the background like a faint hum.

When nighttime fell, he and Kitra would head up to Asherin's tallest parapet and stare up at the stars together, the faint light of a torch glowing behind them. Sometimes he would whip out the sword and, aiming its tip at the stars, slash at the air.

Nothing ever happened.

"I guess it really won't work until Brandegil wakes it up,"

Kitra said one night while they made their way up the steps to their usual spot atop the parapet. "I hope he comes back soon. I wonder what's taking so long."

Lirien wondered what he would do if Brandegil never came back from his trip to Ardeth. What if he was caught and imprisoned, or worse?

When Kitra and he got to the top of the rampart, he rested the sword and scabbard against the wall while he found a place to sit. Then he folded his arms behind his head and laid back, stretching his long body across the stone walkway. Kitra followed suit, laying on her side, resting on her arm, her chin in her hand. They were only inches apart from each other.

The torchlight caught Kitra's hair and made it burn a brighter red. The flickering glow warmed her skin and softened her features, and Lirien stole glances at her strange, beautiful eyes and the long lashes that framed them.

Kitra caught him looking. She met his gaze evenly and held it until Lirien had to turn away, embarrassed. Then Kitra let out a little breath of air and rolled over onto her back, copying his exact pose.

"The stars are quite bright tonight. Perfect for hunting them, don't you think? If all the nights were like this, then it would be easy to catch what you need. The stars, and the moonlight, and the northern aurora. The most beautiful things about the night sky." Kitra turned her head to the side, peering at him. "Your curse is terrible to break, but at the same time, it's lovely, too."

Feeling brave, he signed. *Lovely. With you.*

The corner of Kitra's mouth ticked upward. "I like being with you, too."

You're my friend...

"And you're mine, Lirien. After all we've been through, you don't have to worry about that."

What if more?

She looked at him curiously, in thought. Then she whispered, "More than what we have now?"

He nodded.

"Do you want me to..." she trailed off. Her gaze fell on his lips. "May I?"

He smiled shyly as she crawled on top of him, her tail swishing to the side. His hand slid behind the back of her head to cradle it, his fingers running through her soft, fox-red hair, his other hand gliding down to her waist. He pulled her close to him, pressing her tightly against his body, her strange yet wonderfully wild, sweet scent flooding his senses.

This is what I want, he thought. *At last.*

Her mouth met his, cautiously at first, a touch soft as gossamer. Their kiss lasted only a moment. He looked up at her, eyebrows raised, wondering what he could do next, what she wanted next.

Kitra pulled back a little, her fingertips gently stroking his cheek. She nodded. "More. It's all right."

A fluttery breath escaped him, and they drew together, their lips searching, their tongues exploring the wonder of each other, the heat of their kisses consuming them both.

Their hearts beat like the steady current of a river or the waves that crashed to shore. He thought he would burst from the rapturous joy of it, the nearness of her, the feeling of being safe, of being at home with someone, of wanting and being wanted.

Kitra's fingers walked up his shirt and she gently opened the buttons, her soft flesh brushing across him, welcome against his own. His breath caught in his throat as she ventured over his body, kissing him at his neck, his chest, then down the smooth muscles of his stomach.

His hands shook from nerves, from eagerness, as he

fumbled with the knotted ties at the collar of her shirt. Once loose, he pulled it apart, exposing the tops of her breasts. His lips found the hollow between them, and he kissed her.

Suddenly Kitra let out an airy laugh. Her lips were plumped and pink, glistening in the light of the torch. "We should probably continue this elsewhere," she said with a smile.

You sure? he signed. *Continue?*

"I want to. But you have to want it, too. We will never do anything you don't want, Lirien."

I want you. I want this.

Kitra climbed off of him, quickly adjusting her shirt. He haphazardly fastened only some of his buttons to his top, knowing he would soon be free of it. Kitra held out her hand to him, and with a foxlike grin, wove her fingers with his.

She led him hurriedly down the stairs and to her room, and in the night, they lay together, finding comfort and solace in each other's bodies.

In the morning, he woke to Kitra curled up against him, still fast asleep. His fingers softly combed through her hair, and he thought to himself in wonder what he did to deserve this, to deserve her. He had always dreamed of the moment he could truly become one with someone, and there were times when he was alone in his tower, kept away from the world, when he never thought it would happen. That it was something precious he would never come to know.

His eyes grew misty as his gaze wandered over Kitra's sleeping form. He kissed the crown of her head and thought to himself blissfully, *Let's stay like this as long as we can.*

DURING ONE OF the trainings with Sir Gregory, while Kitra dutifully watched him practice, Lirien nearly dropped the sword as a headache came on quickly. The familiar pain behind his eyes— Queen Aurinda was using the Seer's Helm. Why would she need to? She knew Lirien was in Asherin. Queen Eira should've been there with her, telling her their plan. Was it really necessary for her to keep spying on him?

And that led to another thought, a worry that unfurled in his mind, that somehow Aunt Eira's presence would do nothing to dissuade the Queen from her intentions and obsession with him.

Brandegil's arrival confirmed nothing. He was gone only long enough to make it to Pinemore and back; even with the fur cloak to disguise him, he did not dare to accompany Aunt Eira into Ardeth itself, where he was a wanted criminal for freeing Lirien from the dungeon.

"I left her as soon as I could," he said. "We'll just have to trust that she can keep Queen Aurinda at bay for the time being."

Lirien signed. *Sword. Help me, please.*

"When did you learn to do that?" Brandegil asked. "And so fast!"

"It's mostly spelling and a handful of simple gestures— there are a lot of words he and I don't know," Kitra said.

"You can do it, too?"

"You can learn if you want. It would make it easier. Otherwise I'll just translate for you."

He thought about it for a moment. "Sure. Let me know when I can start. In the meantime, what did he say?"

Kitra explained what Lirien wanted.

"Yes, we can start tonight."

I want to try for the stars.

Kitra translated for Brandegil, and he responded, "Let's do it."

Later, he and Kitra climbed the highest tower of Castle Asherin with Brandegil and Alibrandr in tow. He pulled out the sword and showed Brandegil his movements with it, how the sword was meant to cut. Brandegil eyed the sword with his mouth hanging open slightly, peering at it with reverence.

"You look good," Brandegil conceded after a moment. "But if you need the sword to slice things from the sky, I definitely have to wake it up first. I'm not quite sure how to do it, to be honest. The sword has been gone so long, and it's not like I was in training to join the temple and handle holy relics before I met you. I just know what I've heard about it over the years. Hand it over and I'll see what I can do."

He held the sword out to Brandegil, who only stared at it with awe. His eyes turned wet for a moment, and he rubbed them with his hand and let out a sigh. "All right. I'm going to try it."

He took Alibrandr with both hands and raised it, holding it above his head in a triumphant position, his body and the sword a pillar against the sky. He closed his eyes and stood there still, and nothing happened.

He thrust the sword up into the air again and was met with no response. "This is harder than I thought it would be."

"You can do it," Kitra said. "After everything you've been through to get that sword, I know it will answer you. It just has to."

Lirien nodded, and with shy encouragement, patted Brandegil's arm. It was the first time he'd reached out to touch Brandegil as if they were friends. In that moment, something within him told him that they were brought together for a higher purpose, and just as with Kitra, it was meant to be. Maybe that's why Elythia wouldn't let him escape Brandegil— maybe it knew they were going to end up as allies, as though it had to happen the way it did. After all, neither could have made it this far toward their separate goals without the other.

Brandegil took in a deep breath and repeated his pose with the sword. He stood there, perfectly still, his jaw clenched, the muscles of his cheeks taut, and his brow furrowed. He stayed there, concentrating, until Lirien caught the gleam of sweat on his forehead.

Then Alibrandr made a sound, a soft metallic *shing* that left a faint ringing in the air. It was almost musical, like the note of a song. The sword grew in Brandegil's hands, the blade thickening and stretching into the heavens, as tall as a man, and then taller.

"Oh wow— it's still light," said Brandegil.

Aiming away from Lirien and Kitra, he lowered the sword for a second, then raised it again. He narrowed his eyes at the stars, and then swung across in a swift, supple motion.

The sky rippled like the water of the sea, and the stars trembled.

Brandegil pumped his fist. "YES!"

He gave the sword back to Lirien. Lirien's hand dipped lower at the weight of it. It wasn't heavy, but there was a marked difference once it had grown in size.

"Do it quickly. I don't know how long the sword is going to stay like that," Brandegil said.

Lirien took a breath and sliced the air as hard as he could. To his surprise, there was a bit of a kickback from the rippling air and the power coursing through it.

"Look!" Kitra cried.

Several stars shot out of the sky, falling to the ground with streaks of light behind them, and made pocks in the earth beneath them where they fell. It was beautiful, but not without violence.

The sword immediately shrank back down to its more manageable size, looking like a regular broadsword. Lirien slid it into its scabbard as Brandegil cried, "Hurry! Let's grab them!" He gave him a proud grin.

They dashed down the stairs and out of the castle, counting seven stars in the grassy yard outside of the stone palace. They were much smaller than he expected, each one the size of the palm of his hand.

Without thinking, he eagerly picked one up. He dropped it immediately. Oh God, it burned, how it burned! He looked down at his hand, and it was already pink and peeling.

He shook his head frantically and made an 'X' with his arms — *don't touch!*

"Lirien!" Kitra came to his side, staring at his wounds. "Oh, that looks awful. We've got to get you inside to the physician immediately."

"What about the stars?" Brandegil asked.

Lirien tried to sign with his good hand, and it was more difficult than he expected. *Something to grab with.*

Kitra repeated it to Brandegil, and then, "Do you think my gloves would work?"

Lirien looked them over. They were leather, and he wasn't sure if they could handle the heat. If the stars burned his flesh, it could probably burn through animal skin, too.

Don't try it.

"Maybe there's something in the castle we can use," Brandegil said. "Kitra, take him to find the doctor, and I'll ask around." Brandegil headed through the gate into the castle with Lirien and Kitra following just behind him.

They came in just as Aunt Idela and her retinue passed through the great hall. The three of them bowed to her, and the first thing Idela noticed was Lirien holding his burned hand out in front of him, wincing in pain.

She broke from the line of women and ran up to him. "What happened?"

Kitra and Brandegil explained, and Aunt Idela bade two of her ladies to accompany Brandegil to the kitchens while the Queen herself led Lirien and Kitra to the physician.

The doctor placed a poultice on his hand and wrapped it with great care, including around his fingers.

"What are you going to do?" Kitra asked when he and Queen Idela returned to the halls. "When the time comes to weave the robe? You won't be able to touch any of the threads made from that stuff. You're going to destroy yourself!"

He was more concerned about the children. What was going to happen when one of them put on a robe with molten stars woven through the fabric?

All he could think to do was shrug at Kitra. He didn't know. He had no answers. He didn't want to think about it. Time was running out as it was.

No worry. No time. Continue on.

"Two more things left," Kitra said. "Should we do the moonlight next, or the aurora?"

"About that," Aunt Idela began. "I went ahead and secured a ship for you. The nearest place you can observe the aurora borealis is Perdra, our northernmost island. And although you can see the lights year-round, they're in season now, which means you have the greatest chance to catch them."

Moonlight, too. Same time.

"That's true. It's the new moon now. You'll need to wait a week at least, and by then you'll be in Perdra. You can get them both there." Kitra's fox ears flicked back for a moment, and her tail straightened and lowered. "I wish I could go with you."

He looked at her, eyebrows raised.

"Remember. I'm fae. We can't cross the sea. We dare not go near it. That much salt is poison to us."

Lirien's heart sank. Right, she was right. How long would he be away from her? He didn't want to think about leaving her, not after their relationship had become... well, something much more than he'd hoped.

Will I be gone a long time?

"It will take seven days to get there," Aunt Idela said. "Maybe faster if the waters are smooth and the wind is good."

Kitra looked to him. "Do you think Queen Aurinda can hold herself back that long?"

He shook his head.

"You underestimate my wife," Aunt Idela said. "Eira's still wearing down Aurinda and has kept her at bay thus far. And Lirien, we won't just give you up. Go on your journey. Don't worry about us here."

"I'll make sure the children are well taken care of," Kitra said. "I'll visit them every day."

Lirien nodded, but he also couldn't help but frown. Seven days. He remembered Kitra's warning, that the longer he took to break the spell, the wilder the children would become. Nina seemed to retain an essence of humanity in her, perhaps because she had spent so much time with him and Kitra. He was unsure about Sorin, and as for Sonalie, well... it grew harder and harder to get her away from Lake Karda the more he visited her. She was too drawn to her swan family. *I hope this won't take too long,* he signed.

Brandegil arrived holding different sets of metal tongs and wearing a large, heavy canvas bag over his shoulder. "Cook says this is sturdy enough to hold almost anything," he said, indicating the bag. Then he handed the sets of tongs to Kitra and Lirien. "Let's get those stars quick, before they catch someone else's eye."

Lirien touched Aunt Idela's wrist before signing: *Ship— when?*

"It leaves tomorrow at noon. Don't worry; I'll have my staff ready supplies for you. We can talk more about it in the morning."

He nodded, then leaned in and gave Aunt Idela a quick peck on her cheek. She smiled. "Go get your stars."

Lirien, Kitra, and Brandegil hurried back out to the yard outside the castle, and sure enough, the seven stars still glowed where they landed. Lirien thought perhaps they would cool and become gray solid rock, but it didn't happen. They remained shining white spheres in the lawn.

Brandegil pulled off his bag and held the mouth of it open as wide as it could go. "Drop them in. I don't know if they'll burn through, but it's worth a shot."

Kitra and Lirien set about picking up the stars. His tongs came together at a hinge near the handle, so he could work them one-handed easily. He seized a smaller star with them. He couldn't help staring at it. The glow of the star lit up his face, and it almost hurt to look directly at it for too long. He couldn't blink away the afterimage of the light in his eyes, so he focused on the metal arms of his tongs, waiting to see if the star would melt through them.

It didn't. And when Lirien headed over to Brandegil to drop the star into the bag, he was relieved to see it held fast. The star, it seemed, would only burn flesh.

He sighed. Only flesh.

Lirien and Kitra collected the rest of the stars and put them in Brandegil's bag, and there was still plenty of room for the other things inside of it. He wasn't certain how large the moon-light or aurora would be, but he figured the sword could slice them small enough that the bag could keep them fine.

"Maybe you should hold onto this, spell-breaker," Brandegil said, passing it to him.

He drew the bag over his shoulder. The stars, now that they

were all grouped together, had a surprising amount of heft to them. *Thank you,* he mouthed.

"So, Brandegil," Kitra said, "Lirien's going to be trapped on a ship for two weeks, round trip. He'll need your help with the sword again. Do you think you'll be all right?"

"…I've never been out to sea before," he said thoughtfully.

Elves can go to sea, but fae can't?

"Elves and faeries may be cousins, but their rules don't apply to us. We can go freely where we wish. I just never had a reason to go on the water before."

"I'm sure Lirien misses it, being siren and all." Kitra squeezed Lirien's hand. "Do you?"

He thought about it and gave her a nod. He couldn't help it. As much as he loved exploring the forests, the mountains, and the fields; as much as he had loved parts of this adventure, he couldn't help where he was raised and the things that comforted him. He was growing hungry for the vast blue waters, and although it would also be his first time sailing, he couldn't help but take some delight in the fact that he'd be near the ocean again.

"The coast is a few hours away, so you must be up bright and early in the morning," Aunt Idela said.

"I'll see you off," Kitra added. "I'm so glad Lirien has a friend to go with him since I can't be there."

Brandegil blinked. "Friend?"

"Isn't 'ally' just another word for 'friend?'"

"I'm not so sure about that. I mean, Lirien, I hunted you for so long. And I brought you to that awful Queen. All I cared about was the sword—"

Lirien waved his hands and shook his head. With some difficulty with his bandaged hand, he signed and Kitra interpreted for him: "He says you have been a big help. And friends help each other."

"Is that really all it takes for us to be friends?" Brandegil was suddenly quiet, sounding unsure. He looked off to the side, avoiding Kitra and Lirien.

Lirien signed again. *If you want us to be.*

Kitra repeated it so Brandegil could understand.

"I... I guess so. I guess that makes us friends," he said, still averting his eyes. He scratched the back of his head. "Sure."

"Now that that's settled... want to call it a night?" Kitra said this more to Lirien than Brandegil, and gave him a sly grin.

He could feel the blood rushing to his cheeks. He shouldn't have felt shy around her anymore. They'd already revealed themselves to each other, but suddenly he seemed uncertain about it all, as though all that had passed between them was nothing more than a dream.

"Well... see you in the morning!" Kitra said to Brandegil. She inclined her head ever so slightly at Lirien, who followed her back to the castle.

He couldn't verbalize how grateful he was to her, that she was this great, shining light in the midst of all of the dark turmoil the spells had wrought for him, for the children, for the Queen. When Kitra reiterated that she couldn't go near the sea, his heart sank. Once the spells were broken, he and Kitra would remain apart. He, doomed to die if he wanted to break the spell on the Queen, and she, doomed to keep away from the salty waters forever.

He wanted to savor every moment he could have with her, unsure of how much longer they'd have together.

There was little sleep that night.

CHAPTER 15

Captain Fiona Swagger— Lirien couldn't believe that was her real name —was a loud, booming presence on the *Swiftswallow*. She was a tall woman with dark brown skin and jet-black hair that she wore in multiple braids underneath a large felt hat. She wore a ruffled collar with a wool doublet, leather jerkin, and wool trousers cut just above her ankles, along with a set of decorated leather slippers. She kept a long knife sheathed at one side and a flintlock pistol at the other, and walked the deck with long swinging strides and an imposing posture.

The Queens had told Lirien and Brandegil they could place their trust in the crew of the *Swiftswallow* entirely. The crew didn't know everything, but they knew enough not to harm Lirien or Brandegil for the crimes they had been wanted for. Lirien and Brandegil were safe to travel unhindered and undisguised.

"You're dressed for the weather, I see," Captain Swagger said approvingly, once Lirien and Brandegil boarded. "I've been to Perdra countless times, and you've got to arm yourselves against that shock of cold."

The two of them had been sent to the docks in furs and wool. The temperature at the oceanfront was much cooler and reminded Lirien of the chill in the mountain forests when he'd journeyed through Yanna. At the moment he felt rather warm but wondered how much of the freezing weather he could take once they got there, even in such clothing.

As sailors loaded the ship with wooden crates and trunks of what they'd need for the journey, Brandegil looked up in wonder at the ropes, the masts, and the huge sails they secured.

Captain Swagger smiled proudly, puffing out her chest. She tapped the railing that ran along the sides of the ship. "She's got good bones. She's sturdy, steady, and has made the journey thirty-three times. And I think we can get you there in five days, not seven."

Brandegil seemed absolutely thrilled to be on the boat. He pointed to the crow's nest. "Can I go up there?"

"You're the first Glynnan elf I've seen on a ship," Captain Swagger admitted. "But I bet you're not afraid of heights, being up in the mountains and all."

"Not at all, Captain. And I can climb."

"As you wish, then. Oi, Darshan!" she called to a tall burly man with shiny black hair and reddish-brown skin. "Take him up to the nest!"

"Aye!" he responded with a grin. He offered his hand to Brandegil and gave him an enthusiastic shake. "Come with me."

Lirien stared at the two ascending the tall wooden pillar leading up to the circular platform. There was no way he would ever climb up something that high. True, he'd been higher up in the mountains, but the crow's nest seemed far more precarious. And he couldn't imagine what it would be like stuck up there once the ship started moving on the sea. He pictured himself toppling over and out, and swallowed.

Captain Swagger raised her hand to a young girl passing by, a small thing with soft brown hair, tanned skin, and freckles, who looked no more than thirteen. "Granta," she said to the cabin girl, "show this one to his quarters. When that one—" She pointed up at Brandegil— "makes it back down, take him there, too. You'll be sharing a room. I trust you won't object?"

Lirien shook his head as the captain dug into her coat pockets and pulled out small white sticks of what looked like candle wax. "Take these with you. For your ears. Give a couple to your friend, too. Once we get far enough out to sea, it's siren waters. The wax doesn't always work. If the siren's voice gets inside your head, you're done for. But they help dampen the sound and it makes it a little harder for them to reach your mind."

She peered at Lirien's hair and orange eyes. "The Queen's men told us some of your story, Prince. That you are half-siren. Does their song affect you at all?"

Lirien pinched the air with his thumb and forefinger, signifying only a little bit. Captain Swagger nodded in understanding.

Lirien thought of the night his mother sang. He didn't become obsessed or lose himself in any way, but she did manage to draw him out of his tower all the same. But he figured he wouldn't need the beeswax for his ears and thought it would be best to keep his senses open to detect any singing before the sirens came close.

"Sirens dare not venture near land unless they want to go there to die. If they're on the sands too long, they turn to dried coral stone, a bonelike husk left behind."

Lirien winced, remembering his own variation of the curse.

"If only it were so easy to kill them out there," Captain Swagger added. "This particular group likes the open water and specifically comes for the ships. We have an alert system in place, where two rings of the bell mean we've entered their hunting ground, and three means that you need to put your wax in right quick and head below, and one bell means it's all over. We always have someone on the lookout to try to sight them before they start singing. You have only a few seconds before they've got you hooked." She pointed to the poop deck where several barbed lances were displayed. "But as far as hooks go, we have those, too. We'll be ready for them." She turned to Lirien. "You're not... partial to them, are you?"

Did she mean did he care about them? Lirien was part siren, yes, but he felt no affinity with the creatures aside from what they shared in common— being drawn to music and being drawn to the sea. Would he feel bad if they died? He just didn't know. He wouldn't know unless the time came.

THE TIME CAME QUICKLY ENOUGH. It was their first night at sea, and Brandegil and Lirien were relaxing on their beds when the sound of a bell ringing twice interrupted their repose.

"What's two times mean again?" Brandegil asked.

Lirien wrote in his booklet: *Siren waters. Keep your wax on you. Put it in when you hear three bells.*

"I will." He sighed. "It's boring now. I should've brought something to read from the Queen's library. I'd stay above and watch, but it's just so cold."

Safer down here, Lirien wrote.

"True." Brandegil moved to lie on his stomach and rested his chin in his hands, giving Lirien a sidelong glance. "So... how long have you and Kitra been together?"

It felt like ages, but when Lirien measured it in his mind, it was just weeks. He couldn't believe it. He'd fallen for her so quickly, and she seemed to return his feelings, though whether to the same degree, he didn't know. It was enough that they trusted each other to share their most intimate, private selves, something Lirien would never forget.

"I mean together-together, if you aren't sure," Brandegil said impatiently when Lirien got too lost in thought. "At Castle Asherin? Before then?"

Lirien wrote, *Castle.*

"I knew it!" Brandegil rolled onto his back, facing away from Lirien. "You could do better," he said, his voice low. "I would..." and he trailed off so Lirien couldn't hear his words.

Instead, Lirien heard something dangerous, far away— a familiar wordless song, melancholy and beautiful, in a young man's voice. Lirien's eyes widened, and he rose to his feet. He grabbed Brandegil's shoulder and pointed frantically to his ears, miming stuffing them full with wax.

The bell hadn't sounded, and Brandegil just eyed him curiously.

He doesn't hear it yet, Lirien thought. That meant the crew probably didn't, either. He repeated his gesture again and forced his wax into Brandegil's hands, then ran out of the cabin and up the narrow steps to the deck of the ship. The light from the lamps could only go so far, and Lirien squinted in the darkness of the ocean, seeing nothing. The siren's voice sang out again, along with a new one, a woman's, and then a third. It was the first time he'd heard sirens hunting together in a haunting trio.

He found the bell and rang it three times, then hurried back down the stairs to his room. Brandegil was standing there, motionless. One ear was filled with wax, the other not. The stick of it fell out of Brandegil's hands.

Oh no, oh no, oh no—

Before Lirien could complete his thoughts, something gentle swirled around him, tugging at his waist. He blinked—

He was on the deck again, frozen in place, staring out to sea. He had no idea how much time he'd lost, just standing there.

Confused, he looked at his surroundings. Thanks to his warning, almost everyone was below deck except for Darshan, who was readying a harpoon, and Brandegil, who was leaning perilously over the edge of the ship.

The male siren gripped the ledge with one hand, his whitish blue skin shimmering in the lamplights, his sapphire hair blowing in the wind, his tail hanging down the side of the ship. His other hand cradled the back of Brandegil's head as they engaged in a passionate kiss.

Darshan shouted something and launched the harpoon just as the siren pulled Brandegil overboard. The barbed lance sliced across the side of Brandegil's arm as he went over, and blood stained the ledge of the ship.

With no thoughts in his head except for Brandegil, Lirien jumped in the water.

The freezing cold nearly shocked the life out of him, and his bandaged hand stung from the salty seawater. The two other sirens circled him while Lirien watched Brandegil being hauled away farther out to sea.

The female siren gripped Lirien's chin to turn his face toward hers, but then her eyes widened. Her face twisted into disgust. *What are you?* her voice echoed in his head.

Abomination, the other siren said.

You are no kin of ours. The female siren opened her mouth, revealing a set of needlelike teeth. She chomped down on Lirien's shoulder, and without letting go of him, started to drag him below.

There was a screech from the other siren just as Lirien descended into the dark abyss. A lance, launched from the ship, pierced the siren right through the chest. The ocean filled with blood— the siren's and Brandegil's and Lirien's own —as they all sank into the sea.

The female siren's jaw wasn't loosening its hold on him. Lirien struggled with her, wrapping his hands around her throat to strangle her, squeezing with all of his might. At last, she pulled away from his grip, ripping a chunk from his shoulder. Ignoring the surge of pain, Lirien swam toward the dying siren. He whipped the body around and pulled the lance free, then rammed it through the siren who'd attacked him.

Lirien rose to the surface to catch another breath before chasing down the siren he'd just stabbed.

Monster. It was her last word before her eyes closed and she went limp. He tore the giant lance from her body and came above the water once more, scanning for Brandegil, hoping he wasn't too late.

There!

The first siren held him now above the water, running his hands over him, clutching at his chest. Brandegil's eyes were closed in bliss as another harpoon whooshed past them, barely missing them.

Why is he allowing Brandegil a chance to breathe? Lirien's stomach twisted. *He's either toying with him or the song needs more time to work its magic before he eats him,* he thought.

Seeing Lirien approach, the siren wrapped his arms around Brandegil and dragged him under once more. Lirien followed. He could see the siren's eyes glowing orange in the sea, like a ray of light cutting through dark clouds. That was the only way Lirien knew where to go.

Brandegil sought out the siren's mouth to give him a fiery kiss, and the siren did not close his eyes. He looked right at Lirien.

He is my *prey,* his voice said, reaching into Lirien's mind.

Then the siren pulled out of the kiss, tilting his head back, his body growing in size, his teeth elongating, his jaws coming apart—

Lirien pushed Brandegil aside and jammed the harpoon right into the siren's gaping mouth. Then he grabbed Brandegil across the chest and pulled him to the surface before the elf might take in water, lest he drink in the siren's poisonous blood.

Lirien draped Brandegil's limp arms around his neck and pinned them to his chest with one arm so that Brandegil was loosely hanging on his back as he swam toward the ship. With all three sirens dead, the elf seemed to be coming to. His arms tightened around Lirien's neck, and his voice sounded in Lirien's ear. It came out choking, not from the water, but from tears he tried to hold back, "You saved me. Thank you, thank you."

Once Brandegil seemed surer of himself, he let go of Lirien and swam beside him. They made it to the side of the ship, where Darshan had thrown a rope ladder out to them.

Darshan took the two of them below and fetched the surgeon, who added stitches to Brandegil's arm and Lirien's shoulder. He also bandaged Lirien's burned hand again. Then Brandegil and Lirien stripped out of their sopping wet garments, were given some warm nightclothes, and wrapped themselves in blankets.

Brandegil wiped his eyes as he and Lirien made their way back to their cabin. "I will never be able to repay you."

What was with them, Kitra and Brandegil? Was it a code of elvish, of fae honor that always made them say things like that? Friendship was not meant to be built on a foundation of obligation. They should never have to repay what was freely given.

No need, Lirien mouthed. He shook Brandegil's hand, then placed his own on his heart, lowering his head to him.

The two of them crawled into their respective bunks and Brandegil exhaled shakily. He still sounded weepy. "I've never felt anything so wonderful in my life. Ever. I had no idea it would feel so good, to love another person so completely. And now he's gone. I'm so confused. I know shouldn't feel this way about it, but I do. I'm so grateful you saved me, yet I'm devastated."

Lirien didn't know what to say. He thought the best thing he could do for Brandegil was to listen to him.

"Everything inside of me told me to love him. To give him all of myself. And when he kissed me, I..." Brandegil rubbed at his eyes again. "It was everything I ever wanted."

Lirien grabbed his book and sat on the edge of Brandegil's bed. *Could you...* He crossed it out and tried again. *Were you aware of what was happening?*

"I don't know how I got topside. But once I saw him, I went to him. I don't think I can fully explain it. I couldn't help that I fell for him. Everything inside of me pushed me to show that love, to give that love. And I was... somehow I could see it happening. It was like standing at the end of a dark tunnel, and you watch yourself on the other side of it, performing actions, but unable to do anything to stop it at all."

Did he do anything you didn't want?

"He did what I asked him to." Brandegil's face was no longer red, his eyes no longer wet from tears. He sat upright and swung his legs over the side of the bed. "You're thinking about the Queen, aren't you?"

I'm sorry. I hope you don't think I don't care about what happened to you.

"I'm the first person you can talk to about the siren spell, the only one you know who's experienced it besides the Queen. You want to understand what she's doing and why. Yet, I don't think we can understand it. If the siren song made her fall in love with you for real, why would she be so... twisted?"

Maybe the human side of me couldn't make the spell work completely— after all, humans can't do magic. She claims to love me, pursues me regardless of my wishes, and hurts me when I try to defend myself. If she truly loved me, wouldn't she work harder not to do me harm?

"That's a fair question. Although... sometimes people hurt the ones they love, so..." He trailed off, looking uncertain. "I guess I don't really understand any of this."

Lirien flipped to another page, suddenly wanting to pour it all out of him. *I can't help but blame myself for what happened. I know if I hadn't sung the song, she'd be fine. But another part questions her role in all of this. She threatened to kill me if I didn't bring Father back. She stabbed me and slashed at me until I sang the siren song. What could I have done?*

He stopped writing and sighed, sinking deeper into his thoughts, as Brandegil gave him a sympathetic look.

"I don't think you're to blame, Lirien," Brandegil said gently. "If your only choice was to sing or to die, who wouldn't choose the song?"

Lirien gave him a feeble smile, appreciating Brandegil's words, but the guilt for bewitching the Queen was there all the same. *I'm the only one who can end all of this. But you saw what has to happen to break the siren's spell.*

After a moment, Brandegil asked, "Are you all right? With what happened tonight?"

Lirien shook his head, then let out a long, trembling breath. He'd done it. He killed the sirens. He'd killed his own kind. And the feeling he had for it was unnamable. It was something like regret, and perhaps guilt, and then a little bit of anger, too— anger that it had to be done, that there was no other way to stop the sirens from hunting and feeding. He kept telling himself it was necessary, and then he'd turn around and ask it as a question: was it necessary?

And the words they used against him, "abomination" and "monster," haunted him, too. Was he a monster because he wasn't truly one of them, or because he killed?

Maybe he was both.

As THE MORNINGS and evenings passed, no other sirens disturbed them, but Lirien nonetheless kept his ears open for the hint of any song, ready to ring the alarm bell as soon as he heard it.

Brandegil outwardly seemed like he had processed what happened with the siren, but sometimes a melancholy air was about him— and it reminded Lirien of his father, staring out to sea. But Brandegil didn't peer at the ocean dreamily or in a haze, which Lirien took as a good sign.

One day as they helped the sailors swab the deck, Brandegil spoke out of the blue: "I have to keep telling myself that you freed me from something that was going to kill me. There wasn't love there, not really. I was only something to eat." He dipped his mop in a bucket of water and wiped down the wooden floorboards. "I don't know if I'm ever going to be able to thank you properly for saving me."

Lirien mouthed to Brandegil, *Enough.*

"I can't quite make out what you're saying. Hey, can you teach me to sign when we're below? I've put it off too long. I can't read your lips so well."

Lirien nodded, then pushed his mop along the deck of the ship. He winced as pain coursed through his shoulder and hand. He was in poor shape. What would Kitra say when she saw him again?

Kitra. He missed her. It had only been a few days, but he had been through so much. Brandegil was a fine enough companion, but Kitra brought Lirien comfort, and he needed it after his encounter with the sirens. He wanted to curl up against Kitra, to find warmth in her body, to feel safe in her arms.

He shook his head, pushing her out of his mind. *I'm thinking too much about everything,* he told himself. *I just need to keep things simple and focus on the spell.*

On the sixth day, one day ahead of schedule, Captain Swagger got the *Swiftswallow* to Perdra's major pier. Lirien and Brandegil followed the crew to the seaside inn, aptly named the Aurora. They stayed in a room together with bunked beds, with Brandegil scrambling for the top bed and Lirien grateful for the lower one.

The first several evenings they were on land, the clouds wove together to make a blanket in the sky, hiding the moon and any trace of the aurora. The snows came and went.

Lirien took to nightly walks along the cold, frosty boardwalk, Brandegil sometimes joining him and sometimes leaving him alone when he was lost in thought. Completely at the whims of the weather, wasting day after day, he started to lose confidence in breaking the spell. The longer he was away from Kitra, from the children, the more anxious he became. After all, Kitra had warned him that the longer they took, the harder it would be for the children to change back.

And he knew his time was running out, not only to save them, but for the remaining days he could spend with them. With all of them. In order to break the siren's curse, he had to die. He couldn't decide what he wanted to do about that. His heart would break into pieces in a world without his siblings, without Kitra...even without Brandegil. But he had to endure the Queen's obsession with him in order to see his family again, and even so, Kitra and Brandegil would be lost to him. He was of the sea; they were of the land. It was no use.

He had to savor the time left with all of them. If only he had more.

On their ninth evening ashore, after Lirien had finished reviewing the alphabet and some easy vocabulary with Brandegil, they bundled up yet again to head out, making sure it was high tide. This time, a hole in the clouds opened up and the moon poked through.

Lirien practically jumped into the air when they saw it.

"FINALLY!" Brandegil shouted, and he opened his fur coat to reveal Alibrandr in its scabbard underneath. "Let's go get the moonlight."

CHAPTER 16

Lirien and Brandegil ran along the docks and found an area unpopulated with ships. Lirien stepped up to the edge of the platform with Brandegil just behind him, clutching Alibrandr in his hands.

Brandegil closed his eyes and gripped the handle tightly as he raised the sword triumphantly in the air. It immediately grew in size this time, its blade stretching to the height of a full-grown adult, but Brandegil's arm didn't waver, as if he didn't feel the extra weight that Lirien knew was there.

Brandegil thrust the sword toward Lirien. "I think I'm getting better at it, but I still don't know how long the sword keeps its form after it wakes. Do it as quickly as you can, and good luck."

With his bandaged hand, Lirien had trouble gripping Alibrandr, so he swung it none too gracefully. But it was a steady enough movement. With a swish, Lirien sliced circles around the edges of the moon, where a halo of light had formed around it. It fluttered down like a billowing veil, leaving a strange dark spot in the sky where it once was, a black line around a giant white globe. Then the dark space filled with light once more, like water soaking into fabric.

Brandegil had brought the canvas bag with them for catching the moonlight, leaving the stars safely behind in Asherin, and Lirien had packed the sets of metal tongs, having learned the hard way not to touch such things with his bare hands.

The circular streamer of moonlight continued its slow descent, and he realized it was going to land in the sea. He looked to Brandegil in horror. The water was freezing, the waves a fair size, and he was certain that they'd lose the light easily if they didn't get to it fast enough.

In the bitter cold, Lirien stripped down and dove into the water, nearly seizing up from shock before swimming out as far and as fast as he could, while the shimmering band continued its slow descent from the sky. He treaded water as he waited for the moonlight to hit it.

He hadn't remembered to take anything with him; he had just jumped straight in. His bandaged hand was probably slightly more protected than his uncovered one, so he resolved to seize the moonlight with that.

The moonlight landed on the water, floating on it like a ghost, and Lirien quickly grabbed it. His hand instantly locked in place. A fresh layer of ice coated it, and he tried to move his fingers, finding them stuck to the moonlight. It was so cold that it burned, and the fabric of his bandages offered no protection.

If he could've, he would've screamed from the pain. His mouth opened and he took in water, and choking on it, gagged. Tears fell as he forced his way back to the dock, and he was so weak from his agony that he couldn't bring himself to climb back up onto it.

Brandegil had to haul him out of the water, and he halted when he noticed the state of Lirien's hand, how it was trapped against the moonlight, frozen in place. He grabbed the metal tongs and began to chip away at the ice until the moonlight could fall free. As soon as the gauzy halo came loose, Brandegil opened up the canvas bag and allowed the moonlight to drift lazily down inside of it, careful not to touch it with his bare skin.

Lirien struggled back into his furs and wiped his tears away with his good hand, and the two headed back to the Aurora Inn to warm up as fast as they could. Brandegil unraveled the bandages around Lirien's hand, and the skin there was bright red and waxy-looking, with faint lines where the skin had peeled before. The *Swiftswallow*'s surgeon was staying at the inn with the rest of the crew and wrapped Lirien's bandages yet again after slathering a salve on his skin. By the next day, it was entirely covered in blisters and he couldn't move his fingers or even bend his wrist without severe pain.

"You can't keep going on like this," Brandegil said. "We've got to find a better way to protect you. You need your hands to break the spell, and at this rate you'll definitely lose at least one of them, if this continues."

Lirien was equally concerned with their next step. So far they hadn't seen the aurora lights at all, but when they finally did, Lirien feared he would ruin himself further. Brandegil was right: he needed working hands to spin and weave. And he still couldn't stop worrying about the children and what would happen if they put those robes on. Would they burn and blister, too?

Lirien had to rebuke himself— *I'm getting ahead of things. Just focus. Focus on the aurora.*

They ventured out again that night to check the skies and saw nothing of the northern lights. Lirien, despite his frustrations, took it as a chance to give his wounds time to heal a little.

Then the next night came. There was a commotion within

the inn as Captain Swagger's men talked in wonderment about what was going on in the sky outside, and Lirien and Brandegil ran into the street to look. The nighttime sky had finally cleared and shone almost purple in the strange lights, with shimmering greens and blues and even a touch of pink streaming across the heavens.

Lirien didn't move for a few moments, just staring up at them. Brandegil was frozen in place, too, looking at the aurora borealis with awe. Then he shook himself out of it and pointed to the crest of a hill in the distance. "Let's try up over there, past all the buildings."

It didn't take long for them to clear the small seaside village. They passed through the narrow streets and along a backroad until they came across an empty hillside. The land and sky felt so open to them, and his heart beat faster with excitement. The moonlight had been just as easy to cut from the sky as the stars, and just as difficult to retrieve. Surely the aurora would go the same way for them.

Brandegil was able to transform Alibrandr even faster than before, and he gestured for Lirien to come over. "Can you move your hand at all?"

Lirien's hand, bandaged and wrapped thoroughly, was still in a terrible state. He tried to straighten his wrist and wiggle his fingers, but pain surged through him and he winced.

"Try swinging it with one hand."

The enlarged sword wavered in his left hand. His aim was a little off, and the stars rippled in the sky as he completely missed the aurora. The ribbons of light were harder to catch than he'd estimated, as they appeared and disappeared, snaking along the sky.

"Let me help you," Brandegil said. "I'll steady your hand." He moved as though he was going to stand behind Lirien but then realized he was a bit too tall. Brandegil stood beside him instead, and placed his hand over Lirien's, their fingers interlapping.

"You still have to swing the sword because you're the cursebreaker, but there's nothing that says you can't have help, right?"

He couldn't help but smile. He let go of the sword for a moment and formed letters with his hand.

Brandegil squinted, trying to read them. "F... R... I... END." A little rose crept into his cheeks, maybe from the cold, maybe something else. "If you say so," he said, sounding nonchalant. "Anyway, let's get to it."

Lirien slid his good hand back underneath Brandegil's so he could grip the sword directly. Like sliding a pen across paper, they drew a line in the sky along one of the streaming lights, cutting around it, then they looped the sword back under, slicing it out. Similar to what had happened with the moonlight, they left behind a black patch of sky in their wake until a new beam of light overtook it. The ribbon of aurora fluttered down to the earth, brushing back and forth on the air as it descended. It landed in a glowing pile on the snowy ground, its colors changing from green to blue to pinkish-purple as it descended.

The two of them ran toward it. Brandegil held open the bag of moonlight while Lirien, with some awkwardness, used the tongs with his left hand to scoop the aurora inside.

When Brandegil sealed the bag, Lirien sank to the ground on his knees. His heart rose within his chest— they did it! They got their three impossible things.

Lirien shook his head in disbelief. He thought getting the sword would be the hardest thing to do, and he was wrong. He thought getting the stars, moonlight, and aurora borealis would be unachievable, and he was wrong. The next step, the weaving of the robes— maybe things wouldn't be as hard as he imagined them to be. Maybe spells were indeed meant to be broken.

He wished Kitra were there to bask in their triumph, but he was happy to have Brandegil. He couldn't have done it without him. He rose to his feet, brushed the snow off his knees, and held his arms out to Brandegil, who was jumping in the air, whooping with his fist raised.

When Brandegil turned and saw him gesturing for a hug, he froze. "Uh…" he said, scratching the back of his neck, looking aside. "All right." He clapped Lirien's back while Lirien embraced him gratefully, then Brandegil quickly stepped out of the hug. "Good work," he said. "Let's get some rest and tell Captain Swagger we're ready to go in the morning."

IT WOULD HAVE BEEN an uneventful journey back to the mainland of Asherin if not for the fourth night. Lirien was having a simple, albeit stilted, conversation with Brandegil, spelling out words with his left hand, when he heard a familiar voice singing a sweet, haunting melody. He jumped up, nearly knocking over the card table he and Brandegil were sitting at.

No no no, Lirien thought. *Why is she here?*

"What is it?"

Lirien mimed stuffing his ears, and without waiting for a response from Brandegil, bolted up the stairs and out onto the deck.

The night was cold and the moon half-covered by clouds. Stars lit up the evening sky, thousands of white gems shining against a black tapestry. The sea was surprisingly still, and when he got to the deck, he looked out onto the dark water but couldn't spy any figures within it.

Darshan had noticed his frantic ascent topside. "What is it? Do you hear something?" The crew had replenished their lances in Perdra, and Darshan seized one of them.

Lirien knew he should start ringing the bell. He heard the siren's song; he needed to warn everyone. But... something held him back. He couldn't bring himself to, not when it was *her*.

He raised his hand to Darshan— *wait a moment* —and he leaned over the side of the railing, looking down into the ocean below.

His mother was there, clutching onto the side of the bow, pulling herself slowly upward. Seeing her out of the water, he finally grasped the enormity of her, how much bigger she was than a human. Her indigo hair was matted and wet against her skin, and her tail and fins draped downward along the ship's side. Then her tail seemed to melt away as two human legs were revealed, allowing her to further climb up to the side of the prow. She was just short of meeting the rails when she looked up at him, her orange eyes wide with alarm.

My son. I said you would not see me again, but I came to warn you. The others— the other sirens know about you now. I tried to hide you from them as long as I could. But they know what you are, and what you've done. They are coming for you. They are—

She screeched when Darshan's barbed harpoon pierced her neck, then tumbled into the ocean.

The lance might as well have pierced Lirien's heart, too. His mouth dropped and he fruitlessly formed the word "No!" with his lips. He hadn't expected to react so strongly to seeing her hurt, to seeing her in the throes of death.

But she was his mother.

He was ready to dive in after her when a terrible cacophony of voices, what sounded like a dozen different sirens, started a horrid song that drowned out the sound of Darshan ringing the alarm bell. Instead of the beautiful melody the sirens were known for, the mysterious song that seduced anyone who heard it, they made a discordant choir as they closed in on the ship. Surely it was loud enough to pierce the wax in the sailors' ears.

The crew, and Brandegil, ran up to the deck. Darshan froze in place. Everyone stared out to sea, a glazed look overtaking their eyes. The scream-singing from the sirens' voices got inside all of their heads:

GIVE HIM TO US!

Any warmth left in his body disappeared. He turned to the crew, who started to close in on him. Even Brandegil looked at him with something like hunger.

They're going to push me overboard, he realized. He didn't think he had any other choice. If he had more time, he might grab Alibrandr— even without Brandegil's help to make the sword gigantic, the weapon was still incredibly sharp, able to pierce the scales of dragons. But there was no time, and he couldn't risk it getting lost at sea anyway.

As the crew advanced toward him, he knew he couldn't break free. He seized Darshan's harpoon just as Captain Swagger and Brandegil cornered him. Darshan struck him in the face, and Lirien toppled over the side and into the sea.

Two sirens were on him immediately, and he swung his weapon at them, brandishing it as he was taught with the sword. He stabbed one siren in the stomach while the other grasped the wooden shaft of the harpoon and broke it in half. Lirien's lance was reduced to something like a dagger, and nowhere near as effective.

A scream, shrill and buzzing, hit Lirien's ears, and a monstrous apparition appeared before him. His mother— not in her beautiful siren form, but a creature ready to devour. Even though she was bleeding from the neck, her body had extended and her jaws overpowered her face. She started ripping her fellow sirens to shreds around her.

The sea was more blood than salt.

His mother tore out the throats of everyone who neared them, while he tried to stab as many sirens as he could with his broken lance. But one of sirens grabbed him from behind, its powerful arm wrapped around his neck in a chokehold, and it started dragging him deep, deep below until the burning in his lungs became an all-consuming fire and he lost consciousness in the smothering depths of the ocean.

LIRIEN WOKE up sputtering salt water on the deck of the *Swiftswallow*. He was lying on his back, staring up at the stars in the sky, tears pouring from his eyes as he nearly threw up.

His entire body ached— covered in rips and gashes all over from where the siren bit him. He moved to sit up and saw his mother's corpse next to him, her face beautiful once more. Her eyes were wide open, staring empty and upward, and her giant body was covered in wounds where the sirens had torn her apart. Half of her tail was missing, and it looked like something had tried to eat her stomach. He could see her entrails.

He vomited at the sight of her. Then, wiping his mouth with his sleeve, he struggled to his feet, shaking. Brandegil's arm slid around his back to steady him, and he couldn't help but rest his head against the elf's shoulder. He was relieved to see his eyes had gone back to normal, and every one of the crew around them looked fully aware of themselves.

"This one saved you," Brandegil said. "I don't understand it, a siren saving someone—"

Mother, Lirien mouthed.

"Oh." There was an uncomfortable silence between Brandegil and Lirien, and the crew said nothing. Finally, Brandegil added, "I am so... sorry."

Captain Swagger spoke next. "It was so strange. I knew what was happening, but I couldn't control myself. It was like I was watching myself outside of my body. I could see myself, feel myself wanting to surrender you to them, but it was all at a distance. You all felt that, too?"

"Aye," Darshan said. "It was as though I was hovering above my body, watching it move on its own."

"It was different than the love song they sing," Brandegil said quietly. "All I wanted to do was hurt you, Lirien. I'm sorry that I couldn't withstand it."

"The sirens are gone," Captain Swagger said. "You and this one killed them all. So she saved us, too." She looked to his mother's body. "What do you want to do with her?"

Lirien knew she had to go back to the sea— where she came from, and where she would have eventually died. But just tossing her overboard felt crude and heartless.

He sighed and shrugged, not sure what to do.

"We can do a traditional burial at sea, then."

Darshan laid a tarp over his mother's body, and then several members of the crew gathered around her to lift her off the deck, taking her below.

"Rest for the night," the captain said. "At dawn we'll take care of her." The crew dispersed, most to their hammocks to sleep and some to their posts for the night's watch.

"Let me help you to the surgeon," Brandegil said. "You don't look so good." He draped Lirien's arm over his shoulder and his other arm found Lirien's waist, and he gently walked him below.

IN WHAT SEEMED like the passing of a moment, Brandegil, with great care, shook Lirien awake.

"It's morning. She's ready. Come on," Brandegil said softly.

He and Brandegil headed topside to find the rest of the crew standing around Lirien's mother. She had been sewn into a sailcloth, a huge piece of white fabric to cover her sizeable body, which had been cleaned and prepared for burial. There was no trace of blood on the canvas, just the outline of her form underneath.

He touched her through the cloth, where her heart was. Then he looked to Darshan and nodded, and the first mate let the body slide over the side and into the water with a soft splash.

Two parents, dead. Both lost to sirens, "the monsters that dwell in the seas." Lirien felt alone, until he saw Brandegil looking at him with great sympathy. Thanks to Brandegil, he would soon have his family again. Nina, Sorin, and Sonalie were all still alive and waiting for him. And Kitra was waiting for him, too. But how much time was left with all of them, he was unsure; he just knew it was limited. And that hurt his heart.

He tried to swallow his sadness as he looked to Brandegil, who was there at his side throughout all of this.

Thank you, he signed to Brandegil. *For being here.*

"I got half of that," Brandegil admitted. "But you're welcome."

The trip back to the mainland was faster than the trip to Perdra. The next day was filled with uneventful sailing, which allowed the ship to move unhampered and swiftly on the seas. They reached the harbor by early afternoon, and carriages were waiting for them for the trek back to the castle. Brandegil seemed unsure of what to say to him, so most of their ride was in silence, except for the moment he started unbandaging his hand.

"That looks awful," Brandegil said. "Like you made a handprint with red paint."

Lirien's hand was scabbed up from where his skin had peeled. He gently bent and unbent his fingers to check if they could move, and though they could, it was with some difficulty. He could sign, but it would be a challenge.

When they reached Castle Asherin, the herald announced their arrival to Aunt Idela and Aunt Eira, who had returned from Ardeth while they were gone.

Kitra was there too, and as soon as she saw Lirien, she practically pounced on him, jumping into his arms. "I'm so, so glad to see you. I missed you." She kissed his cheek.

He smoothed back her hair and kissed her forehead, then pulled her back into a tight embrace.

"Are you all right? You look... you look like you've been through a lot," she whispered to him as he let her go.

He signed to her. *We were attacked by sirens. My mother— my real mother —is dead. I don't have it in me to tell you more than that.*

Kitra's eyes widened, but she nodded in understanding. "I'll say nothing of it. Tell me more only if you want to. I'm here when you're ready."

"Did you get what you needed?" Aunt Idela asked. Her face was grave, and Aunt Eira looked equally so.

He nodded and quickly signed, *What about you? What news from Ardeth?*

"Ah... that. I'm afraid it's awful news." Aunt Eira paused. "I don't know how to prepare you for it, so I'll just come right out and say it. Queen Aurinda is drawing up an army. She says

Asherin is housing a criminal, and by refusing to give you to her, we have made ourselves her enemy."

The news blindsided him and Brandegil let out a sharp, "What?!"

Lirien shook his head frantically. Was the Queen willing to let people kill and die to bring him back to her? The grave look on his aunts' faces made the answer clear. Yes, she was— but he wasn't.

I'll do it, Lirien signed. *I'll turn myself in.*

"What did you say?" Brandegil asked.

"You can't do that," Kitra said as she clutched Lirien's good hand.

"No, Lirien," Eira said firmly. "You will not hand yourself over to her. Queen Aurinda is not well. I don't know what she'll... well, no, I do have a mind of what she'll do. But we cannot let her have you."

No one dies for me. Send word I'm coming.

"But what about the children?" Aunt Idela asked.

First I break the spell. Then I'm hers. He let out a trembling sigh, a sound of surrender. *I'll give her what she wants.*

CHAPTER 17

The Queens of Asherin continued to protest Lirien's decision, saying they would be willing to fight for him, but he would have none of it. He was exhausted, and angry at how stupid it all seemed now. All this trouble just for Queen Aurinda to have her way with him— it wasn't worth a war. As much as the thought of being with her disgusted him, he saw no other choice that didn't involve the bloodshed of hundreds if not thousands of soldiers. It wasn't something he could bear, no matter how eloquently his aunts tried to persuade him.

Reluctantly, Eira and Idela sent word to Queen Aurinda of his decision. Now, if only she would wait. *Please wait.*

Lirien had just finished feeding Nina in his room when a knock at his door pulled his attention away. Kitra stood in the doorway, and she looked stricken.

"I'm not taking your decision well," she admitted as she stepped inside his room. "I know you're in an impossible position," she said, her eyes misting up. "I know that. But you can't do that, you can't give yourself to her."

He hesitated, unsure if he was brave enough to say what

was on his mind. He swallowed, and steeling himself, signed: *The only one I'll ever belong to is you.*

Kitra stared at him in shock, and her voice came out quietly: "Oh, Lirien." Her hands met his cheeks, and she held him like that, looking into his eyes. "Do you know what you're saying? What this means? To give your heart to a fae is the greatest pact you can make. We'll never let you go. Do you understand? I don't want you to say something like this unless you are absolutely certain." She kissed him, a gentle touch to his lips. "I am yours because you saved my life. But you give me your heart, and you will always, *always* be mine."

He nodded.

"When you have my heart, you'll know I've accepted yours," she said after some thought. She let go of him as she said it.

That stung Lirien. He didn't have her heart already? After what they shared between them?

It was as though Kitra read his mind. "I like you very much, Lirien. I care about you. Don't doubt that. But I'm of the forest and you're of the sea. When the spell has ended, we'll be separated and never see each other again. I can be with you here and now, and we can comfort each other and care for each other, but it cannot last. Would you give your heart to me, knowing all that?"

He wanted to tell her yes. But he could sense something from Kitra, perhaps something like fear or uncertainty, as though she didn't want to hear his answer. So, he kept still.

"Would you still give me your heart knowing what I must do?" she added, her voice suddenly quiet. The way she spoke was tinged with something dark, something he couldn't quite recognize, and for a moment, he thought her teeth looked sharper than before.

Then he realized: she wanted the Queen's blood.

"You don't have to die," she said, her voice growing

stronger. "You don't have to give yourself up. It's the solution that's always been there."

He shook his head. *She's the Queen, and the children's mother.*

"She is no queen! She's ready to send her own people to die in battle to satisfy her lust. And don't you dare call her mother — she's no mother to you, and certainly not to her own children, whom she gave up on, whom she stopped fighting for, once they all changed."

I can't let you do it.

"You won't be able to stop me," she said, "so don't even try. I will kill her, and not just for you. Have you forgotten what she did to my brother? The reason why I came with you in the first place? That's the pact between us. And it still stands, no matter what else has developed between us. You will lead me to her, or you will burn," she warned.

He touched the spot on his shoulder where Kitra had bitten him when they made their pact. He had forgotten what would happen if he didn't deliver on his end of their bargain. He wouldn't die, but living in agony for the remainder of his days, he might as well.

I'll honor my promise, he signed. But in his mind, he added, *Somehow, I'll save the Queen.*

There was a knock on the door, and Brandegil entered without waiting. His presence relieved Lirien, who didn't know what else to say.

"Is everything all right?" Brandegil asked cautiously, as though he sensed the friction between Lirien and Kitra.

"It'll be fine," Kitra said, sounding nonchalant. "What brings you here?"

"I was wondering what's going to happen next. Today's the day, right?"

Lirien nodded. *We're leaving in an hour. We hope to bring the children with us to Bella Morgana's tower, if the forest will grant us all passage.*

"You and Kitra?" Brandegil asked.

He nodded again.

"So... you don't need me anymore, do you?" Brandegil scratched the back of his head as he asked it, his voice soft.

The sword is yours now. You can go as you wish.

"Well... what if I wish to go with you? You've helped me a lot. I can't forget that. And we've been through so much together. I want to see it through— the spell-breaking, I mean. So, if you'll have me, I'll come with you. To Elythia, at least, if it lets me in. Ardeth is another story."

Lirien smiled with joy and relief. And Brandegil knew exactly what Lirien felt, even without words— neither wanted to part from the other just yet. He held out his hand to Brandegil, and the two shook. Then he bowed his head in thanks.

The three of them parted to finish packing their things for Elythia. When Lirien was ready, he scooped Nina out of her glass case and pointed to Kitra's basket and then his arm: *Which one?*

Nina opted for his arm, clearly her favorite spot, as he thought she would. Kitra chose to load the basket with food from the kitchen, in case Elythia didn't come right away and they'd have to do some walking.

By the time he retrieved Sorin from the stables, Aunt Eira and Aunt Idela had entered the castle courtyard to follow them to Lake Karda, where they would retrieve Sonalie before saying their final goodbyes.

When they got to the edge of the lake, the Queens each gave Nina a little pat, Nina's tongue flicking at their fingers as they pulled their hands away. Then Sorin approached them awkwardly, trying to steady himself on three legs. He lowered his head and brushed his nose across their hands in what could be interpreted as a farewell, and the Queens bade him goodbye.

Last was Sonalie, who took more than a little coaxing to leave Lake Karda. She stayed close to the other swans, one in particular, and their faces were so close together their necks and head made the shape of a heart. Lirien waved her over but she didn't come, and he worried that perhaps she'd gotten more wild since the last time he saw her.

Kitra noticed his distress at being unable to call Sonalie away, so she said in a gentle tone, "Sonalie. It's time for us to go so we can break the spell."

Sonalie wrapped her neck around her swan companion's in an embrace, then flew from the water to Lirien's side. She flapped her wings and honked at Aunt Eira and Aunt Idela, who stroked her downy feathers.

This is it, Lirien signed. *Once the spell breaks, I can't come to Asherin again.*

"Why?" Aunt Eira asked.

Sirens are bound to the seas. When the spell breaks, my curse returns. I can't leave again without dying.

"Oh, Lirien, we never knew," Aunt Eira said. "Why didn't you tell us?"

Maybe it was wrong of me, but I always felt I'd be safer if people didn't know.

"We'll work harder to see you in Ardeth more often, then," Aunt Idela said, and then she leaned in close, whispering in his ear. "And we will do what we can to protect you, your decision or no. We will come to see you are safe."

Until then, this is goodbye.

Lirien kissed the cheek of each aunt.

"Your Majesties," Brandegil said. He tapped the sword in the scabbard he wore at his side. "Alibrandr is back in the hands of the Glynnan elves again, and it is all thanks to you."

"Don't forget your own role in it," Queen Eira said.

"Oh no, I won't," he said with a smile. "I'm going home completely triumphant. I hope they throw a banquet in my honor."

"I'm sure they'll give you more than that."

"Well, thank you all the same," Brandegil said, and he bowed to the Queens of Asherin.

Kitra approached the Queens, lowering her head to them. "The fae never forget a gracious host. If you ever make it to Elythia, seek me out."

The Queens thanked Kitra warmly. The corner of her mouth twitched slightly at the words, but she said nothing. Lirien signed to his aunts one last time. *See you.*

He steadied the bags he wore at his sides— one for the stars that burned hot, and the other for moonlight and aurora that burned cold. He closed his eyes reverently and called for Elythia. The forest had ignored him so many times when he needed it before that he doubted whether or not it would come. Then he remembered Kitra was with him. If all else failed, the forest should welcome one of its own home.

Lirien was right to think so. When he opened his eyes, the trees of Lake Karda had changed from new spring green to the familiar fall colors of Autumn Wood in Elythia. The sun shone brightly in the forest there, and Lirien was relieved they would be traveling in the wood while it was still daylight.

"Oh, wow," Brandegil said, impressed.

"Welcome to Autumn Wood," Kitra said. "My home."

The three of them turned to wave at the Queens one last time, only to find Lake Karda had vanished behind them. Autumn Wood surrounded them on all sides. They ventured farther into the forest, with the stag limping beside them and the swan flying above them, to the final steps in the breaking of the spell.

OVER AN HOUR INTO THE FOREST, the group came across the estate of Lord Iesin and Lady Ariana, with its beautiful mansion tucked in the limbs of trees with mulberry-colored leaves.

"We're almost to Bella Morgana's," Kitra said.

"Who's that?" Brandegil asked.

"She's the one who has what Lirien needs to make the magic robes."

"Prince Lirien! Kitra!" a familiar male voice called out to them.

"Oh! My Lord, my Lady!" Kitra halted and bowed immediately. She tapped on Brandegil's back and he hurriedly bowed. Lirien did so as well.

The canopy where Lord Iesin and Lady Ariana had rested during the Midnight Revel was still set up, and a cluster of fae stretched out along the carpeted floor underneath the flowing fabric and glittering glass. Lord Iesin and Lady Ariana were practically buried in a sea of twisting limbs, surrounded by amorous couples.

Lord Iesin finished kissing a beautiful, shimmering sylph and rose to his feet. Lady Ariana was still embracing a faun when Lord Iesin gently squeezed her shoulder. She stood, smoothing her diaphanous skirts, and smiled at the group. "Ah, you brought many friends," she said, looking over Brandegil with interest. Then her gaze wandered to the white animals that followed them.

Sonalie took a break from flying at that point, landing at Lirien's feet and nudging him with her wing. He stroked the top of her head while Sorin came up cautiously behind them.

"I've been wondering how soon you'd come back to us," Lord Iesin said pleasantly.

"It feels like it was just yesterday when we saw you last. You've caught us in a pleasant moment." He looked the animals over. "This is your family, I take it?"

Lord Iesin walked over to Sorin and placed his hand on the stag's forehead, giving him a loving pat. "What a delightful child," he said with a smile. "This one loves you very much."

Nina poked her head out of Lirien's sleeve, and Lady Ariana looked as excited as a little girl opening presents on her birthday. "I'm so happy to see you again, beautiful one," she said.

Sonalie rose up on her feet, flapping her wings. Lady Ariana laughed. "You're beautiful, too." She stroked Sonalie's soft back.

"And what of you, Glynnan elf?" Lord Iesin gestured to the sword at his side. "Is that what I think it is?"

Brandegil, smiling proudly, unsheathed the sword and raised it to the sky. Now used to it, he woke the sword up easily and it expanded to its impressive size. He swung it away from all of them, and with a whoosh, it sliced a branch off a tree about twenty feet away.

A slew of angry pixies flew out of the tree, and their high-pitched voices, unintelligible, rang out at them.

"Sorry," Brandegil called after them.

"So Alibrandr is back in the hands of its people, then," Lady Ariana said. "You should be proud of yourself."

"Of course I am," Brandegil said with a grin.

"I'd invite you to sup with us in celebration," Lord Iesin said, "but something tells me you'd rather be on your way."

"We've got Bella Morgana next, and then we're on to Ardeth," Kitra said. "This will be goodbye from Lirien, I'm afraid. He won't be able to come back, as the magic on him keeps him close to the shore."

Lirien gave the Lord and Lady both a low bow. To his surprise, each fae took a hand and kissed it.

"If you ever can come back, we'll make you our consort," Lord Iesin said. He smiled, but also looked quite serious as he said it.

Lirien knew the fae were changeable in their moods, and he worried he would offend Lord Iesin by turning him down on the spot. The best he could offer was a noncommittal bow, then he gestured that they would go.

"Farewell, Prince Lirien of Ardeth," Lord Iesin called to him.

"May you break the spell at last," Lady Ariana said.

BELLA MORGANA excitedly opened the door to the group when they arrived at her workshop. She clapped her hands together when she saw the animals with Lirien.

"You did it! You found all of them! Everyone, come on in. The children, too, it's all right. I know you probably don't want them out of your sight." Her gaze settled on Sorin and his missing leg. "Poor thing."

Once they were inside, Lirien took out the cloak of many furs and handed it to Bella Morgana. *Thank you*, he mouthed to her.

"It's in good shape. I appreciate it. I hope you found it useful. Now, show me what else you've got!"

Lirien pulled the bag off his left shoulder and opened it up. Bella Morgana bent over and peered inside the bag, the white light shining in her face. "Those must be the stars."

He signed to Kitra. *How to hold?*

"Ah, yes," Kitra said. "Those stars are very hot. Do you have something we can put them in?"

Bella Morgana grabbed one of her large bowls and set it on her worktable. Lirien took the tongs from Brandegil's bag and one by one placed the stars into the bowl. He held two fingers up to Bella Morgana and mouthed the word, *more.*

She did as he requested, setting two more bowls on the table.

He pointed to the second satchel he wore. He signed, *Cold. Careful.*

He pulled out the veil of moonlight and set it in one dish, then the shimmery, multi-hued aurora in another.

"Beautiful. The robes you make are going to be stunning." Bella Morgana couldn't keep the jealousy out of her voice, but it only lasted a moment. "If you need metal tongs to touch each one, then spinning is going to be a problem for you. I have a special fabric woven from dragon scales that I can use to make you gloves."

Kitra interpreted Lirien's signing for everyone: *What do you want in exchange?*

"Well, you've given me your hair and your fish-scale mole..." She looked him over. "I'm partial to the sunset in your eyes. But if I took that, it would hurt." She thought about it for a moment. "I'll keep it simple. Give me the leavings after you've made your robes, and we'll call it even."

She grabbed her ribbon and measured Lirien's hands and fingers. "This will take some time for me to sew. Do you want to watch?"

He pointed to the children, then to the door.

"Ah, yes, it might be better if you go outside with them for a while. I'll call you in again when I'm done."

The group of them went to the grassy ruins next to the keep. Sorin and Sonalie immediately began to play with each other once they got there. Sonalie flew across the yard to the other end of the stone wall, called out, then circled back to Sorin. She repeated it again two more times, until he took off chasing after her. Sonalie beat him to the other end, but when she turned to fly back around, Sorin broke in a faster run than before and reached the other wall. He'd won their little race, and then they continued it again and again.

It was such a pleasure to see. When Sorin ran, he didn't move with a limping gait; he darted just as fast as any other wild deer in the forest. If Sorin could adapt so well to his injury in his stag form, Lirien hoped his adjustment as a human would be just as simple and quick. It would be his right arm that was missing once the spell was broken. He would have to relearn a few things, including writing. But he knew Kerrick would be up to the task of teaching him once more, and Lirien would spend time with Sorin on that, too.

His thoughts halted for a moment. To make that happen, he would have to truly surrender to the Queen's obsession if he wanted to survive. Although he had made the decision to in Asherin, he wondered how much he could endure her in order to live with his siblings. He pushed the thought aside.

He stretched back on the grass, and Nina took that as a cue to slide off his arm. She slithered across the lawn and followed after Sorin and Sonalie at a surprisingly fast pace for a snake, but nowhere near as quickly as the other two. Still, she raced along with them anyway.

Lirien rested his head on his folded arms. Kitra lay down next to him, burrowing into his side just as he had when she was a fox. She lay her head on his chest, one of her arms draped over his waist.

The awkwardness, and perhaps a little bit of anger, between them had dissipated, although Lirien wondered if Kitra was still thinking about the Queen.

"You two are quite smitten," Brandegil said, sitting next to them.

"Yep. Since Asherin," Kitra said. "But... I think we liked each other before that."

Lirien signed. *When I first saw you. Something there.*

Kitra didn't repeat it for Brandegil. She just smiled and nestled against Lirien.

"What are you going to do after you break the spell?" Brandegil asked.

"Well, he's going to take me to the Queen, and then..." She trailed off.

Lirien signed rapidly, with urgency. *Don't hurt her. Please. The children already lost their father; they can't lose their mother, too.*

"I should've worked harder on the alphabet," Brandegil said with a sigh. "I can't keep up."

"He's telling me not to hurt the Queen. You know, the Queen who has hurt him many times over. The Queen who hurt me when she killed my brother. The Queen who has shown us she will hurt as many others as possible just to get what she wants."

Brandegil's mouth fell slightly open. "I didn't know that. About your brother."

"I didn't really speak of it. I haven't given Kai much of my thoughts, to be honest, but now that Lirien's quest is almost done and our time together is coming to an end, my brother is begging for my attention. For atonement." She buried her face against his chest, almost as if hiding. "There is little our future holds beyond the satisfaction of our pact, Lirien. I know I want to be with you, but there are many things working against us. And one of them is my hatred for your Queen."

Lirien didn't know what he could say or do. Their carefree moment together had taken such a turn, and he didn't want to think about how things would end between him and Kitra, nor what sort of ending was meant for the Queen.

The bite that Kitra had given to him on the shoulder never gave any hint of its existence. It was invisible and easy to forget. But Kitra had already done everything she had said she would, and more, so now fulfillment of the pact was all up to him.

I told you I would lead you to her, he signed. *Please— don't make me have to save her.*

CHAPTER 18

The three of them sat in silence as they watched the children play, until Bella Morgana poked her head out the door of the keep and beckoned them to come inside. The children ignored her, so Lirien assumed they wanted to keep spending time with each other rather than watch him spin the thread and weave the robes. He signed to Kitra, *Please tell them not to leave,* and she did as he asked. Then they went inside.

The dragon scale gloves, a rosy coral color and pearlescent, fit him perfectly. He reached into the bowl of stars and picked up a white glowing globe, and he felt no pain. He let out a sigh of relief.

"Are you ready to start?" Bella Morgana asked as she pulled her spinning wheel out for Lirien.

He nodded. Brandegil and Kitra took their seats at the table to watch him work.

"Remember what I showed you. Touch the star to the spindle first, then you've activated the magic. You can spread apart the star like any other fiber once you've done that step."

Lirien did as she told him, and when he stretched the star in his hands, it took on the consistency of a ball of cotton— a substantial clump, but something soft all the same. It still glowed brightly and he dared not set the material on his knee, so he let the pile of star fluff fall to the floor as he took a pinch of it and wrapped it around the starter strand.

Bella Morgana checked the bobbin and the rest of the components of the spinning wheel, and when she gave her approval, Lirien started pumping the treadle with his foot. He was quite tall for a human, but not enough to reach the pedal, so Bella Morgana tied wooden blocks to his feet so he could reach.

He worked very slowly, much slower than Bella Morgana ever had, but in doing so he didn't make any mistakes. In the passing of the hours, he made skein after skein, more than anything he expected to come from seven stars.

And the best thing about it— once the stars were like yarn, they no longer burned. Lirien tested it first with a quick tap on his forearm. When nothing happened, he pressed it firmly into his skin.

Safe, he signed.

Kitra grinned and hugged him, and he forgot all about the somber conversation they'd been having as soon as she put her arms around him.

"You've made so much," Bella Morgana said, giddy with delight. "I'll have plenty of scraps to make something gorgeous!"

He pointed to the moonlight, already like a fabric in a way, its glowing substance less solid than that of the stars, its appearance like that of a veil. Brandegil brought him the bowl and Lirien pinched the end of the ribbon of light, touching it to the spindle. He repeated everything as he'd done with the stars, and the yarn made from the moonlight had an almost glass-like, transparent sheen to it, still radiant.

Lirien, more confident with his work, sped up his process, but it still took a couple hours to get through it. The moonlight stretched and stretched, allowing him to make a large quantity of yarn from it.

Last came the aurora borealis, which produced the most beautiful yarn. It glimmered with prismatic colors— vibrant green, blue, purple, and pink.

It was twilight when he finished spinning everything. He untied the wooden blocks from his feet and hopped out of the chair at the wheel. When Bella Morgana opened the door to summon the children, he found them huddled together, napping. Sorin was lying down, his legs tucked underneath him, his head on the ground. Nina was coiled next to him, while Sonalie rested on his back, her neck curled around her body, her head burrowed into her feathers.

"What a pretty picture," Kitra said, sounding happy and sad at the same time. "They must really love each other."

Lirien nodded. He wanted to spend the night outside with them, sleeping under the stars. Tomorrow, he would weave his yarn into a fabric and stitch the robes together.

"You can spend the night here," Bella Morgana offered when they went back inside. "I'm going to go back to my house, but my workshop is comfortable enough. I have a blanket big enough for all of you to sleep on, some extra pillows, and some food in my stores you can get into, if you'd like. Consider it a gift for all the remainders you've left me."

He held his hand over his heart for a brief moment in appreciation.

"Make yourselves at home. I'll come back in the morning to show you how to weave." She pointed to her loom at the opposite wall. "That's going to take you much, much longer than spinning. Try days, not hours. But you learn quickly, so I imagine it'll go just as smoothly as it did today."

Lirien tried not to let the disappointment show in his face that the robes would not be ready for the children by sundown tomorrow as he'd hoped. Bella Morgana didn't seem to notice as she showed them where the bedding and food was, then bade them goodnight.

After making supper together, Kitra and Brandegil welcomed Lirien's suggestion that they all sleep outside under the stars with the children. They raided Bella Morgana's pillows and bedding and passed them through a window, letting them fall in a pile on the ground before jumping down into it. Then they dragged everything across the lawn, laying them down within view of the children, but some good feet away.

Before the sun was completely gone from the sky, they collected sticks and made a fire, then relaxed on their blanket, which made a carpet more than large enough for all of them to fit. Each of Bella Morgana's pillows were the length of their entire bodies, so they decided to use them like sleeping bags, sliding in between the pillowcase and pillow. They were certainly going to sleep in comfort, but it was still too early to call it a night.

"Brandegil, when are you going to leave us?" Kitra asked.

"Well, I can't go to Ardeth. I'm a wanted criminal, and I can't risk the Queen trying to take the sword back." He sighed. "I suppose I'll leave for my home in the mountains when Lirien asks Elythia to let us out. I wish you could come with me to see Alibrandr restored to its proper place. You deserve some of the glory, too." He grinned. "There should be plenty to go around. But perhaps you can come visit me someday?"

He looked down and shook his head. *Can't leave the sea.*

"So many curses," Brandegil muttered bitterly. "I guess you'll have to say goodbye to Kitra, too, then. It's too bad. Just when we all started getting on with each other."

Kitra looked sad, a small frown on her face and her eyes

turned toward the ground. Then she quickly shelved that emotion. "Let's talk about something else." She thought for a moment. "Know any riddles?"

Kitra's talented with rhymes.

She smiled with pride. "He says I'm good," she told Brandegil.

"I know," Brandegil said. "You made up a little rhyme about me, remember? Although it was insulting."

"Oh, right."

"What happens when someone doesn't get your riddle right? Do you eat them? I heard tricksters eat them."

"Some do. But I don't like the taste of mortals," she said with a wicked grin. "Honestly, I'm quite kind. I tell them I'll send them back on their way, but then I just use my foxfire to hypnotize them and lead them to Muckward Pond."

"What's that?"

"An oasis of mud in Summer Wood. I get them to walk right into it. Gets them stuck and soaked every time."

"You're like a child," Brandegil said.

"The best tricksters are."

You never sent me there!

"Maybe I always liked you," Kitra said without interpreting. "I thought you were too interesting to pass up."

"Oh, you two," Brandegil muttered.

"Well, no riddles then? How about a song?"

You sing?

"Just trying to think of stuff to do around a campfire. It's always singing and terrible jokes, isn't it?"

"I know a terrible joke," Brandegil said. "What did the dwarf say to the elf?"

Lirien shrugged and Kitra kept her mouth shut.

"'You haven't got a beard!'"

Lirien smacked his forehead.

"WHAAAT?" Kitra cried, offended. "That's so stupid. That's not even— that's like a regular conversation. Nothing clever about it at all."

"I told you it was terrible."

"You told me it was a joke!"

Brandegil chuckled, something pleasant and musical sounding, the first time Lirien ever heard him laugh. "Well, sing us your song, then."

Kitra stood up and made a show of clearing her throat. Her voice, a pure alto, reached out into the forest.

"There once was a tailor
And his friend the sailor,
Who argued fair good and hard.
Who was the smaller,
And who was the taller,
When it came down to the yard?
They each grabbed a ruler,
The fool and the fooler,
Trying their best for the pick.
It was down to the letter
And no one was better—
They each had a sizeable stick!"

"Oh, wow," Brandegil said, rolling his eyes. But he wore a big smile on his face.

"What? It's the perfect campfire song. You're supposed to keep it bawdy. If we had some brew, it'd be even more perfect!" She gave a quick bow and sat back down next to Lirien. "Do you know any songs, Brandegil?"

"Nothing silly like that. I know something my mother used to sing to me. I don't know if you'd want to hear it, though. It's very... simple."

"Oh, come on. I bet you have a right fair voice." Kitra clapped her hands. "Brandegil, Brandegil!" Lirien joined in, matching her rhythm clap for clap. With an embarrassed grin, Brandegil stood up and took his place by the campfire. He sang in a tenor, his voice slightly breathy.

"Fall into a sleep, my boy,
Fall into dreams deep.
For you are my pride and joy,
And you I'll always keep.
Darling boy, please close your eyes.
Rest your weary head.
In the morning when you rise,
Remember what I've said.
I love you so, my dearest boy,
And every day anew,
I'll tell you you're my pride and joy
And I'll always love you."

Kitra clapped for Brandegil, but Lirien hesitated. It would have been nice to have had a mother sing to him growing up, a song of love and affection. He never got it.

Lirien didn't want to get too lost in his thoughts, so he joined Kitra with her applause. Brandegil gave them a slightly embarrassed, quick little bow. He rushed to his seat as Kitra said, "That was quite pretty."

Lirien nodded, then yawned.

"Oh, maybe not the right song for the night, though. Too soon for a lullaby," Kitra said. She turned to him and rested her chin in her hand. "I wish I could hear you sing. Do you miss it?"

He thought about it. He did miss singing, but if he never sang again, that would be fine with him. The aftermath of what he'd done, using the siren's forbidden melody, poisoned his feelings for it.

I like to make music, he signed. *I don't need my voice for that.*

After Kitra had translated, Brandegil asked, "What instruments can you play?"

He mimed each instrument— the lute, the lyre, the recorder, the flute. Then he added, a little shyly but at the same time with pride, *I can usually play any instrument I try.* He figured it was something in him, something on his siren side, that gave him such high musical aptitude. But he couldn't deny that it also brought him joy. If he never got his voice back, he would cope with that just fine, because he had other ways to express himself.

It was the one part of the spell-breaking that he wished wouldn't come true. That conclusion surprised him, how readily he came to it. If it meant giving up his freedom, if it meant being away from Kitra, he didn't want his voice back. He had learned, and was still learning, to live without it.

"That's amazing," Kitra said. "It would've been nice to hear you play."

Lirien ripped out a blade of grass and placed it between his thumbs, pressing his knuckles together, then blew through it, a reedy whistle escaping it. It made such a horrid sound that Kitra started laughing, took the grass from him, and tossed it.

"Bravo," Brandegil said with a grin. "You've outdone us all."

The evening continued on in that way, Kitra and Brandegil trading songs and stories, with more terrible jokes and hideous puns. Lirien contributed here and there, but he was content to just observe them.

Something in him felt wistful. This was the first night they had all come together like this, having fun and getting to know each other, yet he had to consider it was also one of their last nights as a group. Lirien felt like he should enjoy the little bit of time remaining, but as the fire died down and they crept into their bedding for the night, all Lirien could feel was loss. He was going to miss them both very much.

The next morning, Bella Morgana peeked her head over the stone wall and called for them to wake up and come inside. She had brought back food for the children, and as they ate, Lirien, Kitra, and Brandegil followed the giantess into the keep.

"It looks like you have a nice setup out there," she said. "You can leave it like that for the next few nights if you wish. It looks fun."

She gave each of them persimmons for breakfast, making very clear that it was not faery fruit and thus safe to eat, then brought out the loom.

He bit into his persimmon, greeted with the sensation of food, but none of the taste of it. The last time he had experienced flavor was when he'd bitten the Queen and took in some of her blood. Nothing tasted as good as that, and something deep down inside him told him it never would. The voice from before came to him, *Do it. Eat her.* He shoveled the rest of his persimmon into his mouth and pushed the thought away.

"Let me show you how to do this," Bella Morgana said, using a yarn made of simple fibers. She cut it to fill the length and width of the loom and tied it around one of the rods, then inserted the yarn in the loom's notches. She grabbed a sizeable wooden needle and tied another piece of the yarn to it, then attached it to the bottom rod of the loom. She took the needle and began weaving, going over and under each length of yarn. Once she got to the end of the loom, the pattern switched to going under and over as she came back to the opposite side. The weaving alternated as she went, row by row, pushing the woven lines down to the bottom of the loom with something that looked like a giant wooden comb, making sure they were tight enough together. She kept going long enough to show the beginnings of an actual piece of fabric, then pulled it off the loom.

"It's time for you to try. I'll still guide you through it, but you're essentially on your own."

Lirien started with the yarn made of stars. It took an incredible amount of time, with lots of repetitive motions. Pushing the lines down to the bottom and ensuring the weaving was tight enough took more energy from him than he thought, and he started to feel the strain in his arms. When he got to a certain point, he had to fetch a stool to reach the higher rungs, and then he started the process again.

It took him hours, not including the breaks he used to go out and check on the children. He worked until the conversation between Kitra, Brandegil, and Bella Morgana became a dull, lifeless noise in the background. He worked until sweat was on his brow, until his fingers felt locked in place from gripping the needle and comb so hard.

When he'd finished, taking two days to get through it, a gorgeous multitude of fabric billowed before them as Bella Morgana pulled it from the loom and spread it out on her worktable. The fabric was a luminescent, silvery white that glistened with an ivory glow.

The routine repeated itself over the next few days. The moonlight was easier to weave, its texture smoother than the stars, and when he was finished, he'd created something that reminded him of a pearl, with its special luster. It was similar to the stars, and yet not— a perfect fit for Sorin and Sonalie, twins who were similar and different. Sorin would get the stars and Sonalie would get the moonlight, he decided.

The aurora borealis was another story. That yarn was thicker than the other two, and harder for him to push down to make the weaving tight. It took extra effort, but when he was done, he'd truly made the most beautiful cloth he had ever seen. The aurora borealis fabric looked almost liquid in its texture but felt silky to the touch. The shades of pink, green, blue, and purple spread along it like watery dye, shades bleeding from one to the other. It was something fit for a queen — no, something better than that. It would be perfect for Nina.

Bella Morgana practically drooled at the sight of it. "I am so, so glad you are letting me keep whatever you don't use," she said. "I'll definitely have enough left over for at least one gown each. Or maybe a suit. Something for the Lord and Lady would be nice…" She awoke from her daydreaming. "Well, last part, then. Sewing. I have a pattern you can use for them. How tall are they, do you think?"

Since only weeks had passed for Nina, she was presumably the same height as before she transformed into the snake. But Sorin and Sonalie were nearly two years older now, and Lirien had seen in his dream that they'd grown. He tried his best to give Bella Morgana a good approximation of the sizes they'd become.

He spent two days each to cut the pattern, pin the fabric, and sew by hand, working from morning to night. Because they were robes, they didn't have to be elaborate, thank goodness, but hand-sewing was still quite a drain on time. It took a little bit for Lirien to get his stitches small and in a straight line, but once he understood how to do it, he got better and faster.

Once he was finished, he admired his handiwork: simple but beautiful, thanks to the materials he worked with.

"What are you waiting for?" Brandegil asked. "Aren't you going to put them on the children?"

Have to wait. Must be near the ocean when my voice comes back, and my curse with it.

"Bella Morgana, this means it's time for us to go," Kitra said.

Lirien bundled the robes into his satchels while the giantess said her farewells to the group. Then she followed them to the clearing in front of the keep where she doted on the children and wished them well.

At last, when all of the goodbyes had been said, he closed his eyes and bowed in deep respect for the forest and all it had allowed him to do to break the spell. Then he called for it to let them out. And Elythia answered.

CHAPTER 19

Lirien opened his eyes to find himself surrounded by what looked like the tall, thin evergreens of Pinemore, and he felt the sweltering heat of a summer day pressing down on him. Nearby, he recognized a standing stone, one that he and Brandegil had used when they were escaping Ardeth.

"This is goodbye for me," Brandegil said. "I think it's too much of a risk for me to stay here longer. Anyone could come across us at any time, and I won't know if they're friend or foe. I could protect myself with Alibrandr but promised I would not use the sword in violence, and I mean to keep my word."

Lirien nodded. He held his arms open to Brandegil and beckoned him forward. They embraced, Brandegil clapping Lirien's back. "Don't forget me," Brandegil said, his voice soft. "I won't forget you."

He turned to Kitra. "See you, fae fox. If I'm ever in Elythia, I'll try to find you again. Don't send me to the mud pond, though. I won't be happy."

Kitra gave him a mischievous shrug, then pulled him in for a hug. "I'll save a lewd little song just for you," she said.

Brandegil walked up to the stone and held his hand over it. The air rippled and Brandegil turned to them, giving them a wave. Then he stepped on through and sealed the rock behind him.

Lirien let out a sigh. That was it, then. Brandegil would no longer be a part of his life, and more painful partings were to come.

"Now onto the next step," Kitra said. "Are you ready?"

He swallowed. The moment he'd looked forward to, yet the moment he dreaded, would soon be upon them. *I'm so scared*, he signed.

Kitra squeezed his hand. "I'll be with you. I hope it brings you comfort. And you know that I'll protect you."

He knew, but to Kitra, his protection meant the Queen's death. And he hadn't worked out how he could keep the Queen safe, not from a giant, fire-breathing fox.

He didn't want to think about that. The children were probably growing impatient, knowing that soon they would be restored to their human selves. He sped up his pace and led Kitra and the children through the pines until he found the familiar pathway to the stony embankment that led down onto the beach.

Kitra looked nervous as they stepped onto the sandy shore. She kept staring at the water, and the salt in the air made her look sickly, her pale skin taking on a greenish gray hue.

This time, it was he who squeezed her hand. *You're still on land. You should be all right.*

"I'll have to make it quick," Kitra said, more to herself than to Lirien.

They traced the familiar path along the sands toward Lirien's old tower, and as they saw the barbican in the distance, Lirien halted.

The gates were opened and they watched the Queen,

wearing an armored breastplate and riding on horseback, passed through them, followed by a seemingly endless procession of armored soldiers marching in unison. The golden bird perched on the Queen's arm, a leash around its neck, and it whispered words into the Queen's ear that Lirien couldn't hear, but it didn't matter— he knew what the bird was saying: *I love you.*

Elythia, as always, had placed them exactly where they needed to be— and when. Lirien had no doubt where the Queen's army was marching. Her patience with the Queens of Asherin was at an end, and she was prepared to kill anyone standing between her and her obsession.

Lirien waved his arms frantically in the Queen's direction. She didn't notice him immediately, not until Sonalie started honking loudly and flapping her wings, drawing her attention toward them.

Even then, Queen Aurinda moved slowly, shock spreading across her features. She took in the sight of the animals, confused, as if she had forgotten what had happened to the children entirely. Then her gaze met with his, and her face erupted in an ecstatic joy that caused a chill to wash over his skin.

"HALT!" the Queen commanded, and the thunderous sound of the soldiers' marching stopped almost immediately. Then the Queen spoke a few words to the captain at her side, who then began shouting new orders at the baffled troops.

But the Queen had lost interest in her army and her war entirely. She dismounted and rushed toward him, shouting his name, her arms spread open as if she meant to grab and embrace him. The golden bird that had been at her side flew into the air, circling them, all while calling out, *I love you.*

He couldn't help stepping back from the Queen as she flew at him, but she came on nonetheless, wrapping her arms around him and kissing his neck. "Lirien," she breathed, drawing his name out.

Kitra bristled— her face filled with poison, her lip curled, her teeth showing, looking very much like a fox ready to bite. "Get away from him," she snarled.

He shuddered and stepped out of the Queen's grasp. He held his hands up to both women: *Wait.* He then gestured to the children, then the bags at his sides. Turning back to the Queen, he tapped just below his eye: *Watch.*

He took the star robe from his satchel and draped it around Sorin. Everything within him tensed as he held his breath, hoping it would work.

A pillar of light enclosed Sorin and he shrank in size, rising from four legs to two, his antlers disappearing, his skin changing, his face returning.

The Queen paled, her mouth falling open. "What is— Sorin? Is that you?"

Sorin let out a sob as he ran to his mother's side, and she latched onto him, kissing the top of his head. "What happened to your arm?"

Sonalie was next. With some difficulty, Lirien placed her inside the moonlight robe, the sleeves hanging awkwardly over her wings. The same light eclipsed her, and she grew in size as she was restored to her human form. She ran to her mother and Sorin, gripping them tightly.

Last was Nina. She slid off Lirien's arm and onto the beach, leaving an 'S' shape in the sand. He laid the aurora robe out for her and she slithered into it until her head poked through the collar. The light came, and she was a girl again.

She walked to Queen Aurinda and squeezed her mother tightly. The Queen embraced all of them once more, and tears trickled quietly down her face as she managed, "I don't know how... Lirien... you..." She couldn't finish without her voice breaking.

But he didn't pay much heed to her. The bird that had circled them in the air now transformed into a glistening, almost smoky golden light, and it shot toward him. "I love you," it said, its voice echoing. Then it dove into his mouth and down his throat, and he swallowed as if he'd just taken a drink. He felt a fullness that wasn't there before, and with another swallow it settled.

He looked at Kitra, and out his voice came: "I love you," and the words were pure, clear, beautiful and *true*.

Kitra's hand flew to her heart, her eyes wide. "Lirien," she said, her voice hardly above a whisper.

The Queen was oblivious— she thought the words were for her. She abandoned the children at her side and flung herself at him, her eyes huge and glassy, "Oh God, Lirien, tell me again, tell me again how much you love me! I cannot wait for the moment I hold you and—" But she could not even finish the words before gripping his hair violently, shoving her tongue down his throat.

He grabbed her, and his voice came out gentle but firm, trying to calm the Queen. "Please, don't. Not in front of them."

The children stared at her, bewildered. "What are you doing?" Nina cried. "Mother!"

But she didn't listen, and she clawed at him, her hands wandering over him, trying to tear at his clothes.

"Lirien, step away from her," Kitra said, and changed into her giant fox form. "You know what has to be done." She opened her jaws and a ball of fire brewed in the back of her throat.

The children ran in front of the Queen, shielding her. "No!" Sonalie cried out, and Sorin shouted, "Don't hurt her!"

"Get out of the way," Kitra roared.

He stepped in front of the children. "Kitra. Don't do this, don't—"

He let out a pained gasp and doubled over, then sank to the sands.

His legs had seized up, his limbs like stone.

Stone! But—but—no! He was by the sea, he was home! Why was this happening?

Lirien felt the hardness spread over him quickly, his body growing solid and heavy.

No no no no no! This can't be! He struggled to move, to rise up again, and landed on his back.

It didn't make sense. He had come home, he returned to the sea, he—

It came to him then, what Lord Iesin had said when they talked about his curse. "The body remembers."

No. That couldn't be it.

But something inside him told him, *You were cursed to never stray far from the sea. The curse was never lifted, only kept at bay.* He had left the sea, and his body remembered all the time, all the miles, on his journey away from home.

Perhaps this was how the siren curse would end...

He sobbed. His legs were already lost, and his stomach hardened. He felt the inside of him petrify, seizing his lungs and his heart.

He looked to Kitra, tears falling from his eyes, then the children. "I love—"

His heart stopped.

CHAPTER 20

Air flooded into Lirien's lungs and his heart beat ferociously in his chest. He was soaked, the shallow waves of the sea washing over him.

Kitra was above him in her fae form, clutching at her chest, breathing heavily. There was a gaping hole in her shirt there, and blood had stained it thoroughly. A jagged line the size of a fist marred her skin, as if it had been torn open and laced back together.

And that wasn't the worst of it. Kitra's ears, tail, and hair had turned solid white. Her skin was ash, and she looked as though she were in incredible pain, gritting her teeth and wincing.

Sorin and Sonalie were screaming loudly as they gripped their mother, and Nina stood aside, her fright and tears clear upon her face.

Kitra pressed her forehead to his, her skin cold and clammy. "Lirien— you *died*." Her voice was weighted with shock. "You dried up and turned into this weird stone—" Then she winced again, her breathing sharp and shallow.

He took steadying breaths as he ran his hands over his body, now soft, now flesh. "How did I come back?" He couldn't understand any of it.

"I made a havoc stone," Kitra said, her voice thin and airy. "My own."

Lirien sat upright, gripping her shoulders. "What did you do?"

"I gave up half my heart and wished it away so you would live again. I didn't think I could do it, but I put into it everything I had." She tried to stand up, but her legs shook beneath her. "I can't stay here any longer. I don't think I'm going to make it. I have to get back, I need to—"

He understood. He closed his eyes and, in his mind, screamed, *Elythia! Come!*

"Look!" Sonalie cried and pointed at the gilt flowers that popped up out of the sand. The trees of Autumn Wood appeared around the children and all across the shoreline, a bizarre amalgam of forest and sea coming right up on each other, but not touching.

Kitra gave him a kiss on the cheek. She seemed afraid to do more, but he took her by the chin and pulled her in for a delicate kiss on the lips.

"I don't want to say goodbye," she said, "but I have to." She rose to her feet, this time sturdier, and he followed. "I knew this was going to be hard. That's why I didn't want to... well, it doesn't matter now. You have my heart."

"And you have mine," Lirien said.

Kitra broke into a pained smile. "The greatest pact there is," she said. "I'm sorry we cannot be together. That's the way of it, isn't it? Doomed to be apart." She wiped her eyes and turned away from him.

She froze, and then her knees buckled underneath her. Lirien caught her.

"My magic is gone. I can't change. I can't do anything." She took in a shaky breath. "I feel like I'm going to faint."

"You can get there," Lirien said. "I'll walk you right up to the forest." And he did so, one arm around her waist, another around her shoulders. He moved with her slowly and patiently to the edge of Elythia.

"Goodbye, Lirien," Kitra said, her voice breathy. She gave him one last kiss on the lips and staggered into the wood. In a moment, less than the blink of an eye, the forest disappeared with her.

A tear fell down his cheek as he let out a tremulous sigh. Then he turned to the Queen. "She's gone. You don't have to worry about her. I surrender."

The Queen looked bewildered, as if she'd just realized everything that happened. She stared at him in horror, her face pale, then she looked to her children, then back at him again. To his surprise, her face crumpled, and an expression of great pain spread across her features. She wiped at her eyes, seeming older somehow, a shell of herself, as if everything in her had emptied out. Her voice was quiet but wavered. "There must be a reckoning, Lirien. We each must answer for what we've done."

LIRIEN KNEELED BEFORE THE QUEEN, who sat upon her throne, the two of them alone in the vast royal chamber. The Queen clutched the scrollwork carved into the chair's armrests, her knuckles white from the tightness of her grip. That action alone betrayed the calm confidence she wore on her face— the detached tolerance that had always been her way with Lirien before the spell.

"It is over," the Queen said. "When you died, I felt all of it leave me, the desire to be with you, to love you."

Lirien nodded his understanding.

"I won't lie to you about it, Lirien. I cannot love you as a son. I never could before, and certainly not now, after everything that has happened."

He only nodded again.

The Queen rose from her throne and stepped carefully down from the platform. "I can't help but feel disgust when I look at you..." She faltered. "And I only feel disgust when I look at myself. I cannot bear what I have done. What I have done to the kingdom, to the children, and yes, to you." Her eyes wandered to the floor, and she fidgeted with the cuffs of her sleeves, much like how Sonalie would when she was nervous. "The whole time, it was as though I was locked away in a glass box... and I watched myself on the other side of it, a double, a doll, an automaton that looked just like me, that said and did the most loathsome things. It didn't matter how much I screamed and pounded on my glass cage; I couldn't reach myself. I couldn't stop myself. Yet I felt all of it. I felt the most wondrous love, more than anything I had ever felt in my entire life, and it made me so happy, until you refused to return it, and then I felt the utmost despair."

She took a breath, and let go of her sleeves, straightening her posture. Then she clutched his shoulder, her nails digging into him. He could feel the rage through her fingertips. "You did that to me," she said, her voice just above a whisper.

"Your Majesty," Lirien began, and his voice trembled.

The Queen let go of him.

"It's true, I sang the siren song. I used forbidden magic. I'm never going to forgive myself for doing it." He met her gaze evenly, even as his eyes misted up. "But what was I to do? You wanted me to die. You came at me with a knife, you *stabbed me* — and told me to sing."

The Queen stayed silent for a moment. "I... didn't really want you to die. I do not love you, Lirien, but I do not hate you, either. I just— I wasn't in my right mind. I was mad with grief over my husband. I thought if anyone could save him, you could, but you needed to be motivated, you needed to know you couldn't fail. And I admit, I wanted to punish you, too. So, I gave you an impossible task. I was wrong to." She reached out to his shoulder again, only this time she touched it gently and said, "Rise."

He stood up and looked at her, a question in his eyes.

"I made terrible choices while I was under the siren spell, and the people of Ardeth deserve to know why. And when they understand that I was bewitched, they will demand account-ability. One of us must answer for what happened."

"And you intend that to be me."

"Yes. The people cannot be made to hate their Queen. We cannot risk the kingdom falling apart. And so the burden must fall on you."

"Then I am to be... imprisoned? Or is it..." He could not say the words.

"No, I cannot bring myself to hurt you again, not when you have saved my children. You will not face the scaffolds or the dungeons. But you cannot stay here. You will leave Ardeth."

Lirien squeezed his eyes shut. "Banishment, then?" It seemed a cruel fate to be torn away from the children after all he'd done to bring them home. And where could he possibly live, if not the castle by the sea? "Your Majesty, I cannot leave the ocean. I will change to stone again. And what about the children? Will you deny me their company?"

"Follow the shore into Delendra, then. Stay on the sea there.

And as for the children... I will allow them to visit you, in secret. We will make plans later."

"Thank you for that kindness."

She resumed her seat on the throne, and all emotion faded from her face and voice. Lirien recognized her expression as the one she wore whenever she tended to affairs of state— a mask of authority, revealing only a stern confidence. She spoke in the Queen's Voice: "I have one last command for you, Lirien."

Lirien bowed to her. "Your Majesty."

"You will never sing again."

LIRIEN'S HEARING took place the very next morning in the presence of the royal guard, the children, and the entirety of the court. The Queen shared almost all the truth with the people of Ardeth, describing everything that had happened, save for her assaults on Lirien and the threats of death to him, framing it as Lirien's own choice to sing the siren song in his own desperation to save the King.

"Fully knowing such magic was forbidden," she announced. "Given the great harm done to myself and the kingdom, he must pay for what he has done. After all, it was beyond my control."

The Queen made a show of banishing him, giving him one last night to stay in the castle and to prepare himself to leave, and the people seemed satisfied by that. And once again, the Queen stated before the whole of the court, "You will never sing again."

And he accepted her sentencing. He would leave his home and family. And no song would escape his lips again. Save one.

He had come up with an idea of his own, something reckless, something desperate. He had one last song left in him, and he would sing it in secret. His last night was to be spent in his old tower, which had been restored in Lirien's absence. He was given a simple meal of cheese, apples, and a chicken leg for his final supper, which he nibbled on while he packed. He would have delighted in his meal, as his tastebuds at last surged with the flavor of his food, but he had no appetite. He was nervous for what he would do next.

He left his tower for the ocean, into the water and onto an outcropping of rocks far off the shore. He made sure he was a distance enough away that no one could hear him over the crashing waves of the sea, and he kept his voice just above a whisper for what he was about to do.

He thought of who and what he was. He was human, but he was a siren, a creature of magic. And although that magic had backfired horribly, he was still able to call upon it to some degree. And as he had passed his final hours in the castle, there was a nagging thought within him, something that he wanted to try, as foolhardy as it was.

He wanted to give up his voice. And the only way he thought he could do so was through magic.

Every song he ever sang belonged to someone else. What he'd performed for the King, for his family, for others... it was always someone else's words, someone else's tune. The magic that he had triggered, the dark power that drove the Queen to her twisted fixation, wasn't his either. He had used the forbidden melody that belonged only to sirens.

What if he had a song of his own to sing? What if he had a power of his own?

It was worth it to try, as much as he feared the danger of it. As he tried to reconcile the fact that he would no longer be in Ardeth, he couldn't stop thinking of Kitra, how he wanted to be at her side. He remembered Brandegil, too, feeling the pain of his absence as well.

He couldn't stop thinking of the mountains, the rivers, the woods.

He couldn't stop thinking of his freedom, of walking where he wished.

If it meant giving up his voice to have all of that back, it was no loss to him. He had already managed to live without it, and life was different because of it, but it wasn't hard. And he could always continue to grow and learn along the way.

So, when the sun had made its final descent below the horizon, Lirien sang. It was a song he'd written himself, his voice soft and tremulous, quiet and serene, in his own words, in his own way. No rhymes or clever wordplay, but the feelings in his heart:

"You were a gift to me, a golden bird with brilliant wings.
You soared above great heights, and you brought joy.
You gave me words and ways of feeling,
You have lived well.
But now I cut the bonds you have to me.
I give you back to the place you came from.
Be with your kin, again in your place of birth.
I release you."

It welled up inside of him, fluttery and delicate in his throat. He opened his mouth and something gold, shimmery and smoky, escaped his lips.

It again took the shape of a bird, and it turned and looked at him, cocking its head to the side. "I release you," it said.

Then it changed— it lost its wings and fell into the sea. And he glimpsed its golden tail coming up out of the water as it dove below. The light disappeared with the foam, and it was gone.

Lirien swam back to shore and headed to the southwest tower, back to his old room. He grabbed a piece of paper and wrote three notes, one for each of his siblings, then changed into the simple clothing he'd always worn before he was made Prince. Since he was banished, he was certain he was out of the line of succession and had no need for finery any longer. He loaded the bag he'd packed with supplies, food, and some money.

Carrying a candle with him, he hurried through the hidden passages of the castle out to the grand staircase.

He entered Sorin's room first. At the corner table, across from his bed, Sorin's new prosthetic lay. It was an elegantly engraved silver arm, with curling etchings and looping lines all over the metal.

He put his candle aside and woke Sorin.

"Brother!"

He tapped his throat, then waved dismissively. *Gone*, he mouthed.

"What happened?"

He handed him the letter he'd written out. It was the same for each of the children.

As you know, the Queen has banished me from Ardeth, so I must leave. But I will be going someplace farther away from you, a place that wanders where it wills.

"Kitra?"

Lirien nodded. Sorin continued reading. *Giving up my voice was the only way I knew to secure my freedom, to go wherever I please. Elythia may let me out entirely on its own whims, but I will always find you. You are my family.*

Sorin hugged Lirien tight. "You love her, right?"

He nodded.

"Then I guess you have to go," he said, his voice forlorn. "I'm going to miss you."

He smoothed Sorin's hair back on his head and kissed the top of it. As he closed the door, he raised his hand to Sorin in farewell.

He headed on to Sonalie's room. "Whoa, Lirien, what are you doing here?" she asked.

He sat at the edge of her bed and handed her his letter. She read it silently to herself, and her eyes glossed over with tears.

She wrapped her arms around Lirien's waist. "But I only just started being able to hug you," she said before rubbing her eyes. "Your punishment is so unfair! Why do you have to leave? You were gone from us for so long!"

He placed his hand on his heart and held it there, hoping she'd understand what he was leaving for.

He kissed both of her cheeks and she called out in a choked voice, "Goodbye."

The last place. Nina's room.

She was awake, reading by candlelight underneath her covers, and she placed her book on the nightstand next to her bed.

"Hello. Come to say goodbye, then?" Her voice came out softly.

He tapped his throat and handed her the letter.

She read it, a somber look spreading across her face. "I thought this would happen. Not that I thought you'd find a way, but, I mean, that you'd go back to her if you could. I was with you and Kitra the longest. I saw how you looked at her, how she looked at you. I guess I knew what was coming. Please, please, find a way to visit us often. I don't want to be twenty years old when you come back to us for the first time."

Lirien couldn't make any promises, but he nodded anyway. He made a gesture like writing, and Nina opened her drawer and handed him a charcoal stick. *You're going to be a great Queen,* he wrote.

"I know," she said with a smile. "Come back before then."

He pulled her in for a tight hug, then headed to the door. He paused.

Paper, he mouthed.

Nina handed him the letter back and Lirien tore a square of it off, just enough to write a couple more sentences.

When he was done, he ruffled Nina's hair and set out.

His heart thudded in his chest as he stood before the door to the Queen's chambers.

He didn't know what compelled him to say goodbye to her, but he felt like he should.

He knocked on her door and she opened it, looking surprised to see him there. "Lirien. What are you doing over here? You don't have to bid me farewell. I'm shocked that you would want to."

He touched his throat and shook his head.

"Your voice."

He nodded and handed her the paper. His note to her was much shorter.

My voice is gone. Forever. I'm going to Elythia.

She raised an eyebrow at him, looking at his face, trying to read him. "Do the children know?"

Lirien nodded again.

"Will you find a way to visit them?"

He nodded once more. She eyed him in silence, then after a moment, spoke: "Do what you must. I will not stop you."

He paused only for a moment, then he signed to her: *Thank you. Goodbye.*

She tilted her head to the side, not understanding the gestures, then closed her door to him.

He went on his way through the passages and out of the castle, along the beach, past the castle town, and up the stone embankment that led to Pinemore. Once he found a comfortable place, he did what he had always done before— he asked for Elythia to come to him.

The gilt flowers burst from the ground and a hazy setting sun stretched through the trees that made up Autumn Wood. And when he looked behind him, the pine trees that rose high in the sky were gone.

He didn't recognize where he was, but he kept on walking through the wood all the same, passing the familiar pixies and fairies, as well as strange creatures in vivid colors. Some of them recognized him, and lowered their heads to him in acknowledgement.

As the sky and the forest darkened, he came across a reddish-orange light glowing off in the distance amid the trees.

He smiled. *I must— I need to —follow these.*

Lanterns hung from various branches, making a pathway through the wood, the light warm and welcoming.

At the end of the path of glowing fire, a young woman with white hair, a white tail, and white ears stood on her toes, hanging another lantern from a tree branch. She clapped her hands, surveying her work, and when she turned around, she froze. But only for a moment.

"Greetings, mortal," she said with a smile.

ACKNOWLEDGMENTS

I'm indebted to so many people for bringing this book to life. It has gone on a long journey, from being written in Japan to being edited and on submission in the United States. Many eyes have been on this work, and for that, I'm grateful.

First, I'd like to thank my developmental editor Katie Kenyhercz, who was the first to look at the manuscript as a whole and gave me valuable feedback. Next, I want to thank the beta readers from Independent Book Review, Haunted Unicorn Publishing, and Kit 'n Kabookle, who all read different versions but helped me clean the manuscript up every time. On top of that, I have writerly friends like Aisling Cornelius and Jay Barlow to thank for giving me their opinions, which also helped shape the book into what it is today.

I am so grateful to my agent Rick Lewis for connecting with the story and sprucing it up to go on submission. I have always felt like Rick truly "got" the book and have only felt support and care throughout this entire process. Thank you!

I want to thank Kim Ostrom for championing the book and giving me wonderful edits. I absolutely loved working with you and have always appreciated your kind words of encouragement.

Next, Jill Stadler, whose eagle eyes made my manuscript even better than I could have dreamed. Your support is also appreciated!

I also want to give kudos to Tanya Anne Crosby and the rest of the team at Oliver Heber Books. You are an amazing group of people to work with and I felt so welcome when I came on board. Thank you so much!

Lastly, I want to thank my family and friends, who had to endure years of me flitting between thinking I was brilliant to thinking I was absolute trash. I know when I write, it's always an emotional rollercoaster, but your love and strength have kept me going. I love you all.

About the Author

Kristina Elyse Butke writes fantasy filled with magic, dark curses, and true love. Her time living abroad in Wales and Japan inspires her writing through the fantastical settings and creatures she creates. She has an MFA in Writing Popular Fiction from Seton Hill University and when she isn't writing, she indulges herself with reading manga and webtoons, watching anime, and cosplaying. She also enjoys spending time in forests, the more whimsical, the better.

Keep in touch! Find Kristina on the web:
www.kristinaelysebutke.com
Find her on social media all of which you can find here:
https://linktr.ee/kristinaelysebutke.